# HE SANG TO ME

# HE
# SANG
# TO
# ME

*Cover and interior design by Casey Tyler*

*Headshot by Christa Bosco Bosse*

*"This Night Will Be Magic" written by Casey Tyler and Chelsea Tautkus*

ISBN 979-8-9891925-9-5 (pbk)
ISBN 979-8-9891925-3-3 (ebook)

*To Lucy, may you always live your days*
*with the greatest sense of wonder.*

# HE SANG TO ME

# ONE

It's finally happening. I'm here. Call it what you like—The Big Apple. The City So Nice They Named It Twice. The City That Never Sleeps. Some even call it Gotham, though I thought that was strictly reserved for Batman. Regardless, this place is now my home.

*I live in New York City.*

Growing up, we would take our annual Christmastime family day trip to Manhattan. My parents would ogle at the decorated Christmas windows, stand in awe of the bright Rockefeller tree, and buy us all hotdogs at the carts that smelled like sautéed cows. Unfortunately, the city never wooed me as it did them. I would much rather have been snuggled up all cozy under a fuzzy blanket, drinking hot chocolate near a roaring fire, than stomping around the nasty streets of Midtown in the freezing cold with the millions of other people who had come for the day to do the exact same three things my family and I were there for.

My distaste for New York came to a head when I saw a man urinating on a wall in Times Square, and I thought to myself, *This is quite possibly the most horrible place on planet Earth.* My innocent eyes grew wide at the sight, and I vowed never to look up from my shuffling feet again as they navigated these city streets.

But that all changed when I was thirteen, and my mom took me to see my first Broadway show. *Wicked.* This lackluster world I once lived in was turned upside down. When we stepped back onto the pavement after those glorious two-and-a-half hours, it was as if an angel had draped the streets of Manhattan with rainbows, glitter, and sunshine. I became fully enamored with the city. This place I initially believed to be revolting became utterly magical. The men that peed on walls in the middle of bustling crowds only highlighted the beauty and resilience of New York's artistic scene against an otherwise dull and uninspired society.

Ever since that night, I knew there was nowhere else I'd rather live because there was *nowhere else* like New York City.

Give me the rats scurrying across the subway platform on your way to work. Give me the moments when you're smelling a delectable croissant baking one second and stale pee the next. Give me the unidentified liquids lining the streets while you walk to your morning bagel place in your favorite shoes. I'll gladly take the eight-by-eight-foot room that costs more monthly than the mortgage on your parent's four-bedroom home back in Connecticut. I want that same room with never-ending bright lights peering through the window as you drift off to sleep to the lullaby of car horns and ambulances racing by.

Not only did the city get ahold of me, but naturally, so did musical theater. I became obsessed. I began auditioning for every school musical or community theater program in my town, signing up for every singing and dancing lesson I could, and became the quintessential theater nerd I never knew I wanted to be.

The dream of one day becoming a Broadway actress was placed upon me as if the President himself told me it must be done. Nothing would stop me—except, of course, fear, and lack of courage, *and* finances.

"You just need to go for it," my best friend Mickey said while we were enjoying our weekly movie night, painting our nails. Mickey, or "Mick" as I call her, is a vibrant, joy-filled firecracker of a woman with a beautiful caramel brown afro that stops people in their tracks. We met at summer camp ten years ago and have been glued to each other's side ever since.

"You've been talking about it forever, and now is the time, Ms. *Sunday Jane*." I always knew she meant business when she used my full name.

Sunday Jane Truelove.

Some people think I've made it up, but it's real. My parents just really love Sundays. And Truelove, well, I'm not sure of the history of our family name. All I know is that I haven't met mine just yet.

Mick was right, of course, about this being the best time to make a move. The guy I'd been dating broke things off with me only days before. I knew he probably wasn't "the one," but he did hope to buy a brownstone home in Brooklyn Heights, as he also dreamed of living in the city. It was exciting to think that if we ended up together, we might make New York our home base, and I wouldn't have to make the big move alone.

But that plan turned to dust in the blink of an eye. I'm still unsure whether it was the loss of our relationship or the loss of my promised future in New York City that left me with a bigger heartache.

Mick watched the emotion play out on my face as I thought of him. Her eyes were measuring as she blew on the fresh coat of paint on her fingernails.

"You don't need a man to do this," she said. Sometimes it would freak me out how she knew exactly what I was thinking. "Your life right now is set up perfectly to chase after your dreams. And we both know New York—or better yet, *Broadway* is calling your name." Her hands gave a rainbow motion as she mentioned Broadway.

"I know, I know," I replied, and like always, I rolled my eyes at her because she didn't understand what the grueling process of becoming an actress would entail. You have to know people in the business and go through hundreds—if not thousands—of auditions, all while trying to figure out how to get ahold of an Equity card in the first place so you can attend said auditions. It's a mystery I have yet to solve, even after hours of research.

"How about you come with me?" I squeaked with raised brows, and she giggled.

"You can do this by yourself. You don't need me or anyone else." She took my hands into hers, careful not to touch our nails and ruin our fresh manicures.

"Everything you need to make this move is right in here." She pointed to my chest, where my heart began fluttering in a nervous pattern. "You are brave and strong. If anyone can do this, it's you."

Looking back into her eyes, my two potential futures played out through my mind like a projector reel. The first of what it would mean to stay in Connecticut and continue my wonderful but monotonous job as a caregiver. The other of pursuing my dreams in New York as an actress on Broadway. I knew at that moment my hopes of being on the stage—under those dazzling lights, singing alongside some of my heroes—were worth the risks of what uprooting my life would entail. It was time to chase my dream.

The following days after our movie night, I quit my job, found an apartment, packed up my things, rented a U-Haul, and squished between my parents in the front seat on the journey to my new front steps in Brooklyn.

I found my new roommate, Finn, on the internet as I scoured for open rooms in Manhattan, Brooklyn, the Bronx—anywhere in or a train's distance away from the heart of Times Square. After a quick video call, likely to make sure I wasn't a lunatic and to offer me the chance to discern the same, she graciously offered me the space.

Upon meeting her in person, I learned that Finn is a fashion designer for a high-end clothing company in Manhattan. This didn't surprise me. She's light-years ahead of me in fashion. Even her "work from home" outfit was stunning. She wore a checkered, black and white sweater with green, flair yoga pants and makeup that highlighted her brown eyes and auburn hair cut short in a bouncy bob. I felt a rush of inadequacy as I glanced down at my moving clothes covered in paint from different projects over the years. Maybe my outfit would've come across as avant-garde? She didn't seem to care, though. After an introductory hug, she handed me my keys and even lent her hand by bringing some of my boxes up to our fifth-floor apartment.

My parents and I were drenched in sweat within minutes as we walked up and down the narrow stairs. I thought to myself that investing in a gym membership would no longer be necessary because of the arduous trek to my new place; again, it didn't faze me—I'm just grateful to be here.

Once everything was out of the U-Haul, we set up my furniture and organized each section of my room. It was smaller than I anticipated but perfect all the same. After placing some of my favorite Playbills in frames and making a small gallery wall with the help of my dad and a level, Mom and I decorated the largest wall in my room with colorful peel-and-stick wallpaper. When everything was in place—clothes put away, bed made, toiletries in their designated cubby—I gave my parents a tearful goodbye hug and kiss before taking a necessary shower and then flopping on my bed with cozy, clean clothes.

And now, here I sit; staring out of my new window and dreaming of all the wonderful possibilities my future could hold.

My first order of business is signing up for every possible Broadway lottery ticket. Generally, shows reserve a few tickets each night for people to enter and win at the last minute. And this girl can't afford to blow all her savings on Broadway shows—though I wouldn't judge anyone who wants to.

After I finish my lottery entries and scroll through the local callboard for auditions, I get a text from Mick. It's a gif of Miley Cyrus exiting her private jet in *Hannah Montana: The Movie,* shouting, "Hello, New York!" Followed by,

**How's the big city, my girl? All moved in and ready to grace that Broadway stage?**

**Lol,** I respond. **It's my first day, Mick. It might take me more than a few hours to get an audition. But yes! I'm here. My roommate helped me move in—she seems sweet—very normal, and chill.**

**You have to get out there, woman! Glad your roomie doesn't seem like a psycho...yet.**

**For sure. It doesn't look like I'll end up as the star victim of a crime podcast like you initially thought ;)**

**We'll see,** she replies. **However, it might be a good edge to get noticed!**

**I'm good haha.**

**Proud of you for doing this <3**

I tear up at her words because I'm proud of myself too. I've finally made my home in this beloved city where nobody knows me, but maybe—just maybe—one day they will.

"This is where I keep all the dead bodies." My new manager, Gavin, shows me the back storage area of the Williamsburg coffee shop. His

long fingers sweep to the large containers that are all capped, then in a singsong way, he says, "Just kidding. It's cold brew."

I applied for every job I was qualified for in the vicinity of our apartment and stumbled upon an ad for a barista position at a cafe called "Devoción." When I walked in this morning for my shift, I was struck by how gorgeous the cafe was. Plants are used as decor everywhere you look, including a wall covered in greenery that stretches toward the large skylight above. Enormous worn, leather couches sit directly underneath the skylight while delicate, wooden tables and chairs are nestled against the faded brick walls. From what I've read online about this place, the coffee is spectacular, and clearly, so are the vibes. Most of the population studying and sipping coffee within these walls will likely be hipsters.

Gavin walks me through where all the supplies are to restock different items like cups and sugars and where I can find the cleaning supplies for the closing shifts. While he explains more of my role, I study his features. He's a slim, mid-30s individual with a luscious head of hair the same color as his brilliantly bleached white teeth. His locks stick straight up and then veer to the right ever so slightly, making him look even taller than he actually is.

"Don't mix up the sugar and the chemicals to clean up—people don't like that," he says dryly as he looms above me. Because I've worked in coffee shops before, I pick it up fairly quickly, especially about not mixing sugars and toxins.

We head back to the main floor. While he teaches me the register and all the various signature coffee drinks, we trickle in facts about ourselves. I learn that he is an aspiring writer—specifically scripts for theater. He and his husband moved to the city from Portland, Oregon four years ago to pursue their dreams, and he's currently starring in a one-person play he wrote about a rock climber who gets stuck on the side of a cliff during a solo climb.

"In reality, I'm just strapped into a harness that hangs from a truss at the theater's ceiling the entirety of the show whilst clinging to a paper mache rock made by yours truly." He poses for me what he must look like each night as he grasps the cliff—fingers curled like tree roots and one calf in the air, flexed. It reminds me of a statue of a lone, standing horse I once saw in a stuffy museum.

"It's a life-or-death situation, and you don't know which he'll choose," he purrs.

"Sounds gripping," I tease.

He throws his head back, breaks into the most obnoxious, fake laugh, and then deadpans, "I see what you did there." For a second, I'm afraid I may have insulted him, but then a smile forms on his lips.

Because my playfulness has been welcomed, I push further and say, "It also sounds very uncomfortable. You're hanging from the ceiling the whole time?"

"Oh, yes. It's *wildly* uncomfortable," he explains. "But that only makes it more realistic!"

"Okay," I say with uncertainty layered in my voice.

"Let me know if you want to come—I can sneak you in for a good price." He bobs his eyebrows up and down.

Hours later, after many spilled lattes and scorched milks, I'm finally getting back into the rhythm of life as a barista. I notice a familiar face walk up to the counter.

*Oh no. Have my Connecticut acquaintances come to the city to drag me back to the suburbs?*

But as she smiles, I'm brought back to my living room sofa, popcorn in hand, watching the previous year's Tony Awards play out with my mom by my side. This is "Best Leading Actress in a Musical" winner Brittany Oliver. Standing right before me. Her theater credentials flood my brain and I feel like a walking Wikipedia page. I remember she is the star of the new Broadway musical *Belle Époque*. From what I've heard, it's a musical retelling of Shakespeare's *Twelfth Night*. Brittany's character disguises herself as her twin brother in order to join the army in the late 1800s. I have yet to see it, but it's on my list.

My heart races as she stands there, scanning the wall to my left where the list of drink and food options are written. Suddenly, I'm overwhelmed by how warm it is in the cafe. Tugging at my apron that rests on my heated neck, I say, "Hi there, how can I help you?" In my shyness, I stare at the counter between us; my left eye twitches uncontrollably. As inconspicuously as possible, I hit my temple to stop it from spasming and then take a better look at her.

"Can I get a large Americano, please?" she asks with an Australian accent as she looks into my eyes.

"Y-yes, of course," I mumble, adding her order into the computer system. "That'll be $4.55." She taps her phone on the Square reader, and I trip over *literally nothing* as I go to make her drink. Gavin recognizes my nervous energy as a bad case of starstruck and approaches me as I grind the coffee beans. He grabs the portafilter and pops it into the espresso machine, pressing the button to start the extraction process.

"You okay?" he whispers with concern.

"*That's Brittany Oliver,*" I whisper through the side of my mouth.

He opens his eyes wide and mimics my side mouth speaking by saying, "*Yeah, so?*"

"She's a star on *Broadway,*" I hiss.

"I know who she is," he says with a quick laugh. "She comes in here every day for her coffee, Sunshine. You'd better get used to it."

My anxious thoughts become distracted by his words. *Sunshine.* He's already given me a nickname. We're becoming friends, and it makes me so happy because Lord knows I need friends in this crazy city. I give him a sappy smile, to which he responds with a sneer. He then pours the espresso into a cup filled with water and ice and hands it to me. I clutch the plastic cup, doing my best not to crush it as I keep my hands from shaking violently.

"Here's your Americano," I say and successfully pass the drink over the counter.

*Nailed it.*

"Are you Brittany Oliver?" The words tumble out of my mouth like vomit.

"I am," she says smugly.

"You are such an inspiration to me. It is an honor to serve you your coffee."

*What am I, a robot? What's happening to me?*

"Thanks so much," she says with a wrinkled brow and uncomfortable grin. "Well, I'd best be off. It was nice to meet you, Sunday."

For a moment, I'm shaken because she can't possibly know my name, only to look down at my chest and remember that I'm wearing a name tag.

"You too!" I say a little too loudly and feel my ears go red. Gavin is laughing at me indiscreetly. I turn toward him with a scowl. But as my embarrassment slowly disintegrates, joy comes over me because it's only been a little over twenty-four hours in New York City, and I've already encountered one of today's biggest Broadway stars.

*Who else will I meet here?*

# TWO

**H**ow was your first full day?" Finn asks as I close the apartment door behind me and place my grocery bags on the counter.

I let out a happy sigh. "It was the best."

I tell her about meeting Brittany Oliver, bonding with Gavin, and wandering around the streets of Brooklyn. After my shift, I spent two hours passing by different offices, parks, and storefronts with a huge smile adorning my lips. A woman with piercings in places on her face I didn't even think it was possible to pierce saw me, and to my surprise, she smiled back. It seems she understood, to some degree, the love I have for this city.

"I'm about to put on a movie if you'd like to join," Finn says.

"I'd love that. Go ahead and start, and I'll join in a few."

I first need to rid myself of the sweat and stale coffee smell, so after hopping in the steamy shower and scrubbing my body squeaky clean, I change into my pajamas, take my dinner out of the to-go containers and sit on the couch, elevating my sore feet on a chair.

Finn starts the movie, and a vaguely familiar—and quite handsome—face fills the screen. I quickly Google the flick to recall the actor's name.

*Tyler Axel.*

The webpage says he's an avid theater performer, currently starring as the male lead in *Belle Époque* on Broadway alongside Brittany Oliver. My eyes widen.

"Ohmagosh!" I say with a mouth full of Pad Thai as I point at the screen with my chopstick. "That's Brittany's costar!"

"Really?" Finn laughs. "I just watched a preview and thought he looked cute, so I put it on."

"He is *very* cute."

As he graces the screen, I find myself becoming less and less interested in the movie's storyline and more transfixed by Tyler's gorgeous exterior. He is lean but muscular with sandy blond hair that swoops down over his right eyebrow, much like Hugh Grant's in *Notting Hill.* His jaw is somehow strong and sharp, but elegant. Every time he smiles, these adorable wrinkle lines appear near his lips and eyes. He is the very essence of a classically handsome man, but not only that, God graced him even further by giving him eyes that look like two ocean orbs—not like the murky waters of the Atlantic as it crashes upon the New England beaches, but like the Mediterranean Sea—clear and light. They draw you in like a sailor to a siren.

The movie is a coming-of-age story about two friends who grew up together in their neighboring summer lake homes. The timelines switch back and forth from young to old—Tyler is the older version of the male character, and Poppy Zerbo is his era's lover.

I find myself on the edge of my seat toward the end of the film, praying for a happy ending for the two. But instead, they part ways, much to my dismay. I have always been known to despise a sad ending. Why put so much effort into something if it's not going to end happily?

The movie flashes forward, and Tyler has found another partner he has married, while Poppy stays single, pursuing her dreams of teaching young students in Africa.

Once the credits roll, Finn turns to me with a sleepy look and says, "I liked it."

"Eh," I say with slumped shoulders as I slide further down into the couch. "Wasn't my cup of tea. But," I lift a finger, "I *loved* him." I groan, and we both laugh.

A short silence falls between us, and I play with one of the tassels on the pillow beside me before quietly saying, "It's sort of crazy to think that he lives in New York too."

"Oh, I know," Finn remarks and adjusts herself upright on the couch. "I have yet to get used to walking the same streets as some of the most famous people on earth."

"Yeah," I say with a small sigh. "The closest we got back in my hometown to a celebrity sighting was when John Mayer's tour bus drove through to get to his show in Boston that night."

"Back in Pennsylvania, I was lucky if I saw anyone other than a cow on the weekends," Finn says, and we laugh together.

After chatting a bit more, we split into our individual rooms. I'm combing my hair to get ready for bed when I see my phone light up from the corner of my eye. Walking over to my nightstand where it lies charging, I read what it says, and my heart starts to race.

**You've just won two tickets to Belle Époque! Click here to claim your prize.**

*Oh, my gosh. My lottery entries have come through for me.*

"HOLY CRAP!" I scream as I charge out of my room. I stumble toward Finn's and rap on her door.

"What's up?" She peeks through the crack, clearly in the middle of her skincare routine, with a poofy headband pulling the hair away from her forehead and a shiny liquid dripping down her face. Her expression carries a slight concern, as though she's still in the process of sizing me up and wondering just how often I let loose with an outburst.

"I just won two tickets to *Belle Époque* for tomorrow night!"

I glance back at my phone, ensuring I read it right, before lifting my gaze to Finn with a nervous grin. As I quickly filter through the list of friends I have in New York, besides Gavin, Finn is at the top. "Do you want to go with me?"

"Really?" She smiles. "That would be fun. I'm in." Finn is much less enthusiastic than I am, but still, her tone shows a sort of excitement. She rubs her hands together, and I'm not sure if she's scheming or warming the excess lotion that remains on her palms before she says, "Now we get to see Tyler Axel in the flesh and find out if his eyes are that blue or if it was all just movie magic."

"If our seats are close enough to see his eyes, that'll be magic in itself," I chortle.

My heart settles back in my room and pumps again to its normal rhythm. I finish getting ready for bed and drift off to sleep before dreaming—borderline nightmare-ing—about being asked to perform in *Belle Époque* midway through the performance when Brittany Oliver doesn't show up for the second act. My dream confidence gets the better of me, and I know I can save the day. As the actors on stage scramble, I daringly get up from my seat and approach the door to the backstage area. The first obstacle is navigating through the unexpected maze ahead of me. Hundreds of doors are scattered in the area, making it nearly impossible to pick the correct one that leads center stage. After choosing one option, I find myself in the rafters, looking down on the audience from above.

*Well, this isn't right.*

But of course, as dreams do, it plops me on stage without my brain questioning how I got there.

Then I'm face-to-face with none other than Tyler Axel. It's the moment for our final duet. As the pianist begins the intro, all the lyrics escape my mind. I try to speak, but nothing comes out. I can feel fear and embarrassment trying to settle into my bones, but something about being near Tyler makes it all okay.

He sings his portion of the song, and the lyrics are beautiful even though they make absolutely no sense. Tyler walks toward me, grabs my hand, and spins me into a dip. I'm staring into his eyes and feel happiness burst in me like a spring. As he leans in, I pucker my lips and close my eyes…

*BEEP BEEP BEEP.*

My alarm jolts me awake.

*Classic.*

"Are you kidding me?" I say while slapping my phone to shut off the alarm. I slide my comforter back over my head to escape reality. Everything in me wants to pull an *Inception*, throwing myself back into the dream, but instead, I start my day and let the dream end there—unfinished but also wholly unrealistic.

I need *something* to get my mind off the show tonight, or else I'll go stir-crazy in our apartment, so I venture to a free dance class I saw an ad for on one of the telephone poles during my wanderings yesterday. And though it seemed sketchy to trust a pinned-up piece of paper on a pole for a free class, I took the risk anyway—but not before telling Finn the exact location I would be going to and clarifying, "If I don't come back before the show, something has gone terribly wrong."

When I arrive, my first reaction is satisfaction because it does look like a legitimate—and non-sketchy—class. But then I notice that everyone is chatting away in small groups. My stomach drops before I'm entirely through the doors.

*They all know each other.*

While most theater kids grow up to become extroverts who can small-talk their way through any and every awkward situation, this girl cannot. And this dance class is an introvert's worst nightmare.

I find a place to sit and change out of my street shoes into my LaDuca dance shoes while talking myself into walking up to the most friendly-looking group to introduce myself.

"Hey," I say, trying my best to find a break in their conversation but also not allowing myself to stand there without saying anything like a *weirdo*. "I'm new here. My name is Sunday."

"Hi!" a shorter, blond boy with a big grin says to me and holds his hand out to shake mine. "I'm Jacob. I'm the instructor this morning."

He takes the time to introduce me to the rest of the group. There is Rachel, a brown-haired, blue-eyed girl wearing what looks to be an art smock and cargo pants, but she pulls it off nicely. Shelly, a tall girl with glasses, smiles shyly as she shakes my hand. And Lucas, a dark-skinned, incredibly handsome man with hundreds of freckles and the most fascinating eyes that I've ever seen. They're emerald green.

Everyone is surprisingly welcoming, asking me where I'm from and how long I've been dancing.

"I've taken a decent amount of dance classes just because I love musical theater," I say while trying to split my eye contact between a few people in the group, "but I'm definitely more of a singer, actress type."

Jacob's face lights up while Lucas raises a hand in a high five, saying, "Nice. So you suck at dancing too!"

I slap his palm with a confused look, surprised by his blunt nature.

"I'm just friends with all these guys," Lucas says, "so I come to these classes to hang, but I'm beyond awful at dancing."

I let out a small giggle. "Well, you don't have to worry about being the worst today. I'm sure I have you beat."

"I'm excited to watch," he says with a charming grin. I feel my cheeks flush.

We start with warm-up stretches, following Jacobs's lead. Rachel stands in the space next to me, and while we're bent over, stretching our legs, she peers through her own and gives me a wave and a smile.

"This is a fine time to talk, right?" she whispers, still glancing through our legs.

"No, it's perfectly normal." I smile, feeling all the blood rushing to my lips from our hunched position. We stand up straight, following Jacob, who begins doing pliés.

Mimicking his moves, Rachel says, "Okay, so you're into theater. Tell me, what is your current favorite Broadway show?"

Bobbing up and down in the pliés, I scrunch my brow. "That is the toughest question anyone has asked me." I let out a small laugh. It takes me a few seconds to give her an accurate answer. "Currently, I'd say because of my soft spot for Lin-Manuel Miranda, it has to be *Hamilton*. But it changes on the daily."

"Yes, *Hamilton* is amazing! I auditioned to be a dancer in the tour."

"No way," I beam.

"Yes, way. I didn't get the part, but I had loads of fun learning the few dance numbers they taught us."

"That's amazing. I'm going to see a new show tonight, so I'll let you know how it is," I say.

"Which one?"

"*Belle Époque.*"

Her face lights up. "My friend is in that one. One of the ensemble members." Rachel gracefully places her arms in front of her in a big oval, just as Jacob does. I follow suit and feel like I'm hugging a sequoia tree rather than doing an elegant ballet move.

"It's a great show—you'll have a blast," Rachel says. "And it might even end up being your favorite." She winks.

Jacob grabs our attention after being adequately warmed and shows us the routine we'll learn. I'm grateful Rachel is by my side because the combination is not coming quickly. I find myself glancing at her often as a frame of reference for what I should be doing instead of the flailing my arms and legs seem to default to.

As I look around the room, I can see that all the other dancers—including Lucas, who assured me he was wretched at dancing—are doing just fine with the routine. In a moment of pure panic, I hear Rachel whisper, "Can I help you fix your attitude?"

The color drains from my face. I *am* annoyed, but I didn't think anyone else would notice.

"What?" I say, and my voice shakes.

*Well, there goes all the effort I put into making new friends today.*

"I'm sorry... I didn't mean—" I start.

"Your attitude," she says with a smile, and suddenly her expression turns horrified. "OH MY GOSH! I meant the turn! That's the name of the move you're doing."

"Oh!" I laugh and wipe my brow clean of the sweat that has formed from the exertion of dancing and the last moments of utter terror. "Thank goodness. I thought you could tell I was getting upset."

"I'm so sorry. I just wanted to see if you needed help," she says with a giggle.

My heart settles. "That would be fantastic."

Rachel takes the time to show me where my feet should be positioned, and once in place, I attempt the turn again. It feels much smoother and looks a lot cleaner from what I can see in the mirror.

"Great! Yes, that's exactly it," Rachel says with a clap and encouraging smile.

"Thank you. It does feel a lot easier." I continue to do the movement and then say with an embarrassed laugh, "I'm not much of a dancer."

"You're doing great. Jacob puts these classes on every other week—you should keep coming back, and you'll be an expert in no time."

Jacob announces that we'll take a five-minute water break. Rachel walks with me to a bench at the side of the room where our bags lay. As I take a large gulp of water, she says, "I know it's hard to find friends in the city—if you ever want to go out to coffee or grab a bite to eat, I'd love to do that with you."

I grin and nod, still catching my breath from the movements prior. We exchange numbers and then return to our final dance run-through. And my attitude—I must say—is magnificent.

While rummaging through my closet later that night, I realize that my Connecticut style needs to translate better in New York City. Now that I'm here, I want to be bold with my fashion choices—literally and figuratively stepping into what I've always wanted to wear but have been too apprehensive about attempting back home. There's no better place than New York to try the outrageous, and tonight at *Belle Époque*, I want to look my best.

After slipping in and out of multiple outfits, tossing them all to the side, I settle on a white, puffy-sleeve, baby doll dress that I would typically wear with neutral sneakers, but this time, I pair it with black combat boots. Like New York City fashion training wheels—a little at a time.

I curl my hair and part it in the middle, yet another change from my Connecticut-appropriate side part, and let my dark, beachy waves fall to the center of my back. My makeup is natural, minus the dramatic wing-tipped eyeliner I meticulously painted on. I finish the look with minimal gold jewelry and wait in the living room for Finn to finish getting ready herself.

She emerges from her room with high-waisted, wide-legged pants made out of a shiny, silver material that I've never seen used as pants before and a black crop-top tank. She's been in the city for over a year, and her Pennsylvania fashion roots have clearly vanished. She looks *ridiculously* cool. Her hair is in a top knot, and her eyelids have purple glitter tastefully placed on them. I'm not sure if we're in the friendship zone of borrowing clothes just yet, but after telling her I love her pants, I secretly hope she'll let me wear them one day.

"Thank you. They're Manière de Voir," she says and spins around so I can see them from all angles.

"Oh?" I say with raised eyebrows because I'm not sure whether she's referring to the company or the designer's name. I nod and smile.

We take the train from Brooklyn and transfer at 8th Avenue, so we're brought right into the heart of Times Square. After snapping a few selfies together under the giant LED screens that fill the sky and grabbing a quick bite to eat, we go to the box office to pick up our tickets.

"How can I help you?" the box office attendee asks.

"Hi, I won the lottery tickets for tonight's show. They're under the name, 'Sunday Truelove.'"

"Well, congratulations," he says with a kind smile, but his eyes show disinterest. "May I see your I.D., please?"

I dig through my purse and pull out my I.D., sliding it through the half-circle hole between us.

He takes a few moments to study it before returning it and finding our tickets in the small stack behind him.

"Here you go, Sunday," he says as he passes the tickets through the hole. Then he slides his glasses down to the bridge of his nose and gives us a lopsided smirk before saying, "You two are in for a real treat tonight. Enjoy the show."

I can't tell if he's borderline creepy or alluding to the glory of what we're about to witness, so I quickly say, "Thank you so much. Have a good night." We hurriedly step out the door.

On the street, a line of antsy theater fans waits for the doors to open. Glancing around the queue, you can see women in full ball gowns, some in jeans and t-shirts, and others in cosplay costumes of characters from the show. Most look like they can't contain their excitement—bouncing on their feet and speaking loudly with giant grins—while others look like they may have been dragged here by their friends or significant others.

As I make eye contact with one particularly bored-looking individual, I wonder how anyone could dread a night at the theater.

When you step foot into a Broadway show, your entire being is transported to a new world. This phenomenon occasionally happens when you watch an engaging movie or get sucked into a thrilling book, but Broadway *fully* envelops you. While you settle into your seat, you become as much a part of the story as the actors on stage. You can't pause or rewind the story—you're living in it. Once the show is over, the realization that you're simply in a historic building in Midtown Manhattan hits you. But, for those two-plus hours, you are in Paris, or the Underworld, or Oz, surrounded by people from all walks of life and backgrounds, encountering the same story as one body. It's marvelous, and simply thinking about it makes my excitement grow even greater for tonight.

While the line moves ahead, we shuffle along the street, getting closer to the doors. I glance at our tickets to see where we'll be sitting.

"That's odd," I say to Finn. "It doesn't say any seat numbers on here, only 'Gem Seating.'"

"Oh, that is weird," she responds.

"Well," I look up toward the front of the line. "Whatever 'Gem Seating' is, I hope it has a good view."

# THREE

**O**nce our tickets are scanned, we're filtered into the noisy lobby.

"Wanna grab a drink before we head in?" Finn shouts in my ear over the loud chatter around us.

"Yes," I say and nod as well in case she doesn't hear me. Getting to the bar is no easy feat. We weave in and around hundreds of people. Attempting not to lose one another, I grab Finn's hand halfway through our journey until we finally reach the counter.

The menu is short and sweet, but some specialty *Belle Époque* drinks catch my eye. Finn orders the Bordeaux wine while I pick the drink labeled "The Cerulean Night." It's a bright blue-colored champagne with edible silver sparkles floating at the surface. I sigh at the first sip; grateful it's delicious because I will have to work an extra shift at the coffee shop just to compensate for the astronomical price.

While we're mingling in the lobby and enjoying our exorbitant drinks, the ushers posted in front of the auditorium doors swing open the entrances with a smile. Dazzling violet lights spill into the lobby, flooding our vision, and we join the crowd making their way through the aisles.

Everywhere you look, there is beauty and design. From the indigo velvet cushions to the swooping string lights placed delicately on the ceiling. At the front of the stage hangs a large sign of the show's name that twinkles with shimmering lights. A realistic Eiffel Tower stands to the right of the sign, while the Arc de Triomphe is to its left, making you feel as though you've just apparated to France. An eerie yet upbeat instrumental song booms throughout the theater, so much so that I can feel it reverberating inside my chest cavity, my heart thumping to the beat.

We walk to the nearest usher to help us find our seats. A plump man in a black suit with a bright red head of curls grins in our direction before welcoming us to the show. We hand him our tickets, and his face brightens even more after seeing our seat assignments.

"Oh! Gem Seating. My favorite seats in the house. Follow me, please." With a slight bow, he turns and begins to waddle forward, guiding us to our section. We walk past every row until we're directly in front of the stage.

"This is where you'll be sitting." The usher gestures to two seats with a decorated table nestled inches from the stage's edge. My jaw drops. Looking at Finn, she is just as shocked. Our usher gives us a funny look before continuing. "Originally, this is where the orchestra pit would be. But because of the immersive nature of our show, the creators arranged this seating for some lucky audience members. You will be a part of the performance, so please don't stand at any point during the show. Enjoy!" Smiling, he hands us our Playbills and heads back up through the rows.

"Woah," Finn and I both say in unison and laugh.

"This is insane," I say, sitting in my seat and putting my drink on the table before us. Only three tables are in this section; another two girls sit to our right, and an older couple comes into the row directly behind ours, filling the remaining seats.

"Tight squeeze, innit, girls?" the woman says with a thick British accent.

I laugh, "Worth the view, though! Is this your first time seeing the show?"

"It's not. We were here on opening night. First time in these seats. How about yourselves?"

"We haven't seen it," I say. "Wow, opening night—that must've been fun."

"It was," she laughs. "Our son is actually in the show, so we come when we can to support him."

"That's wonderful. Which one is he?" I ask while flipping my Playbill to the cast members' page and handing it to her. "I'll keep an eye out for him."

"He plays Samuel," she says and points to his picture.

"But we usually call him Tyler," the older gentleman says with a mighty dad laugh if I ever heard one—I join him in laughing, and then my laugh slowly falters because he just said *Tyler.*

*I'm talking with Tyler Axel's parents.*

"Oh wow!" I try not to sound too shocked. "It's so nice to meet you both. Your son is incredibly talented."

"Thank you," they both say humbly. I turn to Finn and look at her sideways. Before I can say anything about having just communicated with Tyler Axel's parents, I'm interrupted by the lights suddenly dimming and the music dissipating. Everyone in the crowd goes quiet while a spotlight emerges in the far-left corner of the stage.

Tyler Axel appears out of nowhere, and the crowd comes alive, cheering and applauding. My mouth has become slightly ajar at the sight of him. I hurriedly snap it shut, hoping he hasn't noticed.

He is even more handsome in person than any movie or interview could capture. A green velvet suit jacket curves around his chest and arms, hitting all the right places. A small ascot is tied around his cleanly shaven neck. The high-waisted, Parisian-era-appropriate pants hug his thighs so tightly that I wonder if they have ever split in the show. His hair looks as though his routine is simply raking his slender but strong hands through it, which *works*. One piece gently curls on his forehead as though he's Clark Kent, ready and willing to catch any lightheaded lady that may faint before his magnificent exterior.

He towers above Finn and me while he cracks a small grin for the relentlessly cheering crowd. We're close enough to see the overused parts around his eyes and mouth crinkle into charming lines, and my heart skips a beat.

Without shifting from his place, he stands there, waiting for the noise to cease. After a few moments, he gracefully walks across the front of the stage. All eyes are on him. No one is making a sound. Finn and I look up as he glides right past us, but he doesn't look at anyone—his eyes are fixed on the floor he walks upon. I feel the breeze of him as he passes, and it smells faintly of musk and something else I can't put my finger on.

*These are some fantastic seats.*

Once he makes it entirely across the stage, he pauses. Turning his body toward the audience, Tyler begins to sing the lyrics of the opening number. Suddenly, the lights come up, and the rest of the cast joins him, singing and dancing in an epic mashup of modern-day pop songs.

The show has begun.

It's even better than I could have dreamed, and thank the Lord it's not like my actual dreams, or else I'd be up in the rafters. The dancers jump onto our table during one of the numbers set in the city's local bar, and they sing directly at us—inviting the whole audience to join in. At this range, I can see the lingering marks of lipstick on previously kissed cheeks, scuffs on shoes, and slightly ripped fishnet stockings stretched over strong dancers' legs.

During the show, I can't help but think about Tyler's parents behind us and how proud they must be of their son. His voice is stunning, and he leads the cast with great passion. The talent he displays throughout the story using different vibratos and purposeful cracks in his voice is inspiring and emotion-provoking. Tyler makes you feel like you are witnessing his *actual l*ove story unfold right before you.

His love interest, Brittany, otherwise known as my coffee buddy, is equally as intoxicating. Her voice is angelic, but you can sense turmoil underneath it. Like she knows their story is not going to end well.

Together, their stage chemistry is breathtaking; I find myself wondering whether they are a couple in the real world because keeping your eyes off them is downright impossible.

At one point, Brittany glances at me, and I can see a slight smirk form on her lips as though she knows who I am. It may have been a trick of the light, but I could swear she recognized me. Many of the other actors make eye contact with me as well. It's a sort of thank you from them as though they're saying, *I see you, and I'm so glad you're here.* One of the only people whose gaze eludes me is Tyler. He is so focused on his character's story that I don't blame him for missing me sitting at his feet.

The first act flies by and concludes with a mashup of love songs between Tyler and Brittany. The stage somehow transforms into a believable night sky; a haze billows across the floor while the string lights I noticed earlier take on the appearance of stars hanging from the heavens. While the magnetic couple dance and sing together above the clouds, I drift along with them. It is *magical.*

Tyler spins Brittany into a dip and kisses her passionately before the curtain comes down in front of them, and the crowd breaks into thundering applause. Moments later, the house lights come back on, and Finn and I stare at each other with mouths wide open.

"That was amazing," she says.

"Agreed," I respond. "And I know it sounds weird, but I love that we are close enough to see them spit." We both laugh.

"No, I understand. It's cool that we can see every little nuance of emotion this close." I nod. "What was your favorite part so far?" she asks me.

"Oh, my goodness, how do I even narrow it down?" It takes me a moment to process, mentally thumbing through the scenes of act one. "It has to be the song by Samuel's friend, Antoine, toward the beginning about embracing your uniqueness—a mashup of—what was it... *Born This Way* and *The Middle* by Jimmy Eat World? The songs fit perfectly with their storyline and were so creative. But the last song was incredible too. There were so many good pop songs hidden in there. And how the stage transformed...it was just magical." I get lost in the magic of it again before remembering to ask Finn about her favorite scene. She was equally enthralled with the closing number of act one and comments on the precision of each dancer.

"They make it look so effortless," she says.

We get up and stretch our legs in preparation for the second act. Tyler's parents return to their seats behind us with freshly made drinks from the bar.

"So, what do you think?" his mom asks me as she settles back into her chair.

I look at her with the biggest grin. "If I were you, I'd be here every night."

"She would be if we lived closer!" the dad says, and we all laugh.

"I'm just so proud of him," she says, getting teary-eyed. "He's been dreaming about this since high school and has worked his squishy bum off to get here," she laughs, seemingly attempting to lighten up the emotional sentiment with humor. "It's the most amazing treat for a mother to witness her kids doing what they love."

"He is amazing," I say with an outstretched arm and a squeeze of her hand. She smiles back, all warmth and familiarity despite the fact that we are perfect strangers. "And I'm sure he's so thankful to have such caring parents supporting him."

The lights flicker in the house, indicating it's about time for the show's final act. Finn and I turn our bodies toward the stage. Moments later, the curtain comes up, the cast emerges from the wings, and music bursts out of nowhere.

We're back to the late 1800s in Paris.

I didn't think it was possible, but the second act is panning out to be even better than the first. The first number absolutely blows me away, with a mashup of *I Got a Feeling* and *Don't Stop Me Now*. The ensemble members' tattered dresses as they dance in the makeshift streets are beyond colorful and bright, juxtaposing the joy and freedom the characters feel inwardly with the reality of their outer world. The meticulous choreography of the ensemble, mixed with the impeccable lighting and stage design tempts me to purchase tickets for the next show just so I can watch it all again. I don't want to miss a moment, but my eyes can only take in so much.

And who knew Katy Perry's songs could be relevant in 1879? I'm on the edge of my seat during each number, becoming increasingly disappointed as each moment passes. I know the ending is mere minutes away, invading the timelessness that has enchanted me for the last two hours.

While the storyline is full of hope initially, things take a turn shortly after act two begins. Barricades are attacked, fighting grows to a relentless crescendo, and it's become clear that no one is making it out of here alive. My heart stings for the characters as though they didn't just enter my life mere hours ago.

Brittany and Tyler finish singing their final duet together in an epic number where the dancers leap and move across the stage behind them. The stage takes on a dreamlike quality, shifting hazily away from any war scenery and back into the stars as if they were already crossing the line into heaven.

The swell of music is interrupted by a sudden *bang* that makes me jump in my seat. A harsh silence comes upon the crowd as Brittany stumbles across the floor and falls into Tyler's arms. The orchestra softly plays, and the couple gracefully descend to the ground together, inches from Finn and me. We're both glued to the scene, unblinking and barely breathing. I can see a light sweat glittering on Tyler's forehead as his character grapples with the reality of the situation. His love has been shot and is dying in his arms—his other half quickly fading, along with the entire world they built together.

They look into each other's eyes, clinging to their last moments together. Éléanor attempts to sing her final line to Samuel, but before she can finish, her body goes limp, and she fades into eternity. There are a few gasps in the audience and quiet sobs, but then it becomes so quiet you could hear a pin drop. All that is audible in the entire theater is the weeping that escapes from Tyler's lips.

I can see every emotion playing out on his body and face. Disbelief. Realization. Pain. His veins protrude from his neck and on his hairy blond forearms. Goosebumps emerge on my own arms as I watch him cry out in mourning.

Tyler rests his chin atop Brittany's head with closed eyes as he rocks her body back and forth. Tears stream down his face, lightly wetting her own cheeks. Several agonizing moments pass like this until he slowly but attentively lifts his head from her.

But as he opens his eyes, he doesn't glance at the ceiling or the Mezzanine.

He looks at me.

*Oh, my gosh.*

*He's staring at me.*

Tyler's dazzling blue eyes look directly into mine. My heart begins to race, and my hands feel numb, but I don't dare move a muscle or even blink. I will not risk the loss of this moment.

Time is suspended. Everything slows down. The scenery and the audience around us become unfocused and fade from view. Colors I've never quite imagined or seen before illuminate in his gaze. It feels like I'm spinning, but somehow Tyler's presence keeps me steady.

*Am I dreaming? Did I die? No, this is happening.*

My heart thumps so rapidly that I wonder if he can see it pulsating through my white dress. But I keep his gaze. I feel a look of surprise mingled with innocence on my expression. His face is soft, and his eyes show a tinge of joyfulness even in this horrific stage scene.

He has chosen to look at *me*. Not the ceiling or another person. Me. But there's something more to this than a simple stare. His eyes glint in a way I can't quite understand. This inexplicable connection is small but mighty, becoming more concrete with every passing moment. I sense a tug from him on the other side, and a visceral part of me begins to stir.

Little flecks of blue dance in his iris. And suddenly, it feels like we're floating hundreds of feet above everything surrounding us— just Tyler and me in the sky. We're flying above the mountaintops. The clouds hold us up with them as the brilliant stars shine and flicker around us. We brush them with our fingertips.

I can't help but notice that this place feels like home. It's as if this moment is where we were always meant to be—meant to *live*. Way up here. In the sky. Just how long can we stay in this reverie together?

This is euphoria. This is magic. He has taken this moment to notice me, and it's as though I am fully seen for the first time.

Then, without blinking or diverting his gaze from mine, Tyler softly begins to sing.

He sings to me.

"*My life is full of wonder…all because of you.*"

And the stage goes black.

# FOUR

Finn punches me lightly in the arm after seeing what just unfolded. I stare back at her, completely dumbfounded—one of my eyes might even be twitching. The lights come back up, showing the true extent of our surprise. My heart thumps in my ears, and my cheeks are like the sun's surface. Everything feels like a blur of motion and splotchy colors as the ensemble members take center stage. The outro music fades in and out of my ears as though I'm underwater.

*What on earth just happened? I think I'm in shock.*

The cast bows, and Finn and I rise, joining the rest of the audience in a standing ovation. The ensemble members are feet from us with bright smiles, but my only focus is on the last five minutes of my life.

That is until Tyler and Brittany emerge, walking hand in hand out of the sliding doors that open quickly at the back of the stage. I'm watching Tyler's every move as he steps forward, hoping for another millisecond of his gaze to come across my line of view. I wish I were telekinetic so I could lure his eyes to mine. But he doesn't look back.

He takes his bow by placing a hand on his belly, lurching forward with that beautiful head of hair flopping to and fro and then popping back up. The audience members go ballistic, screaming, and applauding, and a few women scream, "I love you!" He mouths, "Thank you," and then steps back for Brittany to take her bow. With as much effort as possible, he is like one of *The Price is Right* models, honoring Brittany with his arms outstretched. Her bow is much more stylistic and fluid. She curtsies, and the crowd goes just as wild as it did for Tyler.

After the cast dances on stage for a few more moments, celebrating another show, they all exit one after the other. Tyler doesn't acknowledge me again but simply walks off in a strut that melts my insides before running a hand through his hair with a heart-stopping smile toward the mezzanine. I keep my eyes fixed on him until he disappears behind the curtain.

I didn't think it was possible to miss someone you'd never met, but that's the exact sensation I feel with this man who has just flipped my world upside down.

Finn and I turn toward one another, finally able to unleash what has been bubbling inside us for the last ten minutes.

"THAT WAS INSANE," I say to her, grabbing her shoulders and shaking her gently.

She looks at me astonished before saying, "Sunday, he *serenaded* you."

"I know," I squeal, but suddenly, I'm hit with the thought that maybe it was just an accident—like my big head just so happened to be where his eyesight landed. Or maybe he just does this in every show with whoever sits in this seat.

"Do you think he meant to?" I ask.

Finn gives me a funny look. "Definitely. It was way too intense—and intentional—to be an accident."

As we're talking, I remember that Tyler's parents are *directly* behind us, and we're being the opposite of chill with our conversation and expressions. My neck flushes with embarrassment, but as I turn to look at them, the seats are empty. I see his mom walking up the aisle; she turns to me, smiling, almost as though she knows what happened between her son and me. I return the gesture and bring my attention back to Finn.

"I don't even know what to say. That was the best moment of my life *by far,*" I laugh and shake my head in surprise. "I hope I wasn't drooling. He must've thought I looked like a complete idiot." I reenact an exaggerated version of how I felt. Mouth agape, eyes glazed over, head slightly tilted to the right.

"No, I'm sure you looked fine," she giggles. "You really should DM him or something. He clearly thought you were cute."

"I don't know about that," I say nervously.

We reminisce on act two's different songs and dances as we walk through the theater, exit the side doors, and find ourselves back on the street. For a moment, we contemplate meeting the actors at the stage door, but Finn and I both have early mornings with work, so instead, we walk back to the subway—satisfied by the truly magical night.

Opening the Notes app on my phone that houses my bucket list, I type in a new line, "Sing with Tyler Axel." Though it's far-fetched, there's never been a more probable time than the present for this new bucket list item to be checked off, seeing as though I'm roaming the same streets as him each day.

As I slip into bed, I close my eyes, and I'm brought back to my front-row seat in the theater. I try my best to recount every detail to not forget. I visualize myself in front of Tyler. His dazzling blue eyes stare into my soul with a glimmer of joy during such a tragic stage scene. His expression of sadness juxtaposes my wonder and delight. The noise fades around us as he continues gazing. And then he opens his mouth and sings to me. This line will stay with me forever.

*My life is full of wonder, all because of you.*

Falling asleep is easy.

My alarm goes off at 4:45 a.m. the following day, and I grunt until I remember my magical night and cheer up instantly. It's still dark out, though the streetlights stream in brightly as I pull open my blackout curtains. I can see people walking down the street—probably coming home from a long night out on the town.

I dress for my shift, devour breakfast, and head out the door.

Gavin is on with me again, opening the shop. We brew coffee, restock straws and cups, and put various kinds of milk on the counter for customers to use.

"Gavin, you have to hear what happened to me last night," I say as we pull chairs off the tables and set them right-side-up on the ground.

Once I share the whole story with him, he says, "Saucy," with a silly grin.

*Not exactly the reaction I was expecting.*

"Gavin, do you realize what this means?!" I ask.

"Uh, no?"

"WELL, NEITHER DO I!" I shout at the ceiling playfully.

He laughs at me, shouting, "WELL, THIS IS A PREDICAMENT!"

I've only known Gavin for a short amount of time, but I know he understands me. He hasn't judged me so far for being weird or quirky. I'm accepted in his eyes, and that is the best feeling.

We settle down from our silliness, and he asks, "Were you able to get his digits at the stage door?"

"No, we didn't stay," I respond while dusting off one of the seats with stuck-on crumbs from the day before.

He stops in his tracks, "What?! Sunday, what if he went out hoping you'd be there?"

"I knew I had to wake up early for work, so I didn't think it'd be a good idea!" I cry defensively.

"You should know by now that people barely sleep in New York. They go out and don't get in until 5 a.m., only to wake up for work at 8."

He *is* right. I still haven't acclimated to the New York sleep schedule because I greatly appreciate my rest. It's not natural to only get a few hours each night!

"I know, I know," I respond, rolling my eyes. "Well, if we're meant to be together, I trust our paths will cross again."

"Yes, in a city of eight and a half million, you'll definitely bump into him soon," he winks.

I look at him with a side-eyed glance and laugh before we finish setting up the shop.

At around 9:30 a.m., the place is bustling with people working remotely or having a coffee date with friends. Chatter fills the room while Gavin and I weave around one another, making drinks and warming up various baked goods for people to enjoy on their morning commutes.

Brittany Oliver walks up to the counter. She looks hip as ever in a flowy green dress with high-top Nikes and a jean jacket. Gavin is at the register when she places her order, but I can't help weaseling my way into their conversation.

"That'll be $10.95. When you're ready, you can—"

"Hi, Brittany!" I interrupt, and Gavin jumps slightly, giving me an annoyed look. I peek at her order on the screen and begin taking over for Gavin to make her Americano.

"Hi there," she responds politely.

"I went to your show last night!" I call over my shoulder as I get the espresso ready.

"Oh, how fun," she says, unamused.

I note her indifference but continue speaking anyway. "It was magical. I've never seen a show that close before. I'm not sure if you saw me—it's okay if you didn't—but I was in the Gem Seating."

My hands are shaking, perhaps from sampling the different coffees or simply the pure adrenaline one gets when talking with a celebrity.

"I thought I recognized you," she smirks. "I'm glad you enjoyed it."

There is a tone of mystery that exudes from her voice. It makes me wonder if she knows what happened between Tyler and me.

*But she couldn't. Her eyes were closed. She was dead!*

"Oh, *she enjoyed it, alright*—" Gavin says as he waggles his eyebrows. I elbow him in the ribs, and he makes an "oomph" sound.

"Don't mind him," I say with embarrassment. "You were incredible. I'm grateful to have seen the show from that angle. It was a once-in-a-lifetime night."

We stand there for a moment in silence, and I realize I've been holding her completed Americano without handing it over. She gives Gavin an irritated look as though she's telling him, *Get this weirdo to hand me my coffee so I can leave.*

He understands and slowly takes the drink from my grasp before handing it over the counter to Brittany. She lifts the cup to "cheers" with a scrunched-up face, then turns from the counter and walks toward the door.

I feel like an imbecile for saying anything.

Once she's out of sight, Gavin asks, "What the heck was that about?"

"I don't know, but I don't think she likes me very much."

"I guess not, but did you have to elbow me?"

"I'm sorry. It just doesn't seem like she would care about what happened between Tyler and me. And besides, it's probably nothing," I say with an unintentional sigh.

"Well, to me, it seems like she knew what was up. She was clearly hiding something."

A shiver goes down my spine, knowing Gavin also sensed the mystery behind her voice.

*Maybe she does know something.*

Hours later, as I'm leaving my shift and walking the graffiti-covered, vibrant streets of Williamsburg back to my apartment, my phone lights up in my hand. Mick is FaceTiming me. I answer, and her sweaty face fills the screen.

"Sorry I'm so gross. I just got back from a run," she says.

I pop in my headphones and say, "No worries. How have you been?"

"Good! It's been weird not having you here. It's so…quiet," she says while smirking. I've always been a chatterbox. And if I'm not talking, I'm probably singing.

I laugh and say, "You miss me."

"I do. A lot. But I'm so glad you're there, going after your dreams."

"Aw, thanks, Mick. You're so sweet," I say with a pouted lip. "And speaking of dreams, I must tell you what happened to me. It's been a whirlwind."

Trying to recreate the story of last night with only words proves difficult. She doesn't understand the insanity it was at first until I clarify that stuff like that doesn't normally happen in shows. The actors usually just do their thing, singing and dancing. It's not an everyday occurrence that they stare into your eyes and sing directly to you.

"Wait, that's amazing," she says. "This could be the start of an epic love story."

"Oh my gosh, I don't think so," I say bashfully. "I'll probably never see him again!"

"You never know. Plus, most rom-coms are set in New York. It's the perfect backdrop for *romance*," she sighs.

My eyes roll, and I change the subject. "What about you? Any bites on the dating apps?"

"I matched with this guy Ben. He's a basketball player, and he's six-foot-nine. You know I like my men tall," she purrs.

"Wow. You'll always be able to find him in a crowd," I shrug. "Do you guys have any dates scheduled yet?"

"No, not yet. But he seems really sweet."

"That's so great. I'm excited for you!"

One of the beautiful parts about my friendship with Mick is that we can be serious one moment, supporting and loving one another, and then the next flow right back into being silly and teasing each other.

"You found a giant," I say, "and I'm crushing on a man who probably already forgot I exist. Things are looking up! Just like you'll have to do all night when you go on a date with Ben." I chuckle.

"Okay, enough with the tall jokes." Luckily, Mick finds it just as funny as I do.

After catching up a bit more, we say our goodbyes. As soon as we end the call, I'm hit hard with loneliness. Nobody knows me here like Mick does. If I spent the next week inside our apartment, I'm not sure anyone would notice a difference in their life—besides perhaps Gavin, who would question as to why I didn't come in for work.

While I walk the Brooklyn streets alone, heading back to an empty apartment because Finn is away for the night, rather than sulking in sadness, I actively change my situation. Rachel from my dance class comes to mind when I remember what she said about grabbing a meal or coffee. I shoot her a quick text before entering my apartment's lobby.

**Hey Rachel! It's Sunday. I wanted to see if you were up to anything tomorrow night.**

She responds almost immediately, writing back, **Nope! What are we doing? :)**

# FIVE

I text Gavin the following morning. **Hey! Wanna hook me up with two tickets to your show tonight?**

He responds a few minutes later. **You betcha!!! Meet me outside the theater at 6 pm, and I'll bring the goods.** He continues typing, **AKA the tickets ;)**

**Amazing! Looking forward to it.**

I text Rachel and tell her I've got a fun night in store for us. We meet before Gavin's show and have dinner at her favorite restaurant in the East Village, conveniently located down the street from the theater.

It's a molten lava day outside—almost one hundred degrees. And in a city where thousands of buildings keep the air from flowing freely, it feels about a thousand degrees.

Before I head out the door to meet Rachel, I slip into the most minimal clothing I can without looking too risqué. I choose a midi blue dress and tan sandals paired with a wide-brimmed hat, hoping to keep the sun from scorching my skin on the journey.

I find her waiting outside and notice she also has chosen the wear-as-little-as-possible option with a short pink and white striped dress with sneakers.

"You look so cute!" I call as we walk toward one another.

"Thank you," she curtsies with the hem of her dress in hand. "So do you."

We quickly hug, barely touching one another, but our arms still stick together with sweat. Laughing, she says, "New York summers. You never get used to them."

"They're no joke," I say with a wipe of my brow.

We turn and walk into the restaurant. Thankfully the A/C blasts the warmth right off of us, and we both let out a loud exhale of gratefulness, wiping off the cooled sweat that was stopped in its path as it dripped down our temples.

The hostess at the entrance smiles at us with a mouth full of braces and asks, "Table for two?"

I nod, and she continues her spiel, "Would you like to be seated inside or outsi—"

"INSIDE," Rachel and I both bark before she can finish. The hostess laughs and pulls out two menus from her station, motioning for us to follow.

The place is buzzing with locals and visitors alike. It's dark and ominous, but modern wallpaper and rich wood accents make it trendy and stylish.

As we open our menus, I pretend to scope out what I want, when in reality, I checked the menu last night after we made the reservations and picked out exactly what I'd be ordering.

"This all looks so good," I say.

"It really is. I'd highly recommend the enchilada—that's my favorite."

"Oh, yum!" This is the exact item I wanted because they have a vegan version and this dairy-intolerant, animal-loving girl can't eat much else on the menu. "That's definitely what I'm going to get," I say after fake perusing for a few more moments.

We both order margaritas—hers with salt on the rim and mine with sugar—and put our order in for the enchiladas.

After some small talk about our individual days, I ask her what brought her to the city.

"Dance," she says, and her eyes light up. "I moved here as soon as I turned eighteen to go to school for it." She tells me she just graduated from school and now teaches dance at a local studio while auditioning for different theater and dance companies.

"What about you?" she asks before sipping her margarita.

I tell her my dreams of Broadway and find it refreshing as we go deeper in the conversation to be in the company of people who are also pursuing their dreams. When I would tell people back home in Connecticut that my dream was to be on Broadway, they'd always look at me like I was nuts—like I'd be wasting my time and, potentially, *my life*, going after such a far-fetched dream. But here in this city, I'm amongst fellow dreamers. And at least with Rachel and Finn, these dreamers have shown to be very supportive of the ambitions of others. I wouldn't have expected that in a seemingly claw-your-way-to-the-top type of city.

Like a horse blowing air through its lips, I let out a breath of minor regret when our plates are empty because I packed my belly *so* full. But, dang, Rachel was right. The enchiladas were heavenly.

After splitting the check, we walk to the theater, and I text Gavin that we're here.

"Hey!" he says as he pops his blond head out the door a few seconds later. "Come on in before you melt into the cement." He swings open the door and we step inside.

"Chickens are probably laying hard-boiled eggs today," he says. I look at him with a scrunched brow. "You know, because it's so hot?" He smirks.

Rachel and I give him an obligatory chuckle.

I quickly introduce Rachel to Gavin and can tell they'll be fast friends. They start teasing each other immediately.

"Rachel, like from *Friends*, got it," he says.

"Gavin, like Gavin Magnus from YouTube, got it," she replies.

Gavin squints his eyes at her, unsure whether he should be insulted or honored. "*Who?*"

"You know, the famous YouTube star? He's a singer and TikToker too."

Gavin's brow and nose crinkle. "How old are you? Because if we're going to be friends, know that I cannot be associated with any *TikTokers*." He draws out the word and rolls his eyes.

Rachel giggles.

Immediately shifting from his playful antics, Gavin looks at me, half smiling, and says, "Cool hat, Sunshine." He taps the brim, so it falls over my eyes. I put it back in place and shake my head with playful annoyance.

He brings us backstage and shows us around. The theater is quaint and intimate—perfect for such an intense show. After a short but sweet backstage tour, Gavin hands us our tickets so he can go get ready for the performance. Rachel and I walk to the small lobby, waiting for the theater's doors to open.

"Gavin's a hoot," Rachel says as we check out the photos on the walls. Some are dated almost a hundred years ago, showcasing the theater's appearance in the early 1930s.

"He really is," I say with a laugh, still taking in the wildness of these photos. "I haven't known him long, but he's already becoming one of my favorite people. It's going to be fun seeing his creation played out."

A man with circular glasses sitting in one of the chairs on the other side of the room makes his way over to us.

"Were you two just talking about Gavin?" he asks.

"We were," I say. "I'm one of his coworkers."

"Sunday!" the man responds enthusiastically, and I'm shocked he knows me. "I'm Eric, Gavin's husband."

I light up with a smile. "No way, it's so nice to meet you." Shaking his hand, I introduce him to Rachel.

"Nice to meet you both," Eric says.

"I'm assuming this isn't your first time seeing the show," I say.

"Oh no," he chuckles. "Gavin has asked me to come to every single one. I haven't been able to make a few, but since this is the last week, I told him I'd be here every night."

"That's so sweet," Rachel says.

"Yeah, it's a great show, so it's not a big deal. I think you'll enjoy it."

"We're excited," I say.

A couple of theater workers open the doors to the auditorium so we all head to our seats. Gavin has stuck us in the front row after telling me during our last shift, "They are the best seats in the house because you'll really be able to see me sweat it out." Though I gave him a grossed-out look, he bypassed my concern and placed us here anyway.

Sitting down, my mind flashes back to the last theater I was in only a couple of days ago. I can almost picture Tyler sitting on this stage before me, serenading me again. I'm lost in thought when Rachel taps my shoulder.

"You okay?" she asks.

"Oh, yes," I mumble. "Sorry, my brain was somewhere else."

I'd give anything to return to that theater in front of Tyler once again. But tonight is for my friends. I turn to Rachel and spark a conversation, which helps me be present in the current moment. Right before the show begins, I spot Gavin looking at me from a crack in the curtain on the side stage, and he shoots me the goofiest face. I laugh and put my thumbs up to encourage him. He smirks and then disappears behind the curtain. A few minutes later, the lights go down, and the show begins.

As the curtain rises, Gavin is center stage, hanging from the ceiling, and clinging to a makeshift rock that I know he spent hours sculpting. He is shirtless with cutoff jeans, rock climbing shoes, and a harness. That's it. His ivory hair sticks straight up—as per usual.

I can't help but smile as I watch Gavin in his element. He's so good at this. The audience becomes captivated in the first few minutes of his monologue. The story reminds me slightly of the movie *127 Hours*—it's hard to watch, but you can't quite look away.

By the end, we're all on the edge of our seats, gripping the cushions under our bums right alongside Gavin. I feel fatigued in my forearms just by watching and can't imagine how he feels. The turmoil his character experiences is so potent. I find myself wondering what I would do in a situation like his.

*Would I hold on and keep fighting? Or would I give in, letting the inevitable fall take me?*

It's uncertain until the final moments what his character will choose to do. We all watch with growing anticipation and fear. But deciding on the inevitable, Gavin unstraps himself, takes a deep breath, and then lets go of the rock. He falls gracefully and before touching the ground of the stage, the lights fade to black, making it seem as though his fall never subsides, concluding the show.

Applause bursts from the fifty or so people in the audience.

Moments later, Gavin emerges from the pulled curtain with a big smile. He air-kisses Rachel and me as we stand directly before him with tears streaming down our cheeks. We applaud and cheer while he takes his final bow before exiting the stage.

"That was even better than I could have imagined," I say to Rachel.

"It was *so good.* My arms are killing me."

"Mine too!" I cry, and we both laugh.

"You must be so proud of him," she says as we exit our row.

I honestly do feel proud. It's an odd feeling because I barely know him, but something tells me we will be friends for a while.

We move back to the lobby where Gavin told me earlier to hang out for a bit so he could meet us after the show. Reconnecting with Eric, we tell him how wonderful the production was. Once the other audience members have departed, Gavin emerges from a backstage door to meet us. He's freshly showered and in his normal street clothes.

"Gavin, that was incredible!" I sing as I pull him into a hug.

"I'm so glad you enjoyed it." He gives me a big squeeze back.

"Yes, it was edgy and fun and so freaking intense," I laugh while stretching my forearms jokingly.

"Seriously," Rachel says. "At one point, I felt like if I let go of my chair, I would fall into oblivion."

"Yes!" Gavin shouts with his arms in the air. "That's exactly how I want you to feel. You're up there with me, struggling and weighing the different outcomes."

"It was awesome," I say and squeeze his shoulder. "You're incredibly talented, not only in your acting, but your writing is phenomenal. It's only a matter of time before one of your shows will go to Broadway." I wink and add, "I can feel it."

With a little bow and closed eyes, he says. "Thank you, kindly." He turns to Eric, "And it seems like you've already met my husband." He wraps his arms around Eric in a tight embrace.

"Yes, we have," I say with a smile.

"Do you guys want to go out for drinks or something?" Gavin asks.

Rachel and I nod to one another. "We'd love to," I say.

We all make our way out of the theater, and as soon as we step outside, Gavin declares, "It is literally as hot as *hell*." He dramatically turns like the Cowardly Lion who has just encountered Oz and runs back toward the door. Eric grabs his collar and stops him before he can go anywhere. We all laugh while Gavin sulks in temperature-induced agony.

Stumbling upon a cute bar that is jam-packed with heat-exhausted people—everyone looks slightly miserable with pink cheeks and glossy gazes—we make our way in amongst them. Thankfully, the air conditioning is on full blast. After an hour or so, we snag a table and find ourselves laughing and telling stories together.

This is exactly the night my heart needed.

By 1 a.m., we leave the bar. Eric and Gavin join me as I walk Rachel to her subway station. She hugs them and pulls me in last before telling me how much she enjoyed the night.

"My friends and I are having a party in a couple of weeks—you should come by. It's going to be '80s themed," she says while doing the Disco Finger dance.

I laugh and join her in her dancing, saying, "That sounds great— I'll be there."

"And I promise I won't critique your attitude," she says with a wink and bumps my shoulder before walking down the subway station steps. "I'll text you the details!"

Gavin, Eric, and I take an Uber back to Brooklyn. They drop me off at my apartment, I hop out and say to Gavin through the open car window, "Thank you so much for tonight. It was the best."

"You're so welcome," he says with a genuine smile. "See you bright and early tomorrow, Sunshine!"

# SIX

It's been a couple of weeks since my big move, and I find myself searching for any and every side gig imaginable. Although the coffee shop is better pay than I anticipated, it still isn't enough to cover my expenses. So today, I'm officially a dog walker.

I snagged an adorable Border Collie mix named Beans as a client—the client being the owner, not the dog. After quickly getting ready, I head to the L train with the rest of the morning commuters. It's a forty-minute ride to Beans' apartment on the Upper West Side of Manhattan. Popping in my headphones with the noise cancellation on, I pull out my Kindle to read as the train sends me uptown.

Once we hit my station, I exit the train and follow my city mapping app that tells me the apartment is a five-minute walk away. What people had to do before apps that gave you turn-by-turn directions in the city is beyond me. I would never have left Brooklyn if I had lived here in those eras.

Even though I haven't spent much time on the Upper West Side, it has taken me only moments to fall in love with it. Some streets make you feel you've been sent back to the '40s, while others are booming with shops and restaurants that are hip and modern.

But, while the avenues are gorgeous and sprightly, the people here are *very* different from those in Williamsburg. There's a sort of elite quality that makes me feel like I should have dressed up a bit more than my leggings and band tee attire. Women wear fur around their necks even in the summer heat. Oversized sunglasses adorn their faces while bright red and pink lipstick is caked on their mouths. On top of that, they all walk as though you are inconveniencing them solely by walking the same sidewalk as them.

Brooklyn is definitely more my style, people-wise.

After navigating the majestic streets, I stumble upon the apartment. It is a gorgeous brownstone located on 75th Street. As I admire the buildings, I see what looks like Mr. Beans himself propped up on the other side of a window, staring back at me. He reminds me of my dog, Jack, back home. I smile to myself and head toward the large oak front door.

According to the messages in my walking app, the owner left me a spare key under the rug. Once I grab the key and unlock the door, Beans rushes to the small mudroom to meet me.

He is a gorgeous dog with fluffy fur, ears that stick straight up, and a tail that curls like a "C," almost touching his back. I bend to his level and notice his ears and tail go down as he sniffs my hand. He's a bit timid, but I'm sure he will become comfortable soon. I try to stay calm and let him ease into getting to know me, but I cannot help but use my baby voice to soothe him.

"Hi there, munchkin," I say, eleven octaves higher than usual. "Oh, you are such a good boy," he wags his tail slightly and becomes more excited. He lets me scratch his neck and rub his ears, and then finally, he lays on his back, lifting his hind leg to allow me to pet his belly.

"Does that feel so nice?" I say and get down on the floor next to him. "You are such a good baby. I just want to take you home with me," as the words come out, I pray that there are no cameras in this apartment. With a nervous laugh, I backpedal, and my eyes dart around the room. "I'm just kidding…this is your home."

*Real smooth.*

"Okay!" I say, jumping up. "You wanna—" Beans bolts from the ground and rushes to the door. I finish my sentence slowly, "…go for a walk?"

He sits patiently, though his tail is flopping back and forth, brushing the ground like a broom. As I kneel before him, he lifts his paw to help me while I clip his harness around him.

"You are so smart, little guy," I rub his head. After grabbing his leash off the table and locking it in place, we head out the door. Central Park is only a few blocks away, so we head in that direction. It seems like Beans knows we're going to the park based on how he's pulling me along.

The park is booming with runners, families, and other dog walkers on this gorgeous summer day. We walk down a path with trees surrounding us on either side. Beans is sniffing every tree and ensuring he marks his territory on most. I snap a picture of him walking and send it within the app to the owners. After he does his business near a bush and I dispose of it with a doggie bag, we walk past a dog run where I can let him off-leash to play with other dogs.

As we head in, five dogs come rushing over to us right as we're through the gate. They sniff and poke their noses at Beans—it seems to be their way of saying "hello," but I'm just grateful humans don't interact like this when you're new somewhere.

I unclip Beans, and he runs around with those five dogs on his tail. At one point, a Maltese-looking pup slams into Beans' butt and then wipes out on the grass. While Beans continues running as though nothing happened, I chuckle at the poor dog who fell until I notice that dog's owner scoffing at me.

*Whoopsies.*

"Sorry!" I say across the way. They roll their eyes, and I shuffle to the other side of the fenced-in area.

After twenty minutes or so of Beans running with his buddies— jumping into the kiddie pool and then running around the park again— I call him back over to get clipped in so we can walk back to his home.

While walking back through the park, a golden dog runs toward us from the trees on the right. The dog begins pouncing around Beans playfully, while Beans stands idle with his ears back, a little shaken by the unexpected appearance of this dog.

"Woah! Who are you, buddy?" I look around to see if any worried-looking owners are running toward us. It's only a few walkers and me in the area.

"Where is your family?" I ask as I kneel to look at its collar. There's a name on it and a phone number.

*Jasper.*

"Hello, Jasper. Your parents must be worried sick right now." The dog rubs against me as I scratch his ears. I tie one end of Beans' leash to Jasper's collar and hold the rope in the middle, attempting not to lose either pup. Grabbing my phone, I call the number on Jasper's tag. But after a few rings, it goes to voicemail.

As I hear the voicemail beep, I leave a message saying, "Hi there, I think I may have found your dog. I'm in Central Park near the Bull Moose dog run entrance. Please call me when you can. Thanks."

Beans' family expects me to have him back at his apartment in a few minutes, so instead of risking the loss of my new job, I take Jasper with me, keeping my phone in one hand with the ringer on high and the dogs on the leash in the other.

We speed walk our way back to Beans' house, and I sit Jasper in the small mudroom while I get Beans situated in the home because, again, if they have cameras, I cannot have my first dog-walking clients know that I let another dog inside their house.

I say my goodbyes to Beans, lock the door, tuck the key under the mat, and take out my phone to complete the walk in the app, letting the owner know everything went swimmingly.

Jasper and I race back to Central Park. It's a bit of an awkward run since there is no leash for him to be clipped into. We don't get the rhythm right on our trot back to the park, bopping up and down, and many people stare at us with amused looks.

Once we're back in the same general area, there is still no sign of his owner. Settling on a bench near the dog run, Jasper seems utterly unfazed by the whole encounter—he's just wagging his tail and panting with, what looks to be, the biggest smile on his face.

I glare at him with a side-eye, saying, "This must happen to you a lot."

Suddenly, panic starts to rise in my chest.

*What if no one ever calls me back? What if this dog is a wild New York City dog?*

*Is that even a thing?*

As my mind starts spiraling toward the most anxious and unrealistic thoughts, my phone rings with an unidentified New York number.

"Hello?"

"Hi," a man answers with a breathless, nervous tone. "I just listened to your voicemail. You found Jasper?"

"I did. I'm here with him in the park. He's doing just fine," I reply, trying to ease any anxiety he may be feeling and simultaneously feeling my anxiety dissipate, knowing that I didn't just capture a wild dog.

"Oh, thank goodness. I'm so sorry. I couldn't keep up because he was after a squirrel in Central Park. But I'll make my way over there right now—I'm only a few blocks down," he says. "Thank you so much for holding on to him."

"Please don't say sorry. It's really no problem at all. I'm glad to sit with him," Jasper is licking my ankle now. "He's honestly keeping me more company than I am for him, I'm sure," I let out a small laugh. "I'll text you a pin of our location, so you know where to find us."

"That would be great. I'll be there shortly," I can hear him begin to run just by how ragged his breath is. "Thanks again."

"Of course. See you soon."

We hang up, and I shoot him the pin location.

With a steel grip on Jasper's collar, we sit on the bench and wait. I couldn't handle telling the guy that I lost his dog yet again. If a squirrel shows up and he tries to chase it, it will be no match for this girl's grasp.

Minutes later, as I check my emails, I hear, "Jaspey! Hey, buddy!" I look up to find a tall man in sunglasses and a backward baseball cap running toward us from a few yards away. Jasper wags his tail and starts jumping up and down. I am essentially a rag doll as he writhes me back and forth with his strength, yanking me up from the bench toward the man.

"Oh, my gosh. I'm so sorry," the guy says. "I should've waited until I was closer to say anything."

"No worries," I say, laughing.

Jasper jumps up and puts his front paws around the man's neck while he kneels to the ground, hugging his dog back. He clips Jasper's leash back onto his collar, and I'm thankful I no longer have to wrangle the wild bull.

Their reunion is so sweet. Jasper is licking his face like it's covered in peanut butter, and surprisingly, the man lets him. This is exactly how I would be if my dog ever ran away, so I understand.

"Thank you so much," he says after using the back of his hand to wipe the slobber off his cheeks. "I don't know where I'd be if I lost this little guy."

He rises to his feet, removes his sunglasses, and as I look at his uncovered face, my stomach does a 360-degree flip. The crystal blue eyes that sent fireworks inside me only weeks ago gaze back into my eyes once again.

Tyler Axel stands before me with a subtle smile playing at his lips.

# SEVEN

I-it's fine," I manage to stammer out.

*Eight-and-a-half million people, and yet, here we are. Meeting again.*

*In your face, Gavin.*

I pause a moment to take him in fully. He's taller than I realized, towering around six inches above me. And as a girl who is 5-foot, 8-inches, the moments are few and far between when I feel short. His luscious locks peep out from his backward baseball cap, while his gray shirt is tight to his chest—I can almost see the outline of his abs. Butterflies flutter in my belly. I have to force myself to look back up into his eyes and can't help but notice that, by his expression, he seems just as surprised as I am. A small, closed-lip smile forms fully on his face.

"You're Tyler Axel, aren't you?" I say, and I'm shocked that the words fall out of my mouth.

"I am," he says with a little chuckle while his crow's feet dance around his eyes.

"I'm Sunday." I reach out my hand, and he takes it, shaking it gently. "It's nice to meet you."

"You too, Sunday." I shiver as he says my name with his ever-so-slight English accent. He drops my hand. We share an awkward silence for a few seconds, just staring at one another, and then I proceed to word vomit.

"I saw your show the other night!" I attempt to sound casual, but my hands still make dramatic gestures, revealing that I'm not calm *at all*.

It takes all my self-control to avoid saying the blatantly obvious moment we had together, but the thought rushes through me again that maybe he does that each night with the person sitting in that seat. Most likely, I was just another one of his props as he did his job.

"Oh really?" he huffs a laugh that sounds like one solid "HA" before adding, "Thanks so much for coming to see it."

"It was incredible," I say, looking down at our shoes. He wears white sneakers with small grass stains on the toe area. I look back up at him and notice his quick glance at his black wristwatch.

*My time is up.*

His expression carries concern, as though he's contemplating what to do next. "I've got to get this guy back," he says with a thumb pointing behind him. "Rehearsal soon."

It sends a pang of sadness through me, knowing I'll probably never encounter him again. But life must go on. Moments you wish would last forever, move onto the next, and the best you can do is file them away into your precious memories.

"Okay," I say with a smile, concealing my disappointment.

"Thanks again for caring for Jasper."

"Of course. Anytime." My mind turns into spaghetti. "Though I don't mean *anytime*. Hopefully, this will be the last time he runs away from you—not that that's what he did. I know he was chasing the squirrel." *Shut up, Sunday.* "Anyway...it was great meeting you. Have a good rest of your day. Sayonara!"

*Sayonara?*

My lips form a lopsided, semi-scared smile while my eyes widen. I turn from him, walking away as quickly as possible without it looking unnatural.

"Hey!" Tyler shouts from behind me.

"Yes?" I say and turn around slowly.

He takes his hat off and runs a hand through his messy hair. My heart thumps rapidly at the sight and at the anticipation of what he's about to say.

"What are you up to tomorrow?" he asks, wringing his hat in his hands. "I have the day off, and I'd love to take you out to coffee as a sort of thank you for caring for Jasper."

*Oh my gosh.*

"Uh-huh," is all I manage to get out.

"Okay," he says with a quick laugh. "I already have your number, so I'll text you the time and place if that works?"

I nod emphatically.

"Sounds good. I'll see you tomorrow, Sunday." He gives me a crooked grin, puts his hat back on, then turns and walks away.

I stand there in awe, watching his hair bop up and down with every step. After thirty seconds—or perhaps thirty minutes—I walk out of the park in the opposite direction of Tyler and Jasper Axel.

"What just happened?" I mumble to myself while popping in my headphones. This is the second time Tyler Axel has surprised me, not just in small ways.

*Did he just ask me out?*

Jim Carrey's Grinch voice flies through my brain as that thought hits me. *But what would I wear?!*

I quickly search for the nearest Zara and take the B train there.

Before walking into the store, I find a little park with a nice sitting area and grab a seat to FaceTime Mick and tell her about my encounter. The call rings for milliseconds before her face emerges.

"Hey, girl!" she says, and I notice she must be on a walk because the screen is slightly wobbling while she has her—what I call—"movie star" sunglasses on. They make her look like a bug, but she rocks it.

"Mick, you'll never believe what just happened to me." I tell her about my interaction with Tyler, and about six times throughout the story, she interrupts and says, "You're kidding me." Each time I laugh and promise her it's true.

I finish the story by saying, "And then he asked me to go out to coffee tomorrow, so now I'm *freaking out* because I have to talk to him again."

"Sunday—he asked you out on a *freaking DATE*."

"You think that's what it is?" Uncertainty grows in my voice.

"Uh, yeah!" At this point, she takes off her giant sunglasses to look me in the eye. "Girl, trust me."

"Yeah, but I was so weird once I realized it was him. I stumbled over my words and said stupid things—it just seems like he wouldn't be interested."

"He would've left it at that if he weren't interested. He didn't have to go out of his way to ask you to coffee," she assures me.

"What if he's just really nice?" I ask with a hand covering my face, knowing she will call me out on my deflections.

"Enough!" she cries, and then her eyes enlarge. "Wait, do you think he recognized you from the other night at the show? He must have!"

"I couldn't tell. It all went by so fast, and I was so shocked—and his blue eyes. Ugh, they mesmerized me. A purple pigeon with a beret could have landed on his head, and I wouldn't have noticed."

She laughs, "Well, we'll find out more once you go to coffee. And remember, he's just a human. He's no different than the other guys you've dated—he just has a unique job." Her voice squeaks at the end as though she knows this is *anything but normal*.

"Oh gosh, I hope he's different than the other guys I've dated. We both know how those turned out."

"You know what I mean," she rolls her eyes. "I just got back to work, so I have to go, but text me pictures of outfit options!"

"Will do."

Shuffling through the busy New York crowd, I enter Zara. The store is buzzing like most Manhattan shops, but this one is filled with fancy-looking women grabbing clothes off the rack without even glancing at the price tag. Unlike me, who looks at every single one, and holds off on anything more than $40. Because the place is crowded, I try to be like a Navy SEAL—get in, get something cute, and get the heck out.

After a couple of duds, one vibrant blue tank top makes me fall in love. It crisscrosses at the neck, and the fabric curves around my waistline flatteringly. My flare jeans will go perfectly with this top. I snap a quick photo of myself in it and text it to Mick, who promptly responds with five fire emojis and two heart eyes. I suppose that means she likes it.

After returning the rest of my items to the dressing room attendant, I head to the checkout. While waiting in line, my phone *dings,* and I assume it's another text from Mick, but as I look at the screen, it shows an unknown number.

**Hey Sunday! Ty here.**

My heart skips a beat. I start swooning because he not only uses punctuation in his texting, but he also calls himself *Ty.*

*I feel like I'm in his inner circle.*

Ninety percent of me is ecstatic because he *actually* texted me, while the other ten percent is terrified because this is for real, for real happening.

**Want to meet at PlantShed in SoHo around 11 a.m. tomorrow?**

I count to fifteen in my head before replying. Don't want to seem too eager.

**That sounds perfect!**

**See you then :)** he replies.

I double-tap his message and give it a heart.

*Holy crap. Holy crap. Holy craaaaaaaap.*

The woman behind me in line taps my shoulder angrily and points to the register. Apparently, it's been my turn to check out for a few seconds, and I didn't move quickly enough for her.

"Sorry," I whisper and walk to the counter.

Once I'm out of the store, I rush home to tell Finn the news. She is just as shocked as I am and even offers to do my makeup in the morning for the special occasion.

I spend the rest of my evening trying to take my mind off the coffee date by checking out the latest audition boards and submitting my information for the few that may suit me.

*Might as well do all the anxiety-inducing activities at once.*

So far, I'm still waiting for anyone to get back to me on auditions. I might be doing this all wrong—who knows? After typing "How to get on Broadway" in Reddit and YouTube and reading everything I already knew, I close my laptop and pray for an opportunity to arise soon.

The following day, I wake up with pangs of anxiousness in my belly every few minutes as my thoughts return to what lies ahead. I'm too nervous to eat, so I try to at least get down a few bites of toast before getting ready.

Finn plops me down in the spinny office chair she has set in front of a vanity mirror and begins working her magic with my makeup.

"Are you nervous?" she asks as she applies foundation to my face with a squishy sponge applicator.

"I don't think I've ever been more nervous about anything in my entire life," I laugh.

"You're going to do great. Just be yourself, and he'll love you."

Though I've only known Finn for a couple of weeks, she is showing to be one of the kindest people I've ever met. Thank the Lord my roommate didn't turn out to be a psychopath. That would've made for a bad first experience living here.

"Alright, close your eyes," she says, and I follow her direction. She brushes my eyelids with shadow, and for the moment, as I close my eyes, I feel my body relax.

Minutes later, she spins me around toward the mirror and I take in her work. My jaw drops. I look better than I think I ever have in my life. My freckles still shine through, which I love, while my brown eyes pop with a gorgeous gold smokiness covering each eyelid.

"I love it," I say as I lean closer to get a better look. "You have to show me a step-by-step of what you did. I've never looked so good." Doing a vogue pose with duck lips looking at her through the mirror, I say, "Tyler will never be able to resist me."

We both chuckle, and I hug her, saying, "Thank you."

After pulling on my outfit, I slip into a pair of tan, heeled boots I found at a vintage store a few months ago. Some small hoop earrings top off the look, and I'm ready to go.

"Wish me luck," I say to Finn, who works on her laptop in the living room.

"Good luck. You can do this." She gives me an encouraging thumbs up.

I respond with a scared grin, take a deep breath, and walk out the door.

According to my subway app, the train to the coffee shop is experiencing delays, but I'm leaving with ample time. Nothing will stop me from seeing Tyler again.

It takes ten extra minutes, but I make it at a suitable time. An adorable dog sat next to me on the subway, nestled in its little bag, and it helped me get my mind off Tyler. But now, as I approach the doors of the coffee shop, all my nerves come back like a tidal wave.

Finn's voice echoes in my ears, *Just be yourself. He'll love you!*

"You can do this," I say under my breath.

An older man exits the coffee shop, holding the door for me, and I step through with as much confidence as I can muster.

# EIGHT

The coffee shop is wide and airy but has minimal seating as most of it is a flower and plant store. I scan the room for Tyler but quickly find that he's not here yet. In an effort to avoid missing him, I sit close by the door, taking in the scenery. Plants are everywhere, which makes sense since it's called PlantShed. The ceilings have ivy swirling around every nook and cranny. There are cut roses, peonies, and other beautiful flowers for purchase at the counter. Succulents adorn every table, while larger plants like Monsteras and fiddle leafs protrude from each lively corner.

*My green thumb could never.*

Honestly, I have more of a black thumb with an optimism that the plants will learn to thrive even with my forgetful watering.

As the coffee shop fills my lungs with fresh, floral scents, I take it as a welcome reprieve from the smog of the city streets. One large window in front of the shop looks out at the SoHo street, where skateboarders show one another new tricks. Those sitting next to me are quiet at work with headphones in, enjoying a relaxing cup of joe.

I take my Kindle out of my purse to kill time. My heart rate is settling because of how chill the ambiance is here. But even still, every few moments, my eyes shoot up to the door in anticipation for Tyler's long, lean frame to come moseying on in.

Minutes pass, and I begin to think he's blowing me off.

*He's probably just some jerk who wanted to get a naive girl to trek to a cute coffee shop and then leave her hanging. He's probably laughing to himself right now as he takes a load off on his leather couch in his enormous apartment, turning on a funny movie.*

My thoughts are interrupted as I see the door swing open, and I first notice the sandy, silky hair of Tyler Axel. He's wearing a black hoodie and aviator sunglasses. His cuffed, blue jeans reveal under them black, high-top Converse that look like they're on their last leg.

The sight of him takes my breath away. We make eye contact, and he beams at me with a bright smile and crinkle lines forming around his eyes and cheeks.

"Hey," he says.

"Hi!" I say a *bit* too enthusiastically.

I internally remind myself to stay calm while I stand up to greet him, unsure whether to hug him, give him a handshake, or just continue standing there. Luckily, he starts talking, so my decision has been made for me—standing it is.

"Sorry, I'm late," he says and steps forward before pulling me into a hug. I'm taken aback.

*Oh! Hugging it is.*

I can feel the tight muscles in his back as we embrace. He smells musk with a hint of mint. Hopefully I don't make it obvious that I'm full-on smelling him.

"Jasper was barking at the door, so I thought he had to go out, but he wasn't doing his business when I let him out. All that to say, I'm not sure what I'll be coming home to after this," he laughs.

"No worries at all," I say. He removes his sunglasses, placing them in the collar of his sweatshirt.

*What I'd give to be those sunglasses right now…*

*FOCUS, SUNDAY.*

"Shall we?" his hand gestures to the counter, and he waits to move forward until I walk first.

We place our orders. I ask for a medium iced latte with oat milk and a pump of vanilla—my usual. Tyler orders a black iced coffee. When the barista asks the name of the order, he discreetly says, "Troy." I disregard it, acting like I didn't notice.

While we go to the pickup line and wait for the drinks, he asks me what I do for work.

"Right now, I work at a coffee shop in Brooklyn. Oh! And I walk dogs. That's why I was out yesterday in the park. I had just finished a walk."

As I speak, I'm finding it difficult to hold his gaze—his eyes are so *blue,* and my train of thought is slowly derailing.

"Very cool. What brings you to the city? Dreams of becoming a world-class barista?" he asks with a smirk while crossing his arms and leaning against the counter.

"No, that's just a placeholder currently. I'm an aspiring singer, mostly, and pursuing musical theater."

I can't figure out what to do with my hands, so I attempt to shove them into my pants pockets. But that's before I realize *these pants don't have any pockets*. As though it were intentional, I slide both hands down my thighs and then quickly interlock my fingers behind my back, doing my best to be a suave as possible. It isn't working.

Shifting on my feet, I stay in the moment and add, "I love everything about Broadway."

His lips twitch in amusement.

Thankfully, it doesn't seem that he notices I'm buckling under the pressure of talking to him.

"And what about you?" I ask. It feels odd asking about his interests because I already know a decent amount, but I'm dying for his perspective.

"Yeah, I—"

"Order for Troy?" the barista shouts.

"That's us," he smiles and turns toward the barista to grab our drinks.

"Here you are," he says as he hands me my iced latte. "Cheers!" We clink our cups together. "Let's head upstairs—the seating is better."

While we walk up the stairs, I watch his feet go up each step, and it hits me just how wild this is. I'm about to have coffee with a celebrity. Not only a normal, run-of-the-mill celebrity—but a celebrity who is on *Broadway*. And it was his idea to do so!

We walk to a wide-open room with even more plants than downstairs. The far side has the same large window, overlooking the SoHo street. We find a place in the corner, away from the sun streaming through but close enough to still feel the light breeze. I watch the gentle wind rustle his hair. A piece falls out of line, and he runs his hands through it, putting it in its proper place. I could watch him do that all day long.

We settle into our seats, and I wipe my mouth quickly in case there's any lingering drool before saying, "So, you were about to tell me what brought you to the city."

"Yes! Let's see." He looks at the ceiling, contemplating where to begin. "Well, first, I grew up in London. Hence the accent," he goes full-out Old English when he says this, making me laugh. "When I graduated high school, I got accepted into Carnegie Mellon for Musical Theater, and while I was in one of the shows there, a Broadway producer was in the audience and asked to meet me after. She took me under her wing and got me a gig for the North American tour of *Wicked*."

As I try to soak in everything he's telling me, even nodding my head along to show him that I'm actively listening; my senses are unintentionally memorizing everything about him. His voice is so soothing. It's not deep and gravelly like I'd expect from a man of his stature, but instead, it's eloquent and light—as if every word he said could be auto-tuned and turned into a brilliant song. He speaks quickly, grins coming on and off his lips as he remembers memories of his past. And he uses his hands often to emphasize his story—disregarding the cup of coffee in front of him completely, while I use mine as a sort of cop-out, holding it, so I don't have to worry about what to do with my hands again. He leans back in his chair in comfort and continues. "It all kind of just came together after that. I moved full-time to New York, kept booking shows, and started auditioning for movies. Honestly, I was just really lucky."

"I wouldn't say it was luck. You're super talented," I interject.

"Thank you," he says with a sweet chuckle, looking at the lid of his coffee. His humility and kindness surprise me.

"But tell me more about you," he says, reaching across the table to touch my arm briefly. My skin tingles where his fingers landed.

I laugh nervously, "Sorry, this is all so surreal." I look out the window and say, "I was just watching you in a show the other night, and now we're having coffee. I would never have imagined this. New York is wild."

*Thank God for Jasper. Good boy.*

As I take my second sip of coffee, I feel a presence hovering above my shoulder.

A tall woman with bright red lipstick and a poorly cropped-top shirt says, "I don't mean to interrupt, but are you Tyler Axel?" She poises her iPhone at the ready.

Tyler's eye twitches slightly.

"I am," he says with a nervous smile as he looks up at the woman, keeping his eyes on her face rather than the rest she's revealing. If there was any trace of annoyance in the line of his lips, it's gone now. He is the very image of a gracious celebrity.

"Holy sh—" she begins to say, and Tyler clears his throat covering over the remainder of her sentence. She pushes her phone further toward his face, staring at him through her screen. "You heard it, folks! I am here with *the* TYLER AXEL. And, yes. He's just as cute in person!" Tyler's eyes dart to mine with a confused look.

"Can I get a picture?" she asks him.

"Yeah, of course," he says before shaking his head in my direction as if to say, *I'm sorry.*

The woman hands me her phone without looking at me and asks if I'd mind taking it.

"Uh, sure?"

*Are you frigging kidding me?*

She squats down next to Tyler, and I snap a few photos. She keeps changing her position while Tyler remains still as a statue, smiling without his teeth. I continue taking pictures until he turns toward her and says, "It was nice meeting you. I hope you enjoy your day." There is a kindness to his voice and also a sternness, letting her know it's time to move along.

"Thanks so much. Nice to meet you too." She seems to get the message and moves toward a free table. Although she's no longer hovering near us, her presence still lingers. I can see her videoing us from the far side of the room. It feels like I'm in a real-life episode of "Gossip Girl."

*Spotted: Tyler Axel and some brown-haired chick that looks like she's clinging to every word he says. Does he enamor her? Or is she just using him for fame? XOXO*

I scoff internally at my train of thought.

*No way am I using him for fame. That didn't even cross my mind!*

It doesn't matter to me what others may think, but I don't want him to get the impression that I'm using him. Because this would be an easy conclusion most people would come to, I make a pact with myself in this moment that I will never ask Tyler for help with my musical theater career.

"I'm sorry about that," he says. "Usually, I can evade these sightings with the clever disguise of a hat and sunglasses, but I wanted to be able to look you in the eyes."

A chill runs through me.

*Is he alluding to the night at the theater?*

I shake off the thought. "It's no problem at all," I say with a small laugh. "Hence, the fake name when you're ordering? *Troy?*" I raise one eyebrow quizzically.

He looks sheepishly at the table, now using his coffee as a comfort to hold. "If people start to think it's me but hear a different name called, they generally go back to their own business, assuming it's not. You learn these little tricks along the way," he says, twiddling his fingers.

It doesn't feel like he says any of this with pride. It genuinely seems to me as though fame was never something he sought. It was solely a byproduct of pursuing his dreams.

We sip our coffees, and I wonder if that moment we shared at the show is running through his mind, but I can't figure out how to bring it up naturally. So instead, we continue getting to know one another with rapid-fire questions as if we're at a speed dating event.

"Favorite color?" he asks.

"Red," I look at him with narrow eyes and tip my head for him to answer.

"Green. Full name?"

"What are you, the FBI?" I ask with a laugh but proceed anyway. "Sunday Jane Truelove, what about you?"

"Wait, your surname is Truelove? You're joking."

"Nope," I reply with a shrug. "Growing up, we thought it was because we descended from a Native American tribe. My cousin got a tattoo on his leg saying, 'Forever Native,' and then my other cousin—his brother—got a DNA test confirming we are not, in fact, Native American."

Tyler eyes go wide.

"I know. Nobody had the guts to tell him," I say with my teeth barred. "Okay, but what about you? Full name."

"Tyler Pickles Axel."

My eyes narrow in on his. "You're making that up."

"I'm dead serious!" With hands raised in surrender, he says, "My mum just really likes pickles."

At this point, I remember that I actually met his mom when she and his dad sat behind us at the show.

*Do I bring it up? That would be weird, wouldn't it?*

As I'm deciphering what to do, Tyler must think I'm still processing whether or not his middle name is, *in fact*, Pickles because he fesses up and says, "Okay. I lied. It's not Pickles. It's Edward." As he says his middle name, he uses the same exaggerated English accent as before.

"Ah, yes. Edward," I say, attempting the same accent. "How very regal of you to be called such a name."

"Yes, very regal, indeed," he responds, then lets out an exaggerated, monarchical-sounding laugh. I giggle.

Time flies by as we ask each other different questions, like how many siblings each of us has, our dream vacation destination, our favorite artist, and our favorite Broadway show.

We find out that *Wicked* was the show that got us both into musical theater. I saw it with my mom when I was in junior high, while he saw it as a teenager with his school class on the West End.

He tells me how crazy being on tour with *Wicked* was. "It was all so surreal but also *exhausting.* Packing and moving to a different city every few weeks was one thing, but also doing eight shows a week? I had no idea what I was getting myself into. I remember every Saturday night I would say to myself, 'Just one day more.'"

Simultaneously, we both break out our inner Jean Valjean and sing *One Day More* from *Les Misérables.* Pointing at each other with our eyes wide, we begin laughing. My mom and I have spontaneously broken into show tunes for years, and my heart is so joyful now doing it with Tyler.

Talking with him feels like second nature—as though I've known him my whole life. He is a lot funnier than I expected and remarkably quick with his wit. It's a fun challenge to keep up with him.

"So, you're telling me—" he puts his hands on the table before us, parallel like railroad tracks. "In a piggyback ride, you think the *piggy* is the one on the other person's back?"

I can't even retrace the steps as to how we got to this portion of our conversation; I smirk at its absurdity.

"Yes. You see, the person on the ground is carrying said, 'piggy'—so it could, in essence, be called 'A piggy-is-on-my-back ride.'"

He raises an eyebrow.

"Okay, I understand where you're coming from." Tyler looks up at the ceiling with just his eyes, as though he's still baffled but trying to comprehend my reasoning.

"I would think that the piggy would give the ride. Because it could, in essence, be called 'A-piggy's-back ride.'" When he says the word "piggy," he points to himself, and it makes me let out a small laugh.

I percolate his point, tapping a finger up my chin. "Hmm, fair point. But isn't it way cuter to picture a person carrying a piggy versus them riding one?"

"I'm not sure how realistic it is that a person would be able to carry around a 600-pound animal."

"Oh, no—I've always pictured the piggy as tiny. Like Miss Piggy."

"The Muppet?"

"Yes."

"Ah. While that would be more practical," he says, "my argument is stronger because piggyback rides generally aren't smooth, and neither would it be to ride an *actual* pig."

He doesn't know that I've already begun to agree with him from the start of the conversation, but instead of conceding, with a shrug, I teasingly say, "Agree to disagree."

He flashes me a crooked smile and then takes a sip of his coffee, even though there is clearly not much liquid left. As he tips the cup forward, the ice flies to the lid with a 'whoosh' sound. I hope the lack of coffee doesn't mean our time will be over soon. It doesn't seem Tyler is ready to leave, as he's getting more comfortable in his seat.

I've had to pee the last half an hour, but I don't want to get up and have him question whether we should part ways because this date— or whatever you call it—is just too fun. So I ask him more questions and take microscopic sips of my barely there latte.

"What has been the worst thing to ever happen to you on stage?"

He seems lost in his own little world for a moment as he remembers the scene and then begins chuckling to himself before responding.

"When I was in my high school's production of *Into the Woods,* I played Jack. You know, like Jack and the Beanstalk?" he asks, and I nod, knowing the show more than he probably realizes. It's one of my favorites.

"Well, Milky White—the puppet cow—was played by my childhood best friend, Dylan. He turned toward me too quickly at one point, and the Cow's paper mache head flew off, bouncing across the stage," he uses big hand gestures to explain the flying head.

I let out a quick gasp as my mouth drops, and my hand rises to cover it.

"Yeah, I know," Tyler says with a nod. "We both just stood there and stared at each other while the audience did what you just did, but then slowly started laughing." His eyes are becoming teary with joy.

"So I shuffled across the stage, picked up the head, and when I gave it back to Dylan, I said, 'Milky White, get yourself together.' Everyone in the audience cracked up, and we went on with the scene. It was terrifying but amazing."

We both laugh and wipe our tears. His laugh is unhinged and loud. I love it. Some people in the coffee shop start staring, but neither of us cares.

"That is so incredible. Way to go with the flow and bring the audience on the journey with you," I say. "And that is what I love about live theater." I lightly bang my hands on the table to emphasize my passion. "Everyone is in it together. If something goes wrong, you just have to roll with it. It's so uncertain, and that is *so* exhilarating."

"It is," he beams at me and leans back in his chair once again.

"What would you think about having a private tour of one of Broadway's theaters this week?" he asks.

"Are you kidding?" I say, trying not to sob. "I would love that."

"Okay," he gives me a wry smile. "It's a date. How does Friday sound?"

"That sounds perfect."

# NINE

I do everything I can to live in the moment throughout the week, but I only find myself thinking about Tyler. After five hours of talking with him in the coffee shop, which was only cut off because he had to prepare for the show, we said our goodbyes. He pulled me into the coziest hug ever—his arms around my middle and my arms around his neck. Butterflies erupted in my belly. When we parted ways at our individual subway platforms, my mind went a million miles a minute. But once everything settled, I realized I didn't just have a crush on some far-off, handsome actor. *I genuinely like Tyler Axel.* He has won me over in one sitting. Well, two sittings, if we count our first interaction.

His personality is charming but not in a flirtatious, player way, but more so in an endearing way. He asked me questions left and right, listening to every word I said. Active listening is always a win in my book. And we *laughed*—laughed without reservations. It was better than any first date I've ever had, and I'm still unsure if it even *was* a date.

I've wanted to text him about every hour on the hour after we left, but I've been waiting patiently for him to do so first. I just about leapt out of my skin when I heard my phone ding as I ate breakfast in the living room, only to find it was a scam postal service text.

*Of course my package hasn't arrived. I didn't order anything!*

Attempting to reel myself back into reality, my focus has strictly been on auditions. Although I've sent out information to multiple agencies, I've heard nothing back. I've been reaching out for any non-Equity parts, hoping one of them will come through, but still nothing. It's becoming pretty discouraging, but I have to keep reminding myself that I've only been in the city briefly. It's going to take some time and some grinding.

By Thursday morning, "One Day More" becomes the song I can't quite get out of my head—replaying at every lull while it increasingly becomes louder. Gavin and I are opening the coffee shop together, and he's becoming more annoyed every time I break out into the *Les Mis* lyrics.

Once I've spilled the beans to him about my time with Tyler, he grills me.

"So, you're dating a Broadway actor?" he asks while pouring fresh almond milk into one of the carafes.

"I'm not sure," I whisper. "…though he did mention the word *date* when we talked about Friday."

"So...*you're dating a Broadway actor*," he says again with a deadpan expression.

"Maybe!" I can't help but let out the inner teenage Sunday and giggle while jumping in the air slightly.

"Only a few weeks in New York City, and she's already climbed the ladder," Gavin says.

"Ha! No, it's not like that. I mean, all that he's achieved is remarkable, but I genuinely *like him*—from what I know of him." I shrug.

"That's awesome, Sunshine. I hope it works out for you guys," he says while I sip the coffee we've just made. "And if he's looking for a best friend, tell him I'm available. I'm pretty great."

This almost makes me spew out the piping hot coffee in my mouth.

"Will do."

Luckily, the hours fly by with Gavin. According to him, Brittany Oliver always comes in each morning for her coffee order, but today she's a no-show. Maybe she's not feeling well.

*Or perhaps she hates my guts and never wants to see my face again. Unlikely, but not out of the question.*

A few hours later, as I'm grabbing more plastic cups from the storage area, I check my phone quickly and notice a text from Tyler. My heart thunders.

**6 pm work for tomorrow?**

I scream like Rapunzel in *Into the Woods*.

"What?!" Gavin yells as he runs into the room.

I grin. "Tyler texted me."

He touches his tongue to his back teeth, looking at me with annoyance. "Are you kidding? That type of scream is reserved for murderers…and," he pauses, "…and pigeons!"

"Pigeons?" I ask with a smirk.

"Yes. Pigeons."

"Got it. Now, help me figure out what to say!"

Gavin comes over and we both loom behind my phone's screen with big, cheesy grins slapped on our faces.

"How about," Gavin starts, "'Totally, I can't wait to see your handsome face once again. And also, can my best friend come? He's the *coolest*.'" His voice goes low at the last part.

I grimace. "How about 'Perfect.'"

"Yeah, that's good too, I guess," he says quietly.

**Perfect!** I write back.

"An exclamation point?" Gavin says and grabs the phone from me. "That's *way* too eager. What have you done!" he cries.

I glance at him nervously wondering if it does come off as too excited but then a new text comes in and we both let out a sigh of relief.

**Great! Just head to the stage door and text me so I can let you in.**

"Oh, he *likes* you," Gavin drawls.

"How can you tell that from one little text?" Though I try to keep my face neutral, I can't help but smile.

"Intuition." He raises his brow with a smirk. "Now text him back and get back to work!"

I quickly write out, **Sounds good :) Can't wait!** and send it without showing Gavin because who knows what he'd think of a smiley face.

IT'S FRIDAY. Hallelujah!

I spent my entire morning trying not to panic. But I kept reassuring myself that everything felt so natural last time. There really is no reason to worry. It's just Tyler. My new friend…

*…and hopefully, my future husband.*

*No big deal. It's fine. I'm fine!*

I lay the outfit befitting for a night backstage in a Broadway theater on my bed. Though my first instinct is to break out a ballgown, I decide against it. Instead, I pair a vintage Broadway tee from *Phantom of the Opera* with a leather jacket, jean miniskirt, and platform Converse. I would have loved to purchase a new outfit for the night, but this girl has got to eat.

The sun is setting, and the bustling Brooklyn streets are getting busier with bar-goers. I weave through the avenues that are becoming more familiar daily and take the M train into Manhattan.

The theater is on 48th street, right across from Times Square—a place I love to go, even though most New Yorkers love to avoid it. Maybe it will be like that for me one day—but not today. I have a little extra time, so I head to Times Square and take a selfie with the bright screens behind and in front of me, illuminating my whole being.

I post the image on social media with the caption, *Am I a New Yorker yet if I still love Times Square?*

A heart appears on the image seconds after posting it by an account with a blue checkmark.

*Tyler.*

The cheekiest smile comes across my lips. Shortly after, Mick comments on the photo, **SO CUTE! Have fun tonight :)** I give her message a "heart" and check the time. It's just about 6 p.m., so I go to the theater and text Tyler once I find the entrance.

The door opens, and the lightly makeup-ed, smiling face of Tyler Axel appears. I don't think I'll ever get used to his face. I giggle just at the sight of him, but he doesn't seem to care.

"Hey, come on in." He holds the door open for me to enter.

Once it shuts behind us, he wraps his arms around my waist.

"How are you?" he asks.

"A bit nervous, I'm not gonna lie," a quick laugh escapes my lips as we continue to embrace. I didn't expect our hug to be this long, and I'm not sure when to let him go. If it were up to me, we'd stay like this forever—becoming one of those mummified couples who clung to one another as they took their last dying breaths.

*Woah, way too dark, Sunday.*

He lets me go, and I worry he can hear my thoughts.

"There's nothing to be worried about," he takes my shoulders in his hands and gives me a light squeeze of reassurance. "We're going to have a blast. And if there's any questions you have about anything or you need a bit longer to take certain parts in, just let me know." He smiles and I reciprocate the gesture before he leads me to his dressing room.

As we walk through the dark hallways, he asks about my day. I don't dare tell him all I did was try to get my mind off him. Instead, I tell him about my little walk to a vegan donut shop called Dun-Well Doughnuts. His face lights up, and he tells me it's one of his favorite places to visit in Williamsburg.

"You *have to* try the maple French toast one—it's incredible." His eyes roll back in his head to emphasize the point, making me smile.

After multiple twists, turns, and three flights of stairs, we find ourselves in his dressing room. It's smaller than I expected, but just enough room for what I imagine needs to happen in here. On one side is a large mirror with a table in front of it for makeup and hair. A window with a small loft in front of it holds a makeshift bed with pillows and fuzzy blankets. The left wall has his costumes hanging neatly on a rack, and scattered over all the walls are hundreds of papers full of fan art and notes.

"This is where I get ready each night. My favorite place is the bed," he says as he hops onto it and looks at me with a grin. "I nap here when we have two-show days, or I snuggle under the covers when I just need a quiet place to read."

I love that he uses the word 'snuggle.'

"That's fantastic," I laugh and approach his costume rack. As I glance over the multiple outfits, my eyes narrow in on one costume. With a light touch, I run my thumb over the hem of the shirt he wore the night he sang to me. He doesn't seem to notice my enchantment with this particular piece. Perhaps he thinks I'm simply admiring the details.

"That one is my favorite," he says, jumping off the bed and walking in my direction. He comes right up behind me and stands only inches from my back. I can feel his breath tickle my neck as he touches the cloth of the costume next to my fingers. Our pinkies accidentally touch, and it sends a shiver down my spine. I look up at him. He beams down at me.

He clears his throat and says, "Let's go check out the rest of the place."

We walk through the winding staircase to the stage. On the way, we pass a few ensemble members who are all very welcoming.

I try to take it all in, knowing that not many people get the opportunity to see what I'm seeing. One day I hope to be as familiar with a backstage area as he is, but right now, this experience is perfect.

He ushers me through "the wings," the side of the stage where actors wait before entering. There are loads of props and different sets waiting to be used for the show tonight. He shows me his favorite prop, a fake gun that looks too real for comfort. Anytime I've seen a gun in the past, I've clammed up. Thankfully, this one is just a replica—no bullets and no worries that it might go off at any second. Tyler spins it in his hand like he's from the Wild West, and I try not to drool at his suave nature.

"Pretty cool, huh?" he asks once he puts it back on its allotted shelf.

I don't dare touch anything because my mind automatically shifts to worse case scenarios. Like, what if I accidentally put a prop back in the wrong place? Or forget to put it back altogether and ruin an entire scene while the actors shout on stage, "WHERE IS MY PROP?!"?

Shaking off the imagery—knowing nothing will be misplaced if I resist touching it—I grin and nod to Tyler, hoping to move on from this section of the theater.

He smiles at me and picks up a small metal piece that looks like a compass. "Here," he says, tossing it to me. I scramble to grab it in the air, fumbling it in my hands while my heart picks up speed. I safely catch it and feel a drip of sweat on my brow.

Tyler chuckles and says, "You don't have to be so afraid. Look." He tilts a large Tupperware bin full of identical compasses to the one that I hold in my hand.

"Oh, wow." I put the compass back in the bin with the rest and allow myself to freely move in the wings. Grabbing a pair of circular glasses and top hat from another rack, I place them on my head and say with a silly smile, "How do I look?"

Tyler turns toward me, saying, "Lovely. So lovely in fact, I think my heart may stop." He pulls out a blood-soaked flag from another bin and pretends to faint with the flag held high in his hand. We laugh and put everything back in its proper place. He motions for me to walk out onto the stage that is only mere feet away.

When I step out, my eyes get teary as I see a real Broadway theater from this perspective. The vantage point is magical, and the theater looks *massive*—there are probably two thousand seats. Tyler must see how awestruck I am. He grins with his hands behind his back, letting me take the time to soak it all in.

"Wow," is all I manage to get out. I want to say *Holy crapperoni*, but I keep that to myself.

"Sing something," he suggests.

"Absolutely not," I laugh.

"Do iiiit," he teases. "Here, wait." He runs to the far wing and comes back with a handheld microphone.

"Are you serious?" I ask as he hands me the mic.

"C'mon, you know you want to."

"Okay, but you have to close your eyes. And turn around. Close your eyes and turn around and go a little further away." I point to the far side of the stage.

"Noted." He smirks, turns from me, and does everything I ask. Once in the corner, he says in a singsong way, "I'm waiting!"

"Okaaay," I sing back.

With nerves vibrating through my body, I take a deep breath and close my eyes. *Is this actually happening?* The first song that comes to mind is one of my favorites that began my love for Broadway. "The Wizard and I" from *Wicked*.

At first, my voice comes off a little shaky—as to be expected, the first time singing on a stage of this magnitude would make any singer nervous. After a few lines, though, I can shake off those feelings and enter into the character of Elphaba.

While I'm singing, a man pops up on the monitor at the back of the stage and starts accompanying me on the piano from the orchestra pit. The pianist's notes fill the theater alongside my vocals. One of the production managers moves around in the back of the auditorium, and I notice a change in my vocals. He's tastefully utilizing reverb on my voice as they would in a live show. A smile breaks out on my lips, knowing that Tyler has likely arranged for all of this to happen.

While I continue, I envision the theater full of audience members at the edge of their seats, with candy and drinks in hand. I see myself in the Elphaba costume, painted green—ready to take on the world—or, *Oz*. It's all right before me, so close I could taste it.

This is what I was made for.

The final notes sound majestic as the pianist goes berserk, and the production person bumps up my reverb even greater. The song concludes, and I forget that Tyler has been standing here the whole time—I only remember when I hear him clapping in the corner.

"Wow," he says, as he walks toward me.

I'm sure my face is bright red from embarrassment, but also because the end note was *so* high and drawn out.

"I'm not going to lie; part of me was a *little* nervous that you might not be able to carry a tune," he laughs. I drop my jaw and playfully punch him in the arm, pretending to be offended. He holds the place where I hit him with his hand as if he's seriously injured and then softens his face.

"You're outstanding," he says.

"Thank you." My cheeks grow warmer. "And thanks so much for letting me do this. What a fun opportunity."

"Of course, and now it's my turn to sing for you."

My brow wrinkles with confusion.

"Would you like to stay backstage for the show tonight?"

I nod my head slowly. "Uh-huh."

# TEN

Tyler leads us back to his dressing room. As he's fixing his hair for the show, the song "Friday I'm In Love" plays over the loudspeaker for a few seconds before a voice breaks through the music. "It's Friday night on Broadway, folks! This is your half-hour call!" The voice then proceeds to explain little details about the show—who's in, who's out, what swings are stepping in for other members of the cast that aren't present tonight.

Growing up, I was in as many theater productions as possible, but they were obviously less elaborate than this. Everything is structured and mapped out to a T, making little room for errors. But the beauty of live theater is that it is, in fact, live. *Anything could happen.*

We're sitting in Tyler's dressing room as he is steaming his throat and doing vocal warmups. Although I know I shouldn't, I can't help but let a slight giggle leave my lips at the different faces he's making during the exercises. It doesn't stop him from doing them; instead, he looks at me with those big blue eyes and sings even louder and more exaggeratedly, making us both laugh. He is quite a goon for someone so put together on the stage and screen.

"Do you ever get nervous before performing?" I ask.

"Not as much anymore," he says as he puts his steamer back on the counter. "I remember in my first Broadway show, I was such a mess on opening night. Most of my castmates were seasoned actors, so they encouraged and helped me get through. And I knew if anything went wrong, I could lean on them. It's usually like that with a big production—we trust one another. If we didn't, I'm not sure it would work."

"That makes sense." As I say this, Tyler's dresser walks into the room to help him into his costume.

"Oh, hi there!" she says with surprise and jumps slightly. She must not have seen me as I'm tucked into a chair in the corner.

"Hi," I smile.

"Judy, this is Sunday. Sunday, Judy," Tyler motions to both of us while popping a throat lozenge in his mouth.

"Very nice to meet you, Sunday," she says to me with a sweet grin.

"You as well."

She turns to the costume rack and grabs his opening number outfit. After handing him the pants portion, Tyler strips down to his boxers and pulls the costume on. Even though I've been around theater productions and outfit try-ons with many male actors, I can't help but divert my gaze around the room, landing on the ceiling to not stare at him. But that's after *I already have* and noticed his incredibly toned calves. Massive calves, in fact.

He then takes off his shirt so Judy can tape down the cords of his mic to his back. She places the microphone piece so it lands perfectly next to his hairline, and he fluffs up his hair around it to cover over the wire. While looking in the mirror, ensuring everything is as it should be, he notices me looking back at him.

Flashing his signature "closed-mouth" smile that I am becoming more familiar with and falling deeply in love with, I wink at him while making an "OK" sign with my hand to tease him about his shirtless body. He lets out a cackle and looks down at the table. I see his complexion turning a rosy pink.

"All set," Judy says as she pats his back. "I'll leave you to it." She winks at Tyler through the mirror and leaves the room.

"You're funny," he says to me once the coast is clear of Judy. He picks up the rest of his costume that Judy laid out and dresses fully, much to my disappointment.

As he is finishing up the buttons on his jacket, I ask with squinted eyes, "So, have you always had huge calves? Or are you just a major fan of 'leg day' at the gym?"

His mouth turns up at the corners slightly. He looks at me through his long eyelashes as his head is down, still buttoning. "It's genetic. Gramps had 'em, Dad had 'em, and now I am graced with what we call: 'Thunder Calves.'"

He slides the bottom of his pants up and showcases a Thunder Calf, then sits down to slip on his boots.

"Ah, I see, I see," I say, nodding. "You could probably StairMaster your way up to the heavens with those puppies."

"They came in handy with my first apartment in the city on the sixth floor that had no elevator, that's for sure."

"I'm sure they did," I laugh.

He looks at the clock on the wall, and I see the first hint of pre-show anxiety in his face. "Shoot, okay, now don't judge me, but I have to do my pre-show ritual. I've done it before almost every production now. It started as a joke, and then it became a habit." He rubs the back of his neck sheepishly. "Then, one day, I didn't do it, and I forgot the first line to the last song before intermission. So now it's my *I-have-to-do-this-or-else-everything-will-fall-apart* ritual."

"Oh boy," I say with slight fear. "I'm intrigued."

After an extended silence, Tyler nods at me and turns toward the dressing mirror. He grabs his phone from the table and blasts a death metal song. Fixing on his reflection with a piercing gaze, he starts strumming the air guitar.

"You are AWESOME," he shouts at himself. "You can do ANYTHING!"

My mouth drops open while I watch in awe.

One of the ensemble members with rich, black eyeliner adorning his eyes pops his head in the doorway and shakes his head at Tyler. He then looks at me and shouts over the noise, "HE DOES THIS EVERY NIGHT, YOU KNOW."

"I HEARD," I shout back, laughing.

He flashes a cheeky smile, rolls his eyes, then leaves the room.

After about a minute of terrible air guitar, fist pumps, and many cheesy affirmations, Tyler turns the music off.

"That was…something!" I say with a scared grin.

"Don't sugarcoat it."

"That was the weirdest thing I've ever seen."

"Thank you." He bows.

"Places, people!" The loudspeaker's voice echoes through the room.

"Thank goodness," I tease with faux relief. "Enough of that." Tyler throws a pillow at me from the makeshift bed, and I catch it before it hits me in the belly.

"Ha-ha!" I proclaim.

He then walks over to me, lifts me up from my seat—I drop the pillow—and without letting go of my hands, he stands inches from me. I'm definitely blushing. But this feeling is amazing. With narrow eyes, half smiling, he says, "You loved it."

I can't help but grin back at him.

He drops one of my hands and leads me through the hallways to where I'll be watching the show.

Tyler places a chair right at the edge of the wings—one that will be out of the way for all of the different sets but still positioned so I can see the show from a good vantage point.

The lights on the stage go down as Tyler turns and faces me, placing his hands on my arms. For a moment, I'm frozen in place. His face is so close it feels like he might kiss me.

"Break a leg," I breathe in the silence surrounding us. As the music on stage dims, I swallow loudly, hoping he can't hear.

"Thank you," he whispers. It's dark backstage, but I can make out his blue eyes. I feel my breath becoming shallow before he adds, "But these legs are indestructible." With a smirk, he leaves me to my seat, entering the stage as his cue begins.

And the crowd goes wild.

*This is the best night of my life.*

Tyler immediately transforms into Samuel, the soldier in 1800s Paris, right before me.

As cast members circulate me, I do my best to be unnoticeable. I don't want to distract them or cause a stir, so I stay stiff as a board, only moving my eyes to take in what's happening on stage. I feel like a literal fly on the wall—I shouldn't be allowed to see and hear what I am, but somehow, this is reality. I'm mesmerized.

Brittany emerges from the halls and stands beside me in the wings. With a look of confusion and surprise, she whispers, "Hey, Wednesday."

It's not my name, but I don't dare correct her. It's close enough.

*What's another day of the week?*

"Hi! Break a leg," I whisper back with a huge smile.

She quickly smirks after looking me up and down, then waltzes onto the stage.

*Welp, see ya later!*

I shake off the awkward encounter—expecting nothing less from her since she *despises* me—and take in the wondrous view instead. The perk of being side stage is that I not only get to see the actors sing and dance their hearts out, but I also get to see the audience's reactions. The smiles, laughs, and awe on each person's face make my heart sing. Oh, to be an actor on stage and see this view every night. What a rush.

Tyler and Brittany sound even better together than I remembered. Now that I know Tyler and am starting to develop feelings for him, watching him fall in love with a different woman stings a bit, even if *it is* just his job. I find myself looking around the wings each time a kiss takes place between them—studying the crack in the concrete or the tear of the curtain fabric beside me.

As the show continues, Tyler is *on*. He doesn't have a break until intermission. Every fifteen or so minutes, he rushes into the backstage area only to do a quick change, sip some water, and turn back around to enter the stage again. But he looks at me each time he's back here and smiles. I return the gesture and give him a thumbs-up or a silent clap here and there. Anything I can do to encourage him in his performance and show him I am thoroughly enjoying my time backstage.

Intermission comes swiftly, and Tyler and Brittany exit the dark stage on the other side across from me while the audience roars behind the curtain. After a few moments, the lights come back on. Tyler walks toward me, and I see Brittany pull him back by the arm. She starts talking to him, but I can't decipher what she's saying from this far away. After a minute or two, Tyler turns from her and walks in my direction again.

"Hi," he says a little breathlessly.

"Hi!"

"What'd you think?"

"It's…amazing." There are no words to describe what I'm feeling, so 'amazing' will have to suffice for now.

"I'm glad you like it. It's going to be you up here one day. I just know it," he says with a genuine smile so sweet that it makes me want to cry.

"You're very kind," I say while trying to keep my lip from trembling.

"Let me introduce you to the rest of the cast," he says, grabbing my hand to lead me onstage. The other cast members that have passed me going in and out of the stage during the show are all stretching their bodies in preparation for the remaining act. They chat casually with one another as if they didn't just do an hour and a half of intense dancing and nerve-wracking acting.

Instead of announcing my presence to the whole crew, Tyler introduces me to each person individually, which I appreciate. We make small talk with two of his costars who play his close friends in the show.

After fifteen minutes, the show is about to begin again, so Tyler brings me back to my special seat.

A significant dance number begins the second act, and he waits with me before his entrance. Once they finish, he whispers, "That's my cue." He then leans closer, giving me a gentle kiss on the cheek before walking back onto the stage.

I touch my face where his lips met me. Stunned.

Seconds later, while he's in the middle of his scene, we make eye contact across the way, and I can see the faintest smile spread across his lips. This is a moment where the real Tyler breaks forth amid this gorgeous Parisian landscape. I feel my insides crumble to pieces with utter joy as we remain entranced by one another, and then, just like that, he turns his gaze, and he's back to being Samuel for the next hour.

The final scene has me on the edge of my seat. Now, I will find out if he does, *in fact*, just sing the last line of the show to every person lucky enough to sit in that front-row seat.

Brittany lays limp in his lap, he looks up and opens his mouth to sing the line, and a stage manager walks right in front of me—blocking my view.

*Noooooooo!*

I feel like a seagull that's just seen a french fry drop as I try to dart around her, not daring to move my feet for fear of making a noise or, heaven forbid, knocking something over and ruining the moment for the audience.

"*My life is full of wonder, all because of you.*" The melody echoes through the room, and right as he finishes the line, the stage manager moves.

*Classic.*

The show finishes with a bang—literally. Confetti cannons go off everywhere as the upbeat finale song pumps through the theater.

The ensemble members make their way to the front and take their bows before Tyler and Brittany come out one last time. They hold hands and do their final bows. The whole cast dances together before exiting the stage.

Tyler and Brittany continue to hold one another as they move toward me, but Tyler lets go of her as soon as they're away from the audience's view. He stands before me momentarily, letting out a long exhale after the exertion of dancing, and then he draws me into a slightly sweaty, goosebump-inducing hug.

"You were amazing!" I say as he lifts me slightly off the ground, and I let out an accidental "Oh!" at the surprise.

"Thanks so much for coming," he says into my ear, then drops me back down. Looking into my eyes, he adds, "It was fun having you here."

I applaud the other cast members as they walk by, saying they did a fantastic job. They all thank me as they rush back to their dressing rooms to de-makeup and return home to bed only to do it all again tomorrow.

We walk back to Tyler's dressing room. Judy is there to help him with his costume and microphone. While she does that, he wipes off the minimal makeup he has on.

"Do you want a ride back to your place?" Tyler asks me through the mirror.

"Oh no, I'm okay. I don't mind taking the subway," I say, though, I just now realize I haven't done that by myself at night yet.

He must know what I'm thinking because he replies, "On a Friday night by yourself? No, no." He shakes his head emphatically. "This is when all the crazies are out. Let me take you."

I don't want to inconvenience him, but I also know that this means I'll get more time with him. And to be honest, I never want this night to end.

"That sounds great," I reply.

He smiles.

# ELEVEN

After a quick shower, Tyler returns to his dressing room, where I've been sitting. His black shirt has flecks of water soaked into it and I try not to stare.

"Sorry to make you wait," he says as he uses a towel to shake his head dry.

"Are you kidding? I'd much rather be backstage at a Broadway show waiting for you than sitting on the subway, praying I don't get kidnapped."

This makes him let out a chuckle, and I find myself wanting to say more silly things so that I can hear the sound again. Alas, my brain is mush from all the stimuli tonight. A happy mush.

He throws on a green bomber jacket from the coat rack in the corner of his dressing room, and we make our way to the theater's exit. Before we open the door, he turns to me and says, "This might be a little chaotic."

Without a second to compute what he means, he flings the door open, and every fan who was nestled into the theater seats tonight is now lining the narrow Manhattan roadway, pressed up against a metal fence positioned feet from the stage door. The sound that emerges from their mouths is deafening. My face must look as though I've seen a ghost—or many swooning, surprisingly emotional ghosts. Multiple women are literally in tears as Tyler waves to the crowd.

"Unfortunately, I'm not going to sign anything or take photos tonight," Tyler yells to them. "But I'm so grateful you all came. I hope you enjoyed the show! Thank you." He puts his hand on his heart and bows slightly in different directions as people continue to scream at him. I'm standing there watching it all unfold, probably feeling similar feelings to those on the other side of the fence. *Who the heck is she? What is she doing here?*

*What* am *I doing here? How did I get this lucky?*

Tyler takes my hand, continuing to wave to the crowd as we find our way to the spot where the metal barrier opens. People are taking hundreds of videos and photos of us. Unsure of what to do, I just bow my head, watching my feet step one in front of the other, and follow Tyler's lead. A security guard paves the way through the end of the crowd to a black SUV waiting for us. Tyler opens the door, lets me get in, and then slides in after me.

"Where to?" the driver asks. Tyler looks to me.

"Oh! Um, Devoe Street in Williamsburg…" I'm unsure how much of the address you're supposed to give for them to comprehend where you live. "Uh, Brooklyn, please."

"Got it," the man says with a chuckle.

*I guess I could have omitted the 'Brooklyn' part.*

Though there is plenty of space in the backseat—and I have slid into the far side—Tyler has landed in the middle seat, right next to me. His leg brushes up against mine. My body is fully aware of every square inch of his that meets my side. It's like little fires have started in each connection point. I smile to myself, hoping he can't see me doing so in this lighting.

The screaming fans are now fading from view as we embark on our journey to Brooklyn. Our chauffeur definitely missed his calling as a racecar driver because we are *flying*, weaving in and out of Manhattan traffic like we're about to miss a meeting with the president.

It hits me that this trip is taking Tyler well outside of the path to his home, which is most likely on the Upper West Side, seeing as though that's where he walked Jasper. I feel a rush of guilt, but again, I'm grateful for the extra time spent with him, and it seems to me that he is too.

"I lived in Brooklyn when I first came to the city. I miss it," Tyler says and puts his arm on the back of my headrest. I sink a little further into my seat.

"Really? Yeah, I like it a lot." I'm hoping the window doesn't start fogging up next to me with how warm I feel. "It's a lot quieter than Manhattan. I didn't think I'd enjoy it as much as I do."

"Definitely," he replies.

I notice the driver looking back at us in the rearview mirror with a grin, and suddenly, I'm self-conscious about what I might say next. Tyler must also notice it because he whispers his following words. "I'm happy you came tonight. When can I see you next?"

As if the intimacy of a whisper wasn't enough to make me crumble into little, tiny pieces, he then slides his large hand into mine, interlacing our fingers. All the nerve endings in my fingers and palm flicker as if I've just touched a live wire. It feels like there is a jackhammer in my chest, and my body has suddenly turned into an inferno. I wish I could crack a window without making it blatantly obvious I'm overheating.

Any questions I had about whether he likes me flew out the window—the one I don't dare crack open—as he holds my hand.

*Brain, start working. Say something.*

"Some new friends are throwing a party tomorrow night," I whisper back. "I know you have the show, but maybe you could stop by after?" Somehow, I manage to get that out without stuttering or passing out on the floor.

"I'd love that."

"Also, it's '80s themed," I mention, "You don't need to dress up or anything, but if you walk in and see me looking like a dancer from a Richard Simmons VHS, that's why." This makes him let out a cackle that he quickly tries to recover from by clearing his throat.

"I look forward to it."

We head over the Williamsburg bridge. Tyler and I look out the window to watch Manhattan grow smaller. He squeezes my hand, and

I look up at him. The city lights are like a mirror ball shining across his face. I flash him a smile and return my gaze toward the window. The arm he had behind my headrest moves to my lower back. I lean into his chest, becoming more comfortable with our sudden physical intimacy. I rest our interlaced hands on my lap and let out a long breath. It feels like we could stay in this moment forever.

The driver then slams on the brakes. We both are flying forward— our seatbelts catching us before we're thrown to the ground. He honks his horn for a solid 15 seconds, swearing and making rude hand gestures at the taxicab that just cut us off. Tyler and I burst out laughing to the point where we start crying. This glorious, romantic moment was taken away so swiftly by everyday life.

"Apologies for that, Mr. Axel," the driver says while tugging at his collar.

"It's no problem, Bob. Thanks for keeping us alive," Tyler responds. He places his hand on my knee, and then looks at me with a playful, scared smile.

I giggle.

A few minutes later, we arrive at my apartment.

"That one right there with the big bush in front." I point out the window as Bob pulls us slowly up to the building and stops the car. Tyler gets out of his side first and leaves the door open for me to exit on the safe side of the road.

"Thanks so much, Bob," I say as I tap his shoulder while leaving this SUV death trap.

"Hey, no problem!" he says back.

Tyler takes my hand and walks me to the front door. Wrapping me in a hug, I nuzzle my head into his neck and breathe deeply. This time, I don't care if he notices. He smells *so* good.

"I'll see you tomorrow?" he says while still embracing me.

"Can't wait." My voice sounds muffled because my face is smushed up against his chest.

We look at one another, still mid-hug, and he leans forward, but his lips aren't aimed at where I expect. Instead, he kisses me gently on the forehead.

"Goodnight," he says softly.

"Goodnight." We let go, even though I can tell neither of us want to. I buzz into the building, and Tyler walks back to the SUV. He looks back at me, and I mouth, *Good luck,* while pointing at Bob. Tyler laughs and then enters the vehicle.

And that was the last time I saw Tyler Axel.

Just kidding.

Instead of going the easy chips and dip route for an appetizer to bring to the party, I decide to make an apple pie. And what better way to make a pie than dancing around the kitchen listening to the *Waitress* soundtrack while baking said pie? After purchasing apples from the local grocery store a few blocks from our apartment, I begin baking. My mom always made apple pies for holiday events, so after many years of watching her do it, my great-grandma's recipe is ingrained in my mind. I whip up the crust and the delicious filling in no time.

While the pie is baking, Finn walks out of her room amid her workday and says it smells like heaven. A few minutes later, however, I smell smoke. Thankfully, the pie is okay. The oven, on the other hand, is not. I forgot to put a tray beneath the pie (probably because I was too distracted singing my heart out) and now the drippings are on the bottom of the oven, turning black and burning up.

The fire alarm goes off within seconds and I rush to the windows in our kitchen to get rid of as much of the smoke as possible. I grab a chair and hoist myself to the smoke alarm before fanning the area with a towel.

"Hehe, whoopsies," I say to Finn. "Sorry about that."

She laughs and says it's not a big deal.

The drippings stop burning after a few minutes, and I put a piece of tinfoil over the bottom of the oven to catch the rest. After what was supposed to be an hour of relaxing baking, the pie finally finishes baking. I let out a frustrated sigh and get ready to go.

Finn is joining me at the party. We both break out into different outfits, doing a mini-fashion show with each look. After a few duds, we settle on our most '80s-looking outfits with what we already owned in our closets. Not surprisingly—because her closet continues to astound me—Finn emerges from her room in a metallic blue puffy-sleeved dress that fits the vibes perfectly.

I go the Canadian Tuxedo route and dress in my oversized jean jacket paired with a Goonies tee and Goodwill Mom jeans. I pull on my Converse while Finn slips into a pair of colorful, high-top Nike sneakers. We both have curled our hair to the literal breaking point—achieving the highest volume possible.

When we walk onto the subway platform, nobody even glances at us. We're just two eclectically dressed individuals clothed as strangely as everyone else. We're in Brooklyn, after all.

We arrive fashionably late (7:05) and are met by twenty or so wildly dressed partygoers in the gorgeous brownstone apartment in the East Village. Eighties music blasts from the vintage stereo in the corner of the room. There are disco balls hung from the ceiling and variations of blue and purple streamers taped everywhere.

Rachel greets us in the kitchen while heating some nacho dip. She stops what she's doing and says, "Hi, ladies!" before pulling us both into hugs. "I'm so glad you're here."

"Nice to meet you!" Finn says mid hug. "I'm Finn."

I probably should've taken the liberty to introduce them since they only met through me, but Rachel brushes it off by saying, "I'm Rachel. So nice to meet you. Oh my gosh, is that an apple pie, Sunday? It looks amazing!"

I lift the pie to her gaze and say, "It is! It took me all morning to bake—almost burned the apartment down, but we survived."

She laughs, thinking I'm joking. Finn and I quickly glance at each other with a smile, knowing the truth. I walk over to the large food table that is bursting with different chips and dips—just like I thought. I place my pie down in the most open section.

"Please, make yourselves at home," Rachel says. "Some of the people from the dance class are downstairs if you want to go say hi."

"Thanks, Rachel," I respond.

We move downstairs and are greeted by Jacob, Shelly, and Lucas. Finn's eyes twinkle when Lucas shakes her hand as he introduces himself.

*Matchmaker Sunday, take note of that.*

We chitchat with them before the music gets ten notches louder, and somebody yells, "IT'S DANCING TIME! HEAD UPSTAIRS!" And then what feels like hundreds of bodies brush past us, making their way up through the narrow stairwell. The group and I follow, entering the newly created mosh pit of bodies that jump up and down to "Girls Just Want to Have Fun."

After fifteen minutes, Lucas says to us loudly over the music, "Wanna head to the roof?" Finn and I nod. We're both glistening with sweat. A little fresh air will do us good.

We follow Lucas up the stairs and climb a sketchy white ladder leading to a hole in the ceiling. It opens up to the light-polluted night sky of Manhattan. The twinkling lights of the city dance around us, while the fresh air (or as fresh as New York can be) fills our lungs. A gentle breeze keeps us from becoming even more intolerably sweaty.

As if I wasn't already jealous enough of whoever's apartment this is, the roof access has helped me feel that jealousy on a whole other level. I'd camp up here all summer.

After a few hours of talking, laughing, and dancing, my phone buzzes in my pocket with a text from Tyler.

**Just finished the show. On my way!**

**Sounds you soon :)** I write back, realizing I meant to say *Sounds good, see you soon,* but I accidentally meshed it together. He'll get the gist.

I leave Finn on the roof with Lucas, which she seems to be fine with, and I go into the bathroom to get as much dried sweat and glitter from who knows where off of me before Tyler arrives.

I've loaded my bag with all sorts of deodorant, wipes, sprays, makeup, perfumes—anything and everything I could think of to freshen up so I didn't look like a melting monster by the time he got here. It takes me ten or so minutes, but I'm back to feeling my usual self and smelling—might I add—*amazing*.

**Here!** he texts just as I finish up.

I walk to the foyer, navigating through the different clusters of people throughout the main floor. When I open the door, I'm met by a version of Tyler I have yet to see. I first notice the mullet wig he's placed on his beautiful blonde hair. A letterman jacket, white tee, aviator sunglasses, and acid-washed jeans accompany it.

My mouth turns up with joy. "Oh. My. Gosh."

# TWELVE

**W**hat? I always dress like this on the weekend," he says defensively but then breaks out into a huge smirk.

As I stand in the doorway with Tyler in front of me, a rush of clarity comes over my mind. At this moment, I realize *I am definitely falling for this man.* And all it took was a mullet wig. Not only has he accepted my invitation to attend a party with people he doesn't know, but he went even further by decking himself out in '80s attire.

I could cry.

Shaking my head to focus on the moment at hand, I smile and say, "I really hope that's sarcasm. Come on in. You look great."

"You don't look too shabby yourself," he says as he tugs on a curl that hangs on my forehead, and it bounces right back into place when he lets it go.

I wrap him into a hug, standing on my tiptoes so I can put my arms around his neck. He breathes deeply and says, "And you smell *terrific*." A sly smile forms on my lips.

*Mission accomplished.*

"Thank you."

I lead Tyler through the house, asking how his show was while we weave in and around various people. We go up the stairs to get to the roof so he can meet my friends.

"It went well. Roger—the guy who plays Antoine—tripped very noticeably at one point, almost making me break character, but he recovered quickly."

"Oh, so you must have done your pre-show ritual then," I say teasingly before climbing the ladder to the roof. I notice Tyler holding his hands near my legs to catch me if I slip from a rung.

"Sure did," he replies.

Once we're safe to the top, I scope out where the group is and find them laughing in the corner near some picnic tables.

"Hey, guys!" I say amid their conversation. "Sorry to interrupt, but I want you all to meet Tyler." I point my thumb behind me before I realize he isn't there. A group of girls has stopped him and are giggling like lunatics while he glances back at me with a horrified look, mouthing *help*.

"One second," I say to the group before me. Making my way over to the girls surrounding Tyler, I take him by the arm and lean my head against his shoulder. The giggling ceases as soon as they see me, my gesture implying *he's all mine, ladies*.

"Sorry to take him from you girls, but I need to speak with Tyler privately," I say as seductively as I can, grab his hand, and lead us away. I feel silly, but these women are clearly like piranhas, ready to devour at a moment's notice.

"Apologies for that," I whisper to him. "I'm not sure what got into me."

He laughs. "I liked it. And thank you for saving me."

When we walk back to my group of friends, Jacob takes one look at Tyler, drops his jaw, and *then* proceeds to drop his drink. Luckily, it's in a plastic cup which means there's no breakage, just liquid splattered near all of our feet.

"Oh my gosh, I'm so sorry," he says, grabbing some napkins off the nearest table to wipe up the spill. He looks up at Tyler from the ground, "Y-you're Tyler Axel, aren't you?"

I glance around at the group. Finn and Lucas are the only ones who don't seem thoroughly shocked. Finn because she knew he was coming, while Lucas appears to have no idea what a Tyler Axel is.

"I am," Tyler replies, itching his mullet wig.

"It's a pleasure to meet you." Jacob holds out his very shaky hand to introduce himself.

Tyler laughs cautiously and says, "You, too."

The awe at meeting a celebrity doesn't last long for any of them. We can have a regular night after the initial introductions, and nobody else at the party notices that Tyler is in the building. Or on the roof.

After a bit, we all return downstairs and make our way to the makeshift dance floor, forming a small circle. Though professional dancers and movers surround me, I've never cared about how I look on a dance floor—as long as I'm not stuck to a specific routine, I let it all out.

"Push It!" by *Salt-N-Pepa* comes on, and my stank face debuts in New York City. My arms flail about while my body writhes to the rhythm. I feel free.

Tyler makes eye contact with me as he claps, steps to the beat, and then stifles a laugh at my moves. He's learning I'm pretty bold and bright, but I wonder if he realized it was to this extent.

When the song "I Wanna Dance with Somebody" comes on, Lucas grabs Finn's hands and pulls her close to dance with her. She looks at me over his shoulder with an *oh, my gosh* expression, and then her lips turn into the biggest, cheesy grin.

Rachel and I are holding hands, jumping and swaying to the music until Tyler taps her on the shoulder to cut in. She lets go of me with a girlish giggle that turns into a shriek after seeing him.

Tyler bows to me as if I'm the queen allowing him to pursue a dance with me. "Shall we?" he asks in his fake old English accent with one eye half shut.

I curtsy back and speak with the same voice, "We shall." But it comes off more as a grumpy old Englishman. He holds my right hand in one, resting his other arm around my waist, keeping me close. His mullet wig flops up and down, tickling my nose, and it causes me to sneeze.

"Whoops, sorry," he laughs, turning his accent to a southern trucker. "Gotta trim that thing back—it's getting a little out of sorts."

"No, the length is nice," I say. "Before you make any rash decisions, you should definitely *mullet over*."

His eyes squint at me, and then his lips curve up.

"Oh, she has jokes!" he says as his smile lines emerge, and all I want to do is grab his face and kiss every single one because they're so *freaking* cute. I resist. Looking to the side of the room and away from his adorable face to keep my brain straight, I say, "I have all the jokes."

"So, you're beautiful and funny," he says while gently turning my chin back toward him so I'm staring into his brilliant eyes. Warmth creeps up my neck. As I circle his face, he smirks, saying, "That's a deadly combination."

I give him a shy grin before leaning back on his shoulder, and we continue dancing.

After a few songs, Finn and Lucas emerge from the crowd letting us know they're going back to the roof to get some fresh air if we want to join them. It is getting quite warm in this room, and at least for me, I know it's not from all the dancing.

Before heading up, I slice and dish out a few pieces of my pie— taking what's left. It seems like New Yorkers don't see a lot of home cooking, seeing as though they've torn my pie to shreds.

Balancing the plates, I carefully make my way back up to the roof. We find a little section in the empty corner and lean against the edge overlooking lower Manhattan.

Tyler and I share a slice of pie. As the gentleman he is, he lets me take the first bite. When the juicy apples fill my mouth, I'm reminded of home; brought back to our living room, with a fire roaring in the wood stove while my siblings, parents, and I sit on our tan couch laughing and enjoying one another's company.

I'm thrust back into reality as the group before me raves about the pie. "Thanks, guys. I'm glad you like it," I say with modesty, though what I want to say is *I know, right?! It's so good!*

Tyler takes his first bite, and a new glimmer enters his eyes. Everyone else has returned to talking, but he turns to me and says, "Sunday, this is the best pie I've ever had."

"Really?" I say, bashful. "Thank you. It's my great-grandma's recipe."

"Do I detect a hint of liquid smoke?" he asks.

The color drains from my face. I just smile and nod, not wanting to confess my morning of running around the kitchen frantically waving a towel in the air to stop the fire alarm.

"It's delicious," he says, taking another bite. "Tell me more about your family—is this great-grandma of yours still baking pies?"

"No, I never got to meet her, unfortunately. But my mom always made her recipes growing up. Meatloaf, spaghetti sauce, but especially the pies." I tap my fork lightly on the crust.

"Okay, what about the rest of your family?" he asks.

"Well, there's mom and dad, who have been married for over thirty years. My mom is one of my best friends—very supportive and one of the kindest people I know. She's hilarious too. We're very similar—" I snap my mouth shut after hearing the words leave my mouth and registering that they come off as prideful. I make an awkward face, and Tyler laughs.

"Don't be embarrassed. From what I know, that's all true of you as well," he says.

"Thanks," I huff a small laugh. "I also have two sisters and a dog. But I've got to say I miss him the most since moving. He doesn't really get the whole 'video-chatting' thing."

"What's his name?"

"Jack."

"Good strong name for a dog," he says sweetly.

"Yeah, he's the best. But what about you?"

"My parents are still together, and I have a little sister, Haley. She's eight years younger, and she is the sweetest." He shifts his body around on the ledge, facing me. "I'm also very protective of her. Growing up wasn't easy because she has special needs, so kids would tease her or even go as far as bullying her. It wrecked me as a kid. But she's tough. She never let it go too far." I can see the pride in him about his family. He loves them deeply.

"She sounds incredible. I'd love to meet her one day." The words fall out of my mouth, and I stare at the ground before Tyler responds.

"I'd like that too."

Before I can bask in the fact that Tyler just said he'd enjoy me meeting his *family,* Jacob weaves his way over to us and starts asking Tyler a million questions about his career. Although Tyler seems a little caught off guard, he answers each question Jacob asks gracefully. It's nice for me as well, because I'm learning a lot of little details about Tyler that may have taken longer to learn without Jacob. Like what his favorite audition song is or what working on a set with this or that director was like. Even if it's obvious he didn't get along with a particular director or actor, Tyler always finds something positive to say about them. It makes me even more attracted to him than I thought possible.

After about fifteen minutes of endless questions, Tyler's eyes dart to me every few seconds, and I take this as a sign of needing to be rescued.

"Hey, Jacob," I say while grabbing Tyler's arm. "We're gonna get some refreshments downstairs."

"Okay! Sounds great," he says so enthusiastically, but a shadow in his eyes shows me that he understands his questions were a bit too much. I squeeze Jacob's arm to comfort him but also do so as a parting gesture.

After retuning downstairs, I get caught up with some people from dance class while Tyler grabs our drinks and starts talking with a group near the beverages. After a few minutes, we gaze at each other from across the room. Smiling with his eyes, he perfectly executes the Tyra Banks look. I beam back at him. Suddenly I feel like we're Maria and Tony in *West Side Story*, seeing each other for the first time. Falling in love at first sight. All else fades from view except Tyler. The noise dies down; the people become blurry. It's just him and me.

We remain looking at each other for a moment before he nods toward the dance floor, and we both excuse ourselves from our individual groups.

He takes my hand, and we throw our bodies between a mix of people we don't know and go full-out dancing to the song "Come On Eileen." We sing in one another's faces and laugh until our bellies hurt. The rest of our group from the roof joins us, and we all sing-scream the lyrics to "Don't Stop Believin'."

As it gets a little past one thirty in the morning, I watch Tyler let out a tiny yawn. I ask him if he's ready to go, he nods with a small smile, still dancing to the beat. Finn tells me she's going to stay a little longer—things seem to be cooking between her and Lucas.

*Matchmaker Sunday's work is no longer needed.*

We say our goodbyes before heading to the foyer to get our jackets on. As we leave, Jacob runs up to us and says goodbye to Tyler, thanking him for answering all his questions and even thanking him for his presence. Jacob pulls him in for an awkward hug that makes me laugh quietly.

When we leave the apartment and close the door, Tyler and I hear Jacob shout on the other side, "I JUST HUNG OUT WITH TYLER AXEL!"

We look at each other for a moment, baffled, before Tyler does what could only be described as a "spit take." If his mouth were full of water, everything in the five-foot circle around him would be drenched. I am bent over, cackling on the sidewalk while he remains on the apartment steps, grabbing the handrail for dear life because he's laughing so hard. When there is a brief pause in our laughter, I wipe my tears and say as seriously as possible, "He did the same thing to me when I met him."

Tyler shakes his head and mimics what he could only imagine Jacob looking like. With fists in the air, he shouts at the group of walkers who are meandering by, "I JUST HUNG OUT WITH SUNDAY TRUELOVE!" With worried looks, the group starts to pick up their pace, getting as far away from us as possible.

My hands are on my knees, supporting me because my stomach starts hurting from the constant laughter. After a few minutes, I sigh quietly. "I don't want this night to end."

He looks at me, flashing a closed-lip smile, and softly says, "Does it have to?"

# THIRTEEN

There is no dead of night in the City of New York. It's always moving, always breathing. Whether we're in winter's cold or summer's heat, the streets are forever dazzling with lights while hundreds of people flood the sidewalks, walking in pairs, in groups, or alone. Where they may be heading or coming from, you'll never know. Chatter, laughter, singing, and yelling reverberates off the streets while taxi honks and ambulance sirens fill the rest of the space. Music blares in different sections of town from the local clubs and bars, car radios, or boomboxes. No matter what time of day or night you're out, New York will always be awake to greet you. After all, it's known as The City That Never Sleeps.

And for tonight, Tyler and I join in its insomnia.

Walking hand in hand through the narrow streets of the East Village, we make our way to Washington Square Park. Tyler has de-wigged much to my pleasure. His swoopy hair is free to make me swoon once again. Even though we both still have '80s garb draped on our bodies, we look semi-normal walking these streets at night.

There is an eeriness to the park that I've never experienced before in the daytime. Though it's the middle of the night, the place is still saturated with people. The arch looms above us while the fountain sprays us with a light mist from behind. I'm reminded of the Belle Époque stage as we gaze upon the arch here. A thrill goes through my body wondering if Tyler is reminded of our night as well.

"You wanna jump in?" Tyler asks me as he turns his body and points to the water pouring forth from the fountain.

"Isn't that illegal?" As a rule follower, to my core, I have to ask, but also, I would hate to ruin the night by being arrested.

"Nope."

"Huh. Well, in that case, I'm in," I say, and I shrug off my jean jacket.

"Really?" Tyler seems dumbfounded.

"Why not? It sounds like fun!"

He stares back at me, apparently his idea was just a joke, but now he slowly starts nodding. "Okay, let's do it."

We strip off our socks and shoes, leaving them all at the edge where we can see them so they can't be stolen (rule follower and mildly paranoid).

Tyler takes my hand, and we step in. "Oh!" we both say at the same time. In the dark, it looks like the bottom is multiple feet below the water's surface when it's only mere inches. It's a bit anticlimactic as we walk through the ankle-deep, surprisingly warm water.

Hopefully, that's not because it's all pee.

Suddenly, Tyler lets go of my hand, dramatically pretends to trip over his own foot, and dives forward. He catches himself with his arms to avoid injury but then lets them give out so his body is totally immersed in the water. I watch in terror. There's no way I'm lying down in this questionable liquid. Flipping onto his side, with one elbow propping him up, he says, "Hey," and smiles seductively as water drips from his forehead.

"Uh, hi," I say with a laugh.

"You should join me." He pats the surface of the water with a tiny splash.

"Nah, I'm good," I say, shrugging my shoulders and turning from him.

Before I have a chance to run, he's up on his feet and bearhugs me from behind. He lifts me in the air and spins me around, and while I protest with yelps, I become totally soaked through just from his body holding mine.

He puts me down, turns me toward him, and gives me the cheesiest grin.

I curl my lip, trying not to form the smile that the edges of my mouth are so desperately tugging toward. Then I step away from him, lay down in defeat, and playfully make snow angel movements with my arms and legs so I'm just as soaked as he is.

Tyler joins me as we lay on our backs in the warm water. If stars could be seen in this light-polluted sky, we'd admire them from this fountain. I turn to Tyler and find he's inches away, already looking back at me. His eyes move back and forth between mine and then they carefully land on my lips.

*Oh, boy. It's happening.*

His hand gently grazes my cheek, water dripping from his fingertips. I sense him starting to close the gap between us, and then without warning, a bright light shines on both of our faces. Using our hands as shields, we squint toward the light to see what could possibly be blinding us when a voice yells, "Out of the fountain!"

We bolt upwards, and a police officer comes into view holding a flashlight. Blood drains from my head. Automatic nausea.

We're getting arrested.

Perhaps sensing my panic, the officer says, "You're not in any trouble. We just can't have people in the fountain at night."

Relief washes over me. We step out quickly, apologize to the officer, and slide back into our jackets and shoes. The police officer moves along, likely to crush other people's impending romantic moments. Tyler and I don't say anything for a few minutes, both embarrassed and shaken. I break the silence by looking at him with a side-eye glance and saying dryly, "I thought you said this wasn't illegal."

"It's not! I've Googled it before."

His answer sends a sting through my heart.

Why on earth would he have Googled that if not to do this with another woman?

He Sang To Me

"Anyway, it's probably just because they don't supervise it as frequently at night. It's not a big deal," he assures me while bumping my shoulder as we sit on the fountain's edge.

"Okay," bumping him back and shaking off the negative feelings as I remember that he definitely just tried to kiss me.

"I've got an idea," he says.

"Does it involve the police?"

"No, definitely not."

"Or anything that could potentially have anything to do with the police?"

"Nope."

"Okay. I'm in."

We take the 1 train uptown and get a few dirty looks as our shoes squeak through the halls. Our clothes leave a trail of fountain water behind us. Or, you know—pee water.

Of course, the one day I choose to wear a full-on jean outfit is the day that I immerse myself in a fountain. It does bring back some nostalgia though—wet jeans. I'm a kid again on her semi-annual trip to Disney, exiting the Splash Mountain ride. But now Little Sunday has to face the rest of the day with wet underpants and jean shorts, silently sobbing while her inner thighs turn bright red. Yet, in the midst of that, nothing can stop the Disney magic. And that is precisely how I feel at this moment. Though my inner thighs are screaming in pain, I'm sitting on a subway train with Tyler Axel, who is rubbing my thumb with his as he holds my hand in his damp lap. He turns toward me and gives me a slow kiss on the cheek. Heat fills my belly.

I smile and rest my head on his shoulder. I watch him continue to stroke my hand, exuding a gentleness I didn't expect.

"This is our stop," he whispers in my ear after some time. I may have fallen asleep on his shoulder during part of our journey. He lifts me by the hands as the train comes to a halt. We exit and leave the station. I hold onto his arm and attempt closing my eyes while walking, letting him guide me exactly where I need to go until I trip over the sidewalk and decide that closing my eyes will not work on these uneven streets.

After a ten-minute walk, we enter a large building with a doorman who tips his hat to Tyler. Taking the elevator to the sixteenth floor, the doors slide open while Tyler leads us down the hall. From his pocket, he takes out the keys to his apartment. After unlocking and opening the door, Jasper comes romping around the corner and pounces on me with his two front paws—I almost fall backwards, but Tyler puts a hand behind my back before I can do so.

"Whoa, hey, buddy," I say groggily, still waking up. Tyler pulls him down, and Jasper sits, awaiting a greeting from his dad.

"Sorry about that. He's still learning his manners," Tyler says to me before turning to his puppy. "Hi, Jasp." He takes his hand and messes up the fur on his head.

As Tyler turns on the lights, warm, ambient hues fill the space. I'm stunned for a few seconds. The apartment is enormous—probably ten times the size of mine. It's an open-floor concept with the kitchen to the left and a hallway that likely houses the bedrooms and bathrooms to the right. A minimalist living room is front and center, with a large sectional plopped in the middle, facing the floor-to-ceiling windows that overlook Central Park.

"Wow," I say, walking over to the window. "This is spectacular."

Jasper follows me with his nose glued to my leg, sniffing my soggy jeans. When I reach the window, I squat down to give him proper snuggles. We sit on the floor together, and Jasper crawls into my lap, nudging his nose with my hand every time I stop petting.

As we gaze outside, gratefulness rushes through me. I'm looking out over the city I never thought I could live in on my own.

"Do you want to shower and get out of those wet clothes?" Tyler calls while taking off his shoes near the door. "I'm sure I have some clean sweats that would fit you okay."

Still looking out the window in a daydream, I reply, "Yeah, that'd be great."

He comes over to us and sits on my right side. I'm not sure if it's because it's three in the morning and I'm exhausted or what, but I start to tear up. Tyler looks over at me with a hint of worry on his face.

"You okay?"

"What? Oh, yes," I say, wiping my eyes and leaving my trance. "I'm fine." I take a deep breath before continuing. "Moving here has just been such a dream, and now I'm here—not just physically here in New York, but here with you, and it's all so wonderful and overwhelming."

He wraps his arms around me, and we sit there for a few more moments, taking it all in.

"You really should get these wet clothes off," he whispers. "I'm a little afraid that fountain was full of pee."

"I was thinking the exact same thing," I whisper back with a smirk.

Tyler left a towel and dry clothes in the bathroom for me on the vanity. I take the most incredible shower I've ever had because there is a rain shower head and jets on the walls that essentially powerwash me clean. I feel like a new woman when I step out. After drying off, I slip into the clothes he left me—a pair of gray jogger sweatpants, an H&M white tee, and a black hooded sweatshirt. Everything smells like Tyler. I tuck my nose into the sweatshirt's collar and breathe deeply a few times, smiling to myself.

It's a significant temptation for me to fall asleep on the sectional sofa while Tyler takes a turn showering. Still, I resist and instead cuddle with Jasper for a few minutes before Tyler emerges from the bathroom. He wears jeans and a black tee that fits him so well, I find myself staring at his chest.

"So my big idea from before wasn't just to show you my apartment and get clean," he says while shaking out that gorgeous golden hair of his, flecks of water flying everywhere. "I want to show you something."

He takes my hand as we exit his apartment, lock the door behind us, and step into the elevator. Tyler punches the twenty-fifth floor's button. As we stand silently in the dim lighting, backs against the cab walls, I look up to meet his eyes, and my body quivers in anticipation. *Is he going to try and kiss me again?* It feels like the elevator is plummeting dozens of floors—not actually—but that's the sensation my stomach feels as Tyler looks back at me with his ocean eyes circling my face. I sense his body lean closer to mine before the elevator dings and the silver doors slide open. I'm tempted to run my hands over all the floors' buttons so we can ride up and down until we have our moment. Instead, I look through the doors to find an enclosed rooftop that awaits us with a bowling alley and arcade games in every direction imaginable. My jaw goes slack.

"Oh my gosh. This is so cool," I say as we exit the elevator. Running my hands over the edge of an air hockey table, I look back at Tyler who is half smiling as he watches me.

"Isn't it awesome? It's ninety percent of the reason I chose this apartment building. But this isn't what I wanted to show you," he says.

*How could it get better than this?*

He leads me down one of the hallways into a dark room. Once he flicks on the lights, bright blue and purple LEDs illuminate the small room. A television screen is mounted on the back wall while green velvet couches point toward it. Then I notice the two microphones on a stand in the corner.

"Up for some karaoke?" he asks with a sly grin.

"Uh-huh."

"What should we pick?"

*Broadway. Always.*

As I swipe through the booklet of different options, I see a few show tunes I love. I know full well that Tyler has sung the beloved duet, "As Long as You're Mine," from *Wicked* dozens of times, seeing as though he played Fiyero Tiggular. It's a temptation, but I choose a more recent favorite duet from a show I saw months ago in the West End.

"What about 'Seventeen' from *Heathers*?"

"How did I know you would pick a musical number?" he laughs.

"Because they're the best!"

"Okay, okay. 'Seventeen' it is." He searches for the song, clicks it with the remote, and while it starts counting us down, I pretend to crack my neck and do a quick vocal warmup lip trill. He laughs and then does a lip trill as well.

The song begins, and I do my best to get into the character of Veronica Sawyer—the girl who has fallen in love with a menace that is slowly killing all the people around her. Tyler molds himself into J.D., this murderer who convinces himself that he's committed every act of criminal activity solely to display his love for Veronica. It's scary how in-character Tyler can get. I feel within myself the fear Veronica would have felt toward her J.D., but it all quickly dissolves as I look into Tyler's unadulterated eyes and remember this is just Tyler. The man I'm falling for.

Our harmonies mesh so well together that I could burst with happiness and frolic down the streets of New York like a madwoman. Midway through, I realize that I am actively checking off one of my bucket list items—singing with Tyler Axel. I smile and feel myself get a little choked up. But again, it's likely because we've stayed up almost all night, and my brain can't handle this much wondrousness.

During the song's climax, we step toward one another. Tyler twirls me around so my back rests against his chest, and his free arm goes to my opposite shoulder, wrapping me into him. With his breath close to my ear, I hold onto his arm with my mic-less hand, and we sway to the music while continuing to sing.

In the last few lines, when the music goes down and our lyrics become more intimate and low, I turn my body so we're face to face. Tyler gently rests his forehead against mine, and we both use his mic to sing the last line together.

The song ends, and the karaoke screen applauds for us. We don't move from there but continue standing before one another with our foreheads pressed together, each breath slow and calculated.

Tyler drops his microphone to the floor with a clang of feedback from the speaker and brings his big, warm hands to the sides of my face. He gently tilts my head up. We're centimeters from one another. The blue in his eyes glow in the low light. His gaze moves around my face, hovering over my lips. He looks back into my eyes and smiles sweetly before leaning in, closing the gap between us, and kissing me.

It's slow and cautious initially, then grows even sweeter and more passionate. I drop my mic to the floor with another clang and wrap my arms around his neck, fingers sliding into his silky hair. He smiles against my teeth, moving his arms around my back, and lifts me off my feet. I momentarily pull my lips away to look at him and give him the happiest grin before leaning in again while he lowers me back to the floor.

He rests his forehead on mine again, and with a deep breath, he says so quietly that I almost miss it, "I like you."

It's so innocent and endearing, as though he were a young boy saying it on the playground to his school crush.

"I like you." We stand there in silence, basking in the moment before I whisper, "But I have to tell you something,"

"What is it?" he asks with concern, pulling his face back from me.

I stare back at him, a tiny smile playing at my lips. "It was on my bucket list to sing with you." I playfully bare my teeth.

He lets out a cackle. And then says, "Well, check that one off, sister!"

Tyler pulls me in again and kisses me sweetly before saying, "I don't think it will be the last time either."

"I sure hope not," I say under my breath.

We remain in the karaoke room a bit longer and sing more show-tune duets like "Bad Idea" from *Waitress* and "Wait for Me" from *Hadestown*. And I finally convince Tyler to let us do "As Long as You're Mine" even though he rolls his eyes when I suggest it. We kneel together just as Elphaba and Fiyero do in the show and laugh at the cheesiness of it all. I couldn't be happier. Our voices sound like they were made to sing with one another, meshing like the woven fabrics of a meticulously designed frock.

After a couple of rounds of bowling—where, to my annoyance, Tyler wins each game triumphantly—we see a warm light emerging from the windows. Curling up onto one of the couches, we watch the sunrise, concluding this glorious night.

He's silently nestled with his head in my lap and his face toward the rising sun.

"I should probably get back," I say as I stroke his hair with my fingertips. He turns over to look up at me with a big frown. "I know, I don't want to either, but I need to sleep because I have a shift tomorrow and hopefully some auditions this week. And you have a show! Oh my gosh." I didn't even think he'd have to be singing and dancing with his cast for the Sunday matinee in a few hours.

"It's fine, I'll take a nap once you leave, and I'll be golden," he says, putting his pointer finger and thumb in an "OK" symbol and squeezing his lips together.

"Okay, that's good. Alright, in three seconds, we're going to get up," I say with determination. "One…"

"Two…" he groans.

"Three!" He jumps off my lap and yanks me up from the couch. I squeal when he unexpectedly sweeps me off the floor and holds me in a bridal carry. It feels like I'm a damsel in distress in an old movie, and I relish in it. Wrapping my arms around his neck to help alleviate some of my weight, I look into his eyes.

Now that the sun is fully awake, it fills the room with warm orange tones. His face shimmers in the morning light, and I lean in for a kiss. It's sweet and cozy, feeling like home.

"I could stay here forever," I say once our lips part.

"Me too."

"But I really should go." Giving him one more kiss, he carries me back to the elevator, and I giggle the whole way before he sets me down. This time in the elevator, he makes the most of the short journey by leaning us against the mirrored wall and passionately kissing me to the point that I feel like my brain is scrambled eggs.

Once the doors open, I have to shake my head in order to vamoose through the doors and enter his apartment again. I gather up my soggy clothes and other belongings, keeping the clothes that Tyler lent me. It doesn't seem like he minds as he hasn't said anything while we exit his apartment.

*You won't be getting these back, sucker.*

He walks with me through the lobby. And after a lingering goodbye kiss, we part ways. I catch the train back to Brooklyn with a silly grin the entire ride home.

# FOURTEEN

After a much-needed five-and-a-half-hour nap, I awaken to another gorgeous summer day in Brooklyn. You may not be able to hear birds chirping, but you know it's a perfect day when your neighbors are blasting music and breaking out their lawn chairs to perch on the sidewalk while a grill behind them is cooking marinated meat.

Once I left Tyler's place, I realized I had neglected my phone for hours, resulting in many missed texts. The first was from Rachel, saying, **So glad you guys could make it!!**

The next was from Jacob. **It was the best hanging out last night. I hope you didn't think I came off too strong. Tyler has just been my acting idol for years. See you both again soon!**

And then Finn, **sooooo Lucas and I hung out all night!!**

My mouth drops with that one and I do a little happy dance for her.

Shaking off the deep sleep from my body, I respond to them all. First, to Rachel, telling her we were so glad to be there. I console Jacob by writing, **We had a blast! Tyler thought you were so funny.** This may have been a *bit* of a stretch because Tyler and I were laughing at Jacob's quirky comments *about* Tyler. And with Finn, I resolve to wait and hear her story in real life. But based on the snoring and white noise sounds coming from her room, I'm assuming she's still sleeping.

I text my mom and Mick a quick message, telling them that Tyler and I kissed with about twenty-five confetti and heart emojis. They both reply almost immediately with joy and a plethora of heart-eye emojis.

Padding into the kitchen, I whip up a lovely brunch composed of pancakes, oatmeal, and a big bowl of fruit and then go back into my room to indulge. My phone buzzes on my nightstand. Though I assume it's one of the people I just responded to, it's a text from Tyler.

**I miss you.**

My heart practically leaps out of my chest before another text comes in.

**The show is about to start, but I hope you got in a good nap. Can't wait to see you soon <3**

A giggle escapes my lips, and I write back, **I miss you too <3 Enjoy the show. We'll talk after!**

It's been a few days full of utter bliss and wonder, so it's time to hunker down and face reality. I open my email to find that the dozens of self-tapes I've sent out have gotten no responses. Instead of continuing this route, I decide to check audition call boards daily and go to *every* non-Equity audition suitable for me within a twenty-mile radius of New York City. It's about time this dream starts making some headway.

While I scroll through the endless pages of available auditions, one catches my eye. An Off-Broadway run of *Little Shop of Horrors* with the role of Audrey still available. This role was one I've already tackled at my local community theater in Connecticut, so I feel comfortable doing it once again. The auditions are from 2 p.m. to 7 p.m. and I check the date.

*The audition is today.*

My head darts to my alarm clock which reads 1:42 pm. I jump off my bed and dash to the bathroom, grab a handful of makeup products—shove them into my purse—and throw my hair in a loose bun atop my head. Grabbing my audition folder that holds a variety of sheet music and different monologues, I nestle it under my arm, knowing I won't forget it if I leave it there. After pulling on black jeans and a tight black blouse paired with high stilettos—channeling my inner Audrey—I race out the door.

While on the subway heading into Manhattan, I do my makeup and try to get my heart rate down after running up and down the subway steps to make the train. Dropping everything for auditions is likely to become my new norm, but I remind myself that this is why

I'm here—to get my big break in musical theater and become a star on Broadway.

After finishing my makeup, I send Mick a quick text.

**I'm about to go for my first audition. Pray for me!**

Immediately, she responds, saying, **NO WAY! You've got this. LMM how it goes.**

She's become akin to texting 'LMM' rather than 'LMK' for "let me know" because of my love for Lin-Manuel Miranda. Every time she does it, it makes me laugh.

In other news, walking in Manhattan with heels is a trip—*literally.* Next time, I'm one million percent wearing sneakers and slipping into my heels right before I walk into the audition room. These blisters I'm currently forming will be gracing my feet for weeks.

The place where they're holding the auditions is easy enough to find because there is a line of thespian-looking folk wrapped around the side of the building.

*Good thing I ran here!*

Standing behind a younger, black-haired boy with glasses like Seymour's, I catch my breath and start ruffling through my sheet music to find the best fit for this audition.

Typically, you're not allowed to sing anything from the show you're auditioning for, but it's always a good idea to use a song with similar musicality to the show—the same goes for the character. Choosing a song your desired character would likely sing outside their show is always best. It lets the producers and casting directors know you've done your homework and helps them quickly picture you as the character. For instance, if you're auditioning for the role of

Glinda—the perky, girly-girl she is—but audition with the song "I Dreamed a Dream" from *Les Misérables*, sung by a sorrowful woman desperate to reunite with her daughter—you might not get the greatest response.

Audrey is a sweet, hopeless-romantic type who lacks the courage to escape her abusive relationship with a demented dentist. She eventually falls in love with Seymour—a kind, semi-awkward guy— her coworker in the flower shop.

Though it isn't my go-to, the song "Part of Your World" from *The Little Mermaid* stands out because it's almost the same song Audrey sings: "Somewhere That's Green." (They're also both by the same writer, Alan Menken.) Both songs yearn for a place where things are happier, brighter, and full of love.

After humming the song multiple times and doing some vocal exercises, I still haven't made my way inside. The line is moving as slow as molasses, but I can see the front of the door now. I've been here for close to an hour. My song is prepped, my voice is warm, I've calmed my nerves—now I'm ready.

Another half hour goes by, and I'm finally at the door. A woman with jet-black hair in a chaotic, curly bun takes my information. She has a pencil sticking out from the top of her bun, but I notice she begins to write my name on her sheet with the pencil in her hand. The one in her bun is either for fashion purposes or serves as her backup stash. She smiles at me with bright white teeth, and I'm ushered into a room with about twenty other hopefuls, only to wait once more.

I sit there, twirling my thumbs, trying to keep my nerves to a minimum, when Tyler texts me from his intermission.

**How's your afternoon going?**

**It's good!** I reply. Part of me doesn't want to tell him I'm at an audition, so I hold that information back. **How are you? How's the matinee?**

**Great! Do you want to grab dinner tonight?**

Unsure of how long this process will be, I reply, **That would be fun! It might need to be later because I'm in the middle of something.**

**Sounds good. Lights are going down. Gotta go!**

Hearting his message, I hear someone call my name.

"Sunday Truelove?" The man who just stepped through the door with a clipboard looks around the room until I wave my hand. "We're ready for you now."

All that calming myself may have just compressed my nerves inside of me because now they feel like a bomb ready to explode. I follow the man through the doors to a room where a long table rests at one end with five people in chairs lining it. Each has a plastered-on smile covering their evident boredom and annoyance of being here. They introduce themselves briefly and ask me to do the same.

"Hi, I'm Sunday, and I'm auditioning for the role of Audrey," I say as confidently as I can muster and hand the accompanist my sheet music.

"Today I'll be singing 'Part of Your World.'" As soon as the words leave my lips, I see a woman at the far end of the table roll her eyes subtly. It seems I'm not the only one who chose this song today. While I try not to let her obvious irritation sway me as I begin, it still does. My nerves get the best of me, and my voice cracks during my most significant belting moment. I also forget to move around—my feet remain planted in one spot while my arms do all the acting. I probably look more like Ursula, the octopus, than Ariel. On the positive side, I remember all the lyrics!

Once I finish, the producer says, "Thank you, we'll email you." He looks at me with a dry smile and then flicks his head toward the door. I take it as my cue to leave.

*That went well.*

As I exit the building, I blink quickly to stop the tears welling inside me like a blocked fountain. I knew this process would be grueling, but rejection still stings no matter how far along you are in the business.

During my walk and train ride back to my apartment, I shake off the experience. If this isn't my role, then I can live with that. I'll keep trying.

Trudging into my apartment after promptly taking my heels off in our little lobby, I can hear Finn talking with someone, and to my surprise, it's Lucas.

"Oh, hi!" they both say with embarrassment because they didn't hear me walk in. Finn slowly moves away from Lucas's side.

"Hey guys," I say with a bit of a flare, knowing *something* is happening here. They were like conjoined twins while making dinner and only moved away on my account. I give Finn a face that says *I can't wait to hear more.* With a smirk, I tell them their food smells delicious and walk into my room, singing, "Have fun!"

Once I shut the door, I chuck my heels into the back of my closet with urgency as I let out an audible hiss from my lips—never to walk in them again for the journey to or from auditions.

Flopping onto my bed, I begin to journal about my day. Two hours later, I awaken in a dark room—an accidental but necessary nap had come upon me. I look at my phone and see that Tyler had texted me nearly an hour ago about dinner.

**I'm so sorry. I fell asleep. Let me know if you still want to!** I write.

**No worries. I'm still game. Want to meet at The Butcher's Daughter in Williamsburg in an hour?**

**That's perfect!**

I've walked by the restaurant several times in my explorations of our local neighborhood and thought it was *so* cute. Plus, it's only a 10-minute walk from my apartment, so I take some time to wake up and then begin getting ready.

My makeup is minimal but highlights the vibes of the restaurant—glowy and golden. After applying a quick tanner to my legs (those babies needed some TLC), I put on a white tube top, slide into my black midi skirt with a short slit and pair the outfit with chunky black sandals. I curl a few pieces of hair that have become disorderly since my multiple naps of the day and grab my tan trench coat off the rack. I try not to disturb Finn and Lucas, who sit snuggled up on the couch watching a movie. Stifling a giggle, I say, "Bye!" They wave back with sappy grins, and I head out the door.

# FIFTEEN

Tyler meets me outside the restaurant, looking like an absolute *snack* in his green button-down shirt that showcases his lovely biceps and forearms, cuffed blue jeans, and brown leather boots. While running a hand through his hair, he locks eyes with me across the way and grins.

"Hey," he says.

"Hi." I walk toward him, and he wraps his arms around me, giving me a sweet hug at first, and then laying a soft kiss on my lips, leaving me feeling weightless as the smell of mint from his breath lingers. I grin at him as though I'm drunk.

*Drunk on love.*

"How was your day?" he asks.

"It was okay," I respond with a release of breath and turn my gaze to the group walking past us. If I linger too long on my horrid audition experience, I may get choked up again. I return eye contact to him, adding, "I'll tell you more inside. How was yours?"

"Great, but it's even better now." He flashes a smile, and my favorite lines radiate near his eyes. It seems there are even more of them now than when I first laid eyes on him.

We walk into The Butcher's Daughter and sit in the corner near a wide open window. If I could design the interior of a restaurant, it would look exactly like this. The ambient, golden lighting and natural light wood accents are exactly my style. Plants loom above our heads, swaying in the evening breeze.

Our waitress arrives at the table, and after taking one look at Tyler, a wave of panic comes over her expression. Though she quickly hides it, it's clear she knows who he is. He seems to notice as well and prepares for the worst. I pray she doesn't run and grab her phone, asking me to snap a photo of them. But, to our delight, she introduces herself as usual and chooses not to make a scene.

We order some drinks and apps that she shakily places on the table before us. Tyler and I smile at her and thank her multiple times, hoping to ease her nervousness.

"So, tell me more about your day," he says while placing his napkin on his lap.

"Well, I slept for a good portion of it," I respond with a laugh, picking up a carrot smothered in hummus. "I also went in for an audition." His eyes brighten when I mention this. "But it didn't go well," I quickly add to douse any hope he might have that it did.

"Why's that?" He doesn't seem very phased by my response.

I stare at my fork on the table, saying, "I wasn't very prepared, my voice cracked at the biggest part—and I was just a ball of nerves." He nods and listens intently as I tell him more about the experience.

"It's so good you did it, though," he says. "You have to exercise those muscles, and it probably felt like a different ballgame now that you're in the hub of musical theater." Tyler brings his hand across the table and gently grabs mine. "It's all a part of the process and will only get easier as you do it more. But I'm sorry you had a bad experience."

"Thanks," I say and squeeze his hand back.

*I hope he's right.*

"But tell me about your day," I say, wanting to change the subject.

He tells me he was able to take a long nap before the show started, and the show itself went pretty well.

"The audience was unenthusiastic, but that will happen occasionally. Then I hung out with Jasper and took him for a long walk. I picked up some groceries and then hopped on the train to Brooklyn to see you." He smiles.

We continue talking and then feast on our entrees once they arrive. The food is *superb*. I don't usually love dinner dates because they can be so stiff and formal, but Tyler makes our time fun and light.

"Okay, tell me the backstory of that lady there," he says and discreetly points to an older woman with a cane enjoying a glass of wine by herself in the corner of the restaurant. She wears a pair of neon orange circle-shaped glasses, her hair is completely gray, but long and silky, hitting the middle of her back. She wears a dress that is covered in daisies of various colors.

I smile at her kindly when she notices my stare, and she smiles back.

Turning back to Tyler, I tell him of her fabricated life story. "I'd say she grew up in Brooklyn, lived here her whole life. At the ripe age of sixteen, she got a job as a pilot and traveled the world before meeting the love of her life in the Bahamas while they both lounged on the beach. They got married, had five kids, and now, she enjoys a glass of wine each week in a new, hip restaurant to remind herself never to lose the spunk within her and the independence she treasures, being the extraordinary woman she is."

Tyler laughs lightly. "I love that. If I have even a smidgen of her flare when I'm of old age, I'll be doing just fine."

I laugh and pick up a cracker, covering it in vegan cheese. "Your turn. Let's see…" Looking around, I find a group of chatty girls in their twenties. One of them has a tiny dog in her lap. It's a bit rough around the edges as dogs go. Though I think it's just the breed, and it's supposed to be this way; its fur is a mangy white and gray. The poor thing also shakes like a leaf while its pink tongue lolls to one side. But that doesn't stop the owner from adorning it with a loose hanging gemstone collar around its scrawny neck.

"There," I nod in the girl's direction before wiping my mouth with my napkin and quietly saying, "But specifically, the dog. What's her backstory?"

Tyler's lips twitch as he glances at the scruffy pup, making small dimples appear. I think he's trying not to laugh at the sight, and I don't blame him. He clears his throat and puts his tongue to his teeth while pondering the tale of this beggarly dog.

"Well, first. The dog's name was originally Curmudgeon." I pull my napkin to my face and laugh at the name while Tyler continues. "He was born in Mississippi to a lovely family that thought he looked like an old, crusty man—hence, the name. When he was two years old—or fourteen, I should say. Dog years, ya know?—he ran away from home, and traveled to New York City because he desired to be a hat model for Fashion Week."

"Naturally," I say. Tyler smirks.

"After he was scouted by some designers, they told him his dreams would come true, except that after weeks of sewing and creating, none of the hats fit him. They all either covered his eyes or engulfed his entire body. So, the designers kicked him to the curb. He spent his nights begging for food in SoHo until one day, a young girl called Janet picked him up and took him in as her own. She then named the dog "Suzy" before looking under his hind legs. Now he spends his days on her lap or in a Gucci purse being toted around, longing for the runway."

"Aw," I say with a pout. "That's actually really sad."

"Yeah, poor old Suzy," he lets out a sigh. "Her dreams of being a star in Fashion Week could still come true, though. Take a look."

I glance at the shaking dog whose owner has placed a small beret on its head that fits *perfectly*. I gasp and then declare silently, "Yes, Suzy! Chase your dreams." Tyler and I giggle to ourselves.

Once we finish dinner, he pays the bill, writing on the receipt for our waitress: *Thank you so much for a great dinner,* as if to say, *Thank you for not freaking out and instead, simply doing your job very well.*

We walk hand-in-hand, strolling along the quirky streets of Downtown Williamsburg, ending up at one of my favorite places I've been enjoying lately: Domino Park. It's a gorgeous little area that sits to the right of the Williamsburg Bridge and directly across the river from Manhattan. I've only ever seen it in the daytime, but the view at night is even more spectacular.

Walking near the permanent recliner chairs at the park's edge, Tyler chooses an empty seat away from the few groups of people enjoying the views. I'm about to sit in the chair next to his, but he tugs on my hands and lifts me onto his chair and into his lap. With his arms around me, we look across the glowing East River at the twinkling lights of Manhattan.

After a few minutes of soaking in the view, Tyler says quietly, "Promise me one thing."

I shift my body to look at his face and find that he has a very serious demeanor. His brow is slightly scrunched as he looks into my eyes with a new intensity, saying, "Don't give up on your dreams. They're put there for a reason." A beat goes by, and he looks at the view, shaking his head, before adding, "Don't lose them."

I swallow as he looks back up into my eyes. Gazing back at his sincere face, my lower lip starts to quiver. His words feel like a relighting of the flame that burns inside my body. This flame of hope gets dimmer and close to being doused as each self-tape email I send goes unopened. Or each audition goes awry. And after my day, I'm grateful for his awareness of my unsaid thoughts.

"I won't," I whisper back. I take his face in my hands and quietly say, "You are such a gift, Tyler Pickles Axel." A smile forms on my face at his fake middle name, but it returns earnestly again. "I'm not sure why I get the privilege of knowing you, but I'm so happy I do."

The edges of his mouth pull up at the corners, and he leans in even closer, kissing me slowly on the right cheek, then left, then my forehead, and finally landing on my lips. My whole body feels warm as he delicately tugs on my lower lip with a smile.

Seconds later, we both hear his phone buzz in his pocket and pull away. Tyler's mom is FaceTiming him.

"Do you mind if I answer?" he asks, and I shake my head in response.

The screen lights up with his mom's face. She's wearing large, blue eyeglasses and holds the phone upward so Tyler gets a great view of her nostrils. He's positioned the phone where she can only see him. I lean farther away so I'm not in the frame.

"Hey, Mum! How are you?"

"Hi Honey, I'm doing well. How are you?"

"Good! I want you to meet someone." A fearful expression finds its way to my face, but before I can object, he's already placed my entire face in the camera's view. "This is Sunday." I flash a lopsided smile and wave.

Her eyebrows scrunch together, and she moves her face closer to the phone, "Wait a second. Don't I know you?" And then, all of a sudden, her appearance turns bright with the pieces falling together. "Yes, that's right. We sat near each other at the show recently. How are you, darling?"

"Yes, we did," I say and look at Tyler, who is in utter shock. I do what I only know to do and laugh at the situation. "I'm doing well, thanks for asking," I say before returning my gaze to the phone.

"Wait, Mum. You already know who this is?" He points to me.

"Yes, Honey. We talked about you all night at your show! Sunday is a gem. But when did you guys meet? I thought you said you didn't know him, sweetie," she says, a bit confused, because I did not, in fact, know him that night.

"We met a few days later at a dog park," I say with a grin, basking in Tyler's confusion and shock. It's pretty fun.

He shakes his head while closing his eyes like an Etch A Sketch erasing its drawing. "Okay, well. Mum, I'm glad you two have already made your acquaintance, though my mind is blown. Anyway, what's up?"

"I just wanted to see if you'd like to visit sometime soon. It's been a few months, and your sister misses you."

"Hi, Tyler!" A voice calls from somewhere else in the room. Moments later, a brown-eyed girl with bangs comes into view.

"Hi, Haley," he says with a smile. "I miss you a lot."

"I miss you too." She then makes a funny face and asks, "Who's that?"

"This is Sunday, my—" he hesitates before continuing, but then after a quick beat, says, "My girlfriend." He looks at me with a furrowed brow and a shrug as if saying, *is that okay?* I nod back.

*FINE BY ME!*

"Hi, Sunday!" Haley says to me.

"Hi Haley, it's so nice to meet you." I smile.

"Tyler, when are you coming home?" she asks.

"I'm not sure, you guys," he says as his mom and sister both squish into view. "I want to see you, but the show makes it difficult. Maybe I can take a day off soon and make my way out there. But you can always come here too. Sunday and I can show you around."

Everything within me wants to run around the park with my arms flailing about in utter joy because he sees us together in even the weeks to come, but all I allow my outer body to do is present a small smile, nodding at the sentiment.

"Yeah, that sounds good. Maybe we'll make a trip in a week or so. I'd love to see you again Sunday," his mom says with a smirk.

"That sounds good, just let me know," Tyler responds.

"Will do. Well, I'll let you both go to enjoy your evening. Bye, Sunday!"

"Bye, Sunday!" Haley adds.

"Bye, you guys!" I say.

"Love you, Honey," Tyler's mom says to him with an echo of the same from Haley seconds later.

"Love you both. Tell dad the same. Talk to you soon." He blows them kisses before hanging up and then turns to me with the same look of shock as the minutes prior.

"Um, what?!" he says as I sit cross-legged between his legs. "When were you gonna tell me you met my parents?"

Letting out an embarrassed laugh, I say, "I feel like I went too far past the line of when it would have been appropriate and normal to bring it up, and then we crossed into the territory of weird and stalker-ish this late into our, uh…relationship?" I say while looking at my unpolished fingernails. "So I figured it would be better to keep it to myself."

He cackles and suddenly narrows his eyes at me, "What else don't I know?"

*Besides the fact that we've never talked about our first encounter at the show that meant* everything *to me...nothing.*

"Nothing," I say with the inflection of my voice rising at the end as if there's something else, but then repeat it flatly after clearing my throat, "Nothing."

"Okay," he laughs. "Speaking of our relationship, would you like to be my girlfriend?" He says it so casually that once I register what he's asking, a shiver is sent from my head to my toes. He seems to enjoy my look of surprise as much as I enjoyed his discomfort. Though he had already said the word "girlfriend" to his sister, I wasn't sure if he meant it. Now I know.

"Yes, I would," I say as clearly as possible, and it comes out *so* weird and robotic.

We both laugh, and he holds me closer, saying, "I was hoping you'd say that, darling."

"Mmm...yes, dahling," I mimic him with a fake British accent.

"Are you making fun of my accent?"

"Poppycock! I fink your accent is very lovely, babes." I say before adding a sultry look. "Care for a snog?"

He laughs with one big "HA."

He doesn't know I talked with an accent for *weeks* after returning from England. It's a miracle that this is the first time he's heard me speak like this. Once I spend time with his family again, it'll take a lot of self-control not to talk like I'm originally from Essex.

"Anyway, I like your parents a lot, and your sister seems so sweet," I say.

"It's nice you've already met my parents—that takes the pressure off for the next time," he teases me with a wink.

*True, but I'll still be a nervous wreck.*

Tyler's phone buzzes once more, he lifts it and tries to move the screen from my view, but I've already seen what his mom texted him:

**Don't you lose her. She's one of the good ones.**

# SIXTEEN

Unlike our night prior, Tyler walks me into my building at a reasonable hour. We're standing in the hallway outside my apartment door, and I can't seem to wipe the grin off my face. Mostly because of Tyler and how wonderful he is, but also because of the interaction with his mom and sister—especially that sneaky text I shouldn't have seen—but did see—that his mom sent him. It's nice to know she enjoyed my company just as much as I did hers that night in the theater.

*It always pays to be kind to strangers!*

We hold onto one another, not quite ready to let go and say goodnight.

"Tonight was fun," he says.

"It was."

"Before I forget, I have a show in a few weeks at 54 Below. I'd love for you to come."

54 Below is a gorgeous little restaurant where legendary Broadway artists sing while people enjoy dinner and drinks. I've always wanted to go, but I haven't been able to get tickets to my favorite performers' shows because they always sell out so fast.

"Tyler," I reply with a certain seriousness and pull away from our hug. "You are continually checking things off my bucket list without knowing it. Seeing a show at 54 Below is another item I have yet to tick."

He smirks, "Is there anything on there that's not Broadway related?"

"Not really."

*Definitely not telling him that the most recent addition I've thought of adding is to be a costar alongside him in a Broadway production...*

"I'd like to see this list you speak of," he says, looking at me slightly sideways.

With hesitation—or trying to remember if anything mortifying is listed—I take out my phone and let him take a gander. While Tyler is looking through, one item makes him laugh, and he covers his mouth with his hand.

"What!" I say, leaning over to see which one he's chuckling at.

"This one—*pack two suitcases: one full of warm weather clothes and the other cold, go to the airport, close your eyes, and pick a vacation spot on the map.*"

"What's wrong with that?" I argue.

"Nothing! It's cute."

My eyes narrow in on him.

"I'm not trying to be mean…it's just so *specific*…and doesn't seem very realistic."

"Well, you're *definitely* not coming on that trip," I say sassily.

Looking back down at my phone with a teasing smirk, he says, "That's okay. You'll have a blast by yourself in the middle of the ocean."

My mouth drops, and I flick him in the arm with my finger. "Rude." I take the phone away from him. "You no longer have the privilege of looking at my bucket list."

"I'm sorry." He raises his hands in surrender. "I promise I won't make fun of them anymore. Let me see it again, please."

"Nope! Too late." I say as I put the phone behind my back and lean against the apartment door. He places his hands on the doorframe beside my shoulders and gives me a slow, intoxicating kiss. My eyes remain closed, and I sigh, "Okay, fine." I hand him back the phone.

"Thank you." He scrolls a bit more and then bites the tip of his thumb, smiling once again.

"What is it now?" I roll my eyes.

"No, I just like that you put in here: *Get married* and *Have a baby,*" he says without looking at me. "It's nice."

A chill runs through my body as I look at his handsome face. He'd better get out of here before I change it to *Marry Tyler Axel and have all of* his *babies.*

"Thanks," I say. "I should get to bed, though. It's getting late." I slide the phone out of his hand.

"Yeah, you're right," he says, almost as though he's returning to reality after daydreaming. "Goodnight, Sunday."

"Night, Tyler," I say, still leaning against the door—unsure of whether my legs could keep me up if I weren't. He leans in for the last time and kisses me gently while wrapping an arm around my waist, my body melts into his. After a few minutes of fireworks going off in my belly, he smiles and kisses my forehead, saying, "Sweet dreams." Then turns and walks down the stairs.

I stay stuck to the door, envisioning what it would be like to achieve all of my bucket list items with him by my side. Picturing a life with him stirs something inside of me.

*This could be everything I've ever dreamed of.*

The following week, it's back to the work grind—literally. Grinding coffee beans.

Last week, I'd seen Tyler almost every day, which was *the best*, but this week, we've spread our times together a bit more to settle back into our normal routines.

Finn and I had a fun girl's night a few days ago where we squealed about our boys and how cute they are as we painted our nails while a cheesy rom-com played in the background. She and Lucas have quickly made their relationship official and are now boyfriend and girlfriend. We giggled for one another as we told the stories of our first kisses with our boys. Lucas took her to the Met museum for a late-night perusing of the art pieces and kissed her in front of her favorite Monet painting. It sounded brilliantly romantic. I told her about Tyler and me in the fountain, thinking our first kiss would happen there until we almost got arrested, and how he kissed me in the karaoke room in his apartment building. It was a fun bonding night for us girls, and we resolved to make it a weekly tradition to keep up with the latest happenings between our men and us.

Gavin and I have the afternoon shift at the coffee shop, and we're working the front counter together. It's been a while since I've brought him up to date on the latest news with Tyler and me, so I tell our story in between customers.

"And then he leaned forward and was about to lay one on me—"

"Hi, I'd like a small Americano, please," the customer at the counter says.

I ring her up as quickly as possible, saying, "That'll be $3.89 whenever you're ready." Like the Flash, I'm popping her espresso into the machine and blasting the espresso-filled cup with hot water from the spout before handing it back to her with precision.

"Thanks," she says, and gives me a judgmental face with how fast I'm moving, but I ignore her and continue the story for Gavin.

"And THEN, just as our lips are about to touch, a cop says, 'HEY, YOU TWO, OUT OF THE FOUNTAIN!'" I reenact the moment with my best New York cop impression, exaggerating to a large extent with finger guns and everything.

Gavin's eyes bulge, and an awkward smile forms on his lips. I think he's afraid of me, but I'm too high on adrenaline and coffee to care.

"But then, he takes me to his apartment," I purr, and Gavin's eyebrows raise with curiosity.

"Oh? Tell me more," he says with a sultry smile that makes me laugh.

"Nothing crazy happened. But we did kiss," I say with a girlish giggle.

To my surprise, he meets my girlish giggle and gives me a tween twirl, saying, "You did?!" Then he shrieks a little. At first, I think he's making fun of me, but when he doesn't stop, I know he's serious.

"Sunshine, I love this for you. When is the wedding?" he asks while grasping my forearms.

"I have no idea," I sing to him. "But…" I cover my mouth and say with a hidden smile, "I think I'm falling for him." This makes Gavin shriek again.

"What's going on in here?" A familiar voice asks from the other side of the counter. While Gavin and I still hold one another, we turn our faces slowly to the person speaking.

Tyler.

*Dear God, I pray he didn't hear the last two minutes of our conversation.*

My face turns the shade of a lobster, and Gavin audibly gasps. We both give Tyler a worried Cheshire Cat smile, releasing one another, and I make my way to the other side of the counter with my insides feeling like Jell-O as Tyler wraps me into a tight hug.

"Surprise!" he says in my ear.

"Hi," is all I can manage to say. I have to take off my girlish excitement like a sequined jacket with which Gavin and I just danced around the room and morph into cool-as-a-cucumber Sunday.

Gavin reaches over the counter and takes Tyler's hand, morphing out of his teenage swooning and into full-adult swooning of the man standing before him.

"Big fan," Gavin says while shaking Tyler's hand rapidly. "I'm Gavin."

"Tyler. Nice to meet you," he says kindly, but then his face turns a little funny as he tries to pull his hand away at the appropriate time, but Gavin keeps him in a tight grip. Once Tyler can get it loose, he rubs and shakes his hand, keeping his gaze on Gavin. He then turns back to me with a confused smile that quickly fades. "I don't have a show tonight, so I wanted to take you out once your shift ended."

My insides firming up from their prior Jell-O-ing, have returned to full-fledged Jell-O. I *love* surprises, and he has no idea. This is the best day.

"Really?!" I say, raising my eyebrows with the cheesiest grin. "I get off in forty-five minutes if you don't mind waiting."

"No problem at all. I brought a book!" He takes out an old copy of *A Tree Grows in Brooklyn* from his back pocket and then gives me a quick peck on the lips before lingering near my ear and whispering, "I missed you." My face flushes again as his breath tickles my cheek.

"I'll be over here," he says, pointing to a chair in the corner. I smile, nod, and get back on the other side of the counter to continue my barista-ing. I'm shaking with surprise for the next forty-five minutes, trying not to spill the drinks or trip over my own feet, but I do both multiple times.

Once we finish our shift, Gavin and I are relieved of our post by the baristas scheduled for the night. I walk over to Tyler's table after running to the bathroom and doing whatever I can to make myself look as presentable and cute as possible, but nothing can hide the fact that I'm wearing grubby work clothes, and smell of stale coffee.

Tyler looks up at me from his book, through his eyelashes, and says, "You look beautiful." I grin and look toward my shoes, which are covered in spilled coffee splotches.

"Ready?" he asks.

"Ready."

As we approach the door, Gavin catches up to us. With a grandpa's voice, he asks, "So, what are you two crazy kids up to tonight?" and then proceeds to choke on his spit.

Tyler and I stifle a laugh, but Gavin laughs for us—though I can tell he's embarrassed.

"I have a little surprise date for Sunday," Tyler says, and I beam at him.

"Sounds saucy," Gavin responds with his eyebrows high.

Tyler pauses for a moment before saying to Gavin, "Would you like to join us?"

Gavin's facial expression looks like Tyler just asked him to go on an all-expense-paid vacation with him. I giggle. Before he answers, Gavin looks at me as if to ask if it's okay if he joins. I nod enthusiastically.

"Y-yes," he says to Tyler.

The last guy I dated couldn't care less about my friends, so this action from Tyler sends a warm feeling throughout my whole body.

We take the subway to an undisclosed location that's still in Brooklyn. Walking the dark alleyways, Tyler leads us to a Goodwill store. Both Gavin and I wear puzzled faces.

Gavin jokingly whispers to me, "You'd think, as a celebrity, he'd bring us somewhere a *bit* more upscale." I laugh and put my finger up to my lips to shush him.

When we walk in, the fluorescent lights burn our eyes. We're all squinting as we adjust, and Tyler walks ahead of us at the entrance before turning to explain his plan.

"Okay, you're probably wondering why I've brought you here," he says with his hands clasped before him.

"Uh, ya." Gavin says.

Tyler smirks and continues. "I saw this video where you walk through a thrift store and close your eyes while pointing down the aisles until the other person tells you to stop." He acts out the motions. "Whatever you land on, you have to wear the rest of the night."

"Oh my gosh, I saw that too!" I say with a clap of excitement.

Gavin still doesn't look convinced, but I grab his arm and push him toward the aisles.

"Let's do Sunday's outfit first." Tyler points to the row a few yards away. "Women's tops are over there." We all walk over, and I run to the far end while they wait on the other side. I cover my eyes with one hand and point with the other while walking straight ahead. After a dozen or so steps, they yell, "STOP." My hand lands on a soft, fluffy top. I open my eyes to find a colorful sweater with different types of embroidered cats on it. They both start cracking up, but little do they know I may have purchased this shirt outside of the game. It's adorable.

Onto my pants, I graze the aisles again. My fingers land on a pair of stretchy leopard leggings. "Awesome," I say with an approving nod.

We hit up the shoes next, and to my unfortunate luck, I grab a pair of two-sizes-too-big hot pink pumps. My feet throb in agony just at the sight of them.

Gavin is next. He pulls out a blue, 4XL shirt of some 2011 5k race. Classic thrift store. The pants he grabs are neon orange scrubs, and his shoes are very cool cowboy boots, to which he opens his eyes and says, "Um, I'm wearing these every day."

Tyler races through the aisles before we can say stop, so he has to return and start over. He lands on a plaid, button-down shirt that would be very sexy on him if it wasn't a size extra small. While trying it on in the aisle, the buttons barely close while the sleeves stop at his forearms. Gavin and I still pump him up, saying it looks great. He walks toward us, showcasing the top like a model during fashion week.

The pants he lands on redeem the shirt. They're baggy black jeans with the most oversized pockets I've ever seen. He whimpers a little when he pulls them from the rack, knowing he will look the worst out of all of us.

We run back to the footwear, and he grabs a pair of old hiking boots that look like they should have been thrown out or burned rather than donated here. But they fit him! So at the least, he'll be comfortable, unlike me in my sky-high pumps.

After checking out, we enter our separate dressing rooms and put the outfits on. My top smells like it was soaked in an older woman's perfume, and my leggings are itchy. So much so that I wonder if the original owner covered them in itching powder for a good laugh as they donated them.

Once I'm situated, I walk out of the dressing room and burst out in laughter as Tyler and Gavin stand before me in their garb. They take one look at me and start cackling. We're all hunched over, holding our bellies from giggling so much. Every time I glance at Tyler, I begin to snort. His baggy jeans and teeny top look horrible, but he's a good sport about it.

"You look like my old Kindergarten teacher, Mrs. Hornstock," Gavin tells me as he wipes the tears from his eyes.

Between laughs, I say, "Did you go to school in prison?"

While we walk toward the exit, Tyler turns to me and whispers, "You still look beautiful." A smile cracks on my lips, and I look into his eyes—which are in my direct line of view as I'm practically the same height as him in these heels. His gaze is full of admiration even as I wear this hideous attire. Shaking my head in disbelief, I hold onto his arm with a delighted grin. The Goodwill cashier's eyes follow us as we exit, and he covers his mouth to stop himself from laughing.

"Have a good one!" Tyler shouts back and raises his arm to wave, but his shirt hikes up practically to his nipples. I tug on it to get it back down into place while we both chuckle, holding onto one another as we walk through the doors.

After we compose ourselves on the street, Gavin says with a breathy voice, "Where to?" He then poses as though he's on the cover of *Vogue*.

"I know just the place," Tyler replies.

"As long as it's within a few yards, I'm in," I say with reluctance as I point to my heels. There's no way I'll be able to keep up the standard forty-minute walk for a new location in New York City with these bad boys. "If not, someone might need to carry me."

Tyler laughs and then turns his back to me, saying, "Hop on."

As Gavin struts ahead, I quietly say in Tyler's ear, "Thanks, Piggy." A gasp escapes his lips.

"You knew I was right this whole time! The piggy is *totally* on the bottom."

"Of course. But I wasn't going to concede so quickly," I say, kissing him on the cheek. His face flushes, and a smile cracks on his lips. My favorite laughter lines emerge, and I can't help but give him another few kisses near his mouth and eyes. My lips only make the line grow deeper, making me never want to stop kissing him.

"What're y'all doin'? C'mon, let's get goin'!" Gavin hollers after hiking up his pants and walking how he thinks a cowboy would. He looks more like a toddler with a full diaper. Waving an invisible lasso, he shouts, "Yeehaw!"

Tyler whispers to me, "What have we done?"

The boys walk, and I ride a few blocks until we reach a small pub. Tyler gently lowers me to the ground before we walk in. As we take our seats at the bar, the bartender gives us a funny look, but looking around the room, it's pretty wild that we don't stand out *that* much.

*Brooklyn, I tell ya.*

We order a couple of rounds of drinks, and though we look like morons, I couldn't be happier. Gavin is quickly becoming one of my favorite people the more I get to know him, and Tyler amazes me every day. I'm falling for him quicker than I ever thought was possible. Our story feels like a fairytale. And seeing both of them interact makes my heart swim with joy. I'd gladly give up my time alone with my boyfriend for this.

"I'm a little upset," Gavin says.

"Why is that?" I ask while popping a pretzel into my mouth from the small bowl on the bar counter.

"How come when I dress like I'm an escaped prisoner with a hankering for stylish cowboy boots in Brooklyn, no one bats an eye? But when I break out my Speedo in Hawaii on vacation with my husband, everyone on the beach looks at me like I've just stepped on their hamster?"

Tyler mistakenly takes a drink as Gavin finishes his sentence and sprays out lager all over the table before breaking into a loud cackle. He wipes up his drippings with a napkin and apologizes.

Before it gets to be too late in the night, we make our way back to Williamsburg. Gavin tells us how much fun he had before parting ways and returning to his apartment.

Tyler and I stand in front of my building, still in our ridiculous clothes, as he draws me in for a sweet kiss.

"I've been wanting to do that all night," he says as he leans his forehead on mine.

"I've been wanting you to do that all night," I laugh.

He holds me tight, and suddenly, one of the buttons from his shirt shoots off into the bushes. We both are stunned and then slowly start laughing together. "One second," he says, letting go of me. Doing a Hulk sort of move with his arms flexed in front of him, he grunts and the entire back of his shirt shreds open, much to my delight.

"Oh!" The sound escapes my mouth before I can take it back. "He's so strong," I say under my breath. With a chuckle at my embarrassing reaction, he removes the teeny, ripped shirt and slips it back into the Goodwill bag, before putting his own shirt back on.

"That's better," he says and returns to hold me.

I have an early shift tomorrow at the coffee shop, so I say goodbye before I want to. The truth is, I'd stay out with him all night, every night.

As I walk up the stairs back to my apartment, I reminisce about the laughter and fun we had tonight, hoping this could be the start of many more similar nights with my favorite boys.

# SEVENTEEN

Waking up the following morning, my head is pounding, my throat is on fire, and my nose is clogged to the point where I have to breathe with my mouth open or no air will enter my body. I was supposed to be working the opening shift again at the coffee shop, but after my alarm went off at 5:45 a.m., I couldn't even stand up to get ready. My head started spinning while I was vertical, so after texting Gavin and letting him know that I was sick and wouldn't make it in, I laid back down and fell asleep almost immediately.

It's around 10 a.m., and I just woke back up. Every part of my body is achy and sluggish.

Gavin had texted me hours earlier, saying it was not a problem and that he hoped I felt better. Another text comes in from him as I'm scrolling on my phone.

**Brittany Oliver was just looking for you.**

*That's weird. Maybe it was to apologize for calling me Wednesday when I saw her at the show.*

Another text from him dings. **I should say, she was looking for "Wednesday." But don't worry. I set her straight.**

*Ah, guess it wasn't to apologize.*

**That's weird. Did she say what about?** I ask.

**No, she just asked about you and then dropped it when I told her you were sick.**

**Huh. Well, I'm intrigued.**

**So am I!** He writes back. **Also, guess what I'm wearing ;)**

**Your new cowboy boots?**

**YOU KNOW IT! I'll leave you to rest, though. Feel better!! And tell my new best friend I say hiii.**

This makes me cough out a laugh. **Thanks, Gavin. And I will lol.**

It takes immense effort to get up, but I know I should get some food in me. After using the bathroom—clutching onto every surface as I walk by for fear of passing out—I make a light breakfast of toast and jam and roll back into bed only to take a few bites of the bread and then toss the plate back on my nightstand.

My phone lights up from the edge of my bed. A text from Tyler.

**Morning, darling. How are you?**

**Hey,** I type out "babe," "honeybun," and "cutie," erasing them all because I haven't settled on a pet name for him just yet and stick with "hey."

**I'm not great. Woke up feeling sick.**

We had wanted to spend time together this afternoon after my shift, but I know I'm not up for that in my current state. I'm about to type out that I won't be able to make it today when a FaceTime call comes in from him.

I look like an absolute mess right now, and I'm tempted to try and fix my hair before answering, but I don't even have the energy for that. Tyler is about to see me in my most raw form. I swipe to answer, and the camera shows me even worse than I imagined—my face is pale with blotchy red spots, and my frizzy hair sticks out from my gray hood in various directions.

"Hey," I say. This is the first time I've talked today, and it sounds like I have rocks stuck in my throat. I try to clear it, but it doesn't change.

Tyler is sitting on his sofa with Jasper next to him in the frame—they both look like a million bucks.

"Hey," he says, empathy in his tone. "I'm so sorry you're not feeling well. What can I do to help?"

My mom is the only person I've ever accepted help from when I was sick. And that wasn't even accepting it as much as her forcing her way in to help. Trueloves are not generally ones to ask for help, so I brush off his offer.

"I'm okay. Thank you, though." I try to showcase a smile so he can see I'll be fine, but it comes off as strained and awkward.

He laughs lightly and says, "You look like you could use a hand. Why don't I come over and bring you some soup? We can watch movies all day."

"No, it's really okay. I don't want you to waste your free time today on me—or have you get sick yourself."

"Sunday, first of all, it's not a waste. And second, I'm pretty sure if you're sick, then I'll be sick soon enough, seeing as though we swapped saliva last night," he says, and a smile tugs at his lips. My face goes even redder than this sickness is making it. I cover it with my sleeved hands. "I want to help you," he says sweetly. "I'll be there in an hour, okay?"

"Okay," I reply with reluctance, but inside, I'm relieved and thankful for his care.

"See you soon."

We hang up the call, and I look around the room to see if there's anything I wouldn't want him to see. No rogue undergarments are lying around, and all my other clothes are nestled nicely in their drawers. We're looking pretty good—though it's not like I have the energy to get out of bed to clean up anyway.

An hour later, Tyler shows up at my door with vegetable soup, ginger ale, vegan snacks, and various medicines.

"I wasn't sure exactly what was going on, so I brought the mother lode," he says, holding up the bags as I hang on the door, trying not to collapse. Once he puts the bags down on the counter, he puts an arm around me and leads me back to my bed, tucking me in.

I hear him rummaging around in the kitchen, and after a few minutes, he comes back with a tray holding a bowl of warm soup, a glass of water, and a variety of snacks surrounding it.

"Mademoiselle, your dinner," he says with a thick French accent that makes me laugh, but then it quickly turns into a coughing fit. "Whoops, no more jokes or laughter for you, missy," he grimaces and pats my feverish head. I sit up straighter in the bed, and he lays the tray on my lap.

"You're burning up. Take this," he slides two ibuprofen from the tray and places them in my hands. As I sip the water and take the pills, I ask, "Did you make yourself anything?" A steady fountain of snot shoots from my nose, and I quickly grab a tissue to stop the flow.

"No, I'm good," he assures me as he nestles onto the bed next to me, careful not to spill anything from the tray. "I ate before I left. But don't you worry about me. I'm here to help you."

"Okay," I take a big spoonful of soup. The warm broth feels like heaven on my throat, making me sigh with pleasure.

"How is it?" he asks.

"So, so good. Thank you."

He smiles and kisses me on my temple. "What would you like to do? Movie marathon? Read? Sleep?"

"Hmm," I ponder, and the sound is like gravel rolling around in my windpipe. "What if you told me a story?"

"A story, huh?" His lips turn up on one side.

"Yes, a nice story with a happy ending," I say while nuzzling myself deeper into the pillows behind me before taking a slurp of soup. I look at him with babydoll eyes.

"Okay, let's see," he looks around the room, contemplating what to say.

"I've got it," he starts. "So, when I was younger, my family and I had this cat named 'Tail.'"

My brow furrows. "Your cat was named 'Tail'? As in T-A-L-E or T-A-I-L?"

He has the audacity to give *me* a funny look when I ask this—though it may be because I've shoved tissues up my nostrils and kept them there to stop the flow.

He continues. "T-A-I-L. Like the appendage at the rear of an animal's body."

"But why?"

He raises an eyebrow and looks at me, "Well, if I told you that, I'd give away the story's ending, wouldn't I?"

"My apologies. Go on," I motion with my hand for him to proceed.

"This cat was the best. He was originally our neighbor's cat, but they couldn't care for him any longer, so we offered to house him. My sister was playing with him the day we brought him home, and I noticed she was waving around something long and fluffy on the ground while the cat was chasing it."

My eyes narrow in on him as he continues. "And as I got a better look, I realized the cat's tail had fallen off, and my sister was using it as a toy for the cat to chase."

With my head still pounding, I can't tell if I'm hallucinating what he's saying or if this is real. "*What?*" I bark.

"Yeah, we found out later that a bunch of families didn't want him because he lost his tail, so when we got him from our neighbor, they had glued on a fake tail to his butt so we wouldn't be turned off to house him. And that's where we got the name 'Tail.'"

"You're joking." I stare at him with skepticism.

"Yup," he says with a grin.

"So his tail didn't fall off?"

He shakes his head, "No, we just named him that because my sister thought it was cute." He pops a handful of cashews from my tray into his mouth and laughs. I slowly shake my head, a smile forming on my lips.

"That's your idea of a happy ending?"

"No, but I knew it would make you smile." He taps my bottom lip gently.

"You know, you're a little too good at lying," I say as he wraps his arms around me, and I rest my head against his chest.

"That's sort of my job," he responds with a small laugh, and I look up at him. His expression has changed to serious, realizing the potential effect of what he has just said.

"How will I ever know you're telling the truth?" Though I'm teasing, part of me is concerned by this. Dating an actor is riskier than I would have thought because this could all be some evil game put on by the person you're falling for.

"When it comes to things more serious than a cat's tail, you can trust me." His blue eyes flash between mine with a new gravity to them before he leans in and gives my forehead a kiss.

Hours later, after a few naps, sneezing fits, and trying to get some more food in me, we watch an episode of *Friends*. On my nightstand, I see my phone light up. Mick is FaceTiming me, and I answer.

"Woah, what's going on with you?" she asks with concern as the camera shows my state again—somehow, it's gotten even worse. God bless Tyler Axel.

"I'm sick," I say, then point the camera to Tyler. "But Tyler is here taking care of me!"

"Hi, Mick," he says with a light smile. "Nice to meet you virtually."

"Oh, hi! You too. Thanks for taking care of my girl. I'm sure that took some convincing," she says as she glares her eyes at me, knowing I would never ask for help in a situation like this.

"Sure did," he replies and puts his arm around me. "But we'll have her back to her old self in no time."

"That's great," she says. "Sorry you're not feeling well, Sunday."

"Thanks, Mick."

"But I'm calling because I was just scrolling on my phone and came across this video—here, let me send it to you." She starts tapping her screen. A few moments later, a link comes through. Tyler and I watch the video of a 20-something girl talking in her bedroom with the caption, "Who is this b****?" And as she's talking, photos of Tyler and me from the last few weeks flash across the screen.

My stomach drops. There are multiple images of us: the first is when we walked out of the stage door at his show the night he let me stay backstage. Another from when I was leaving his apartment in his sweats at six in the morning after we stayed up all night. And the final photo is a very clear shot of me through the window of The Butcher's Daughter last week at dinner.

My skin tingles with disgust and fear. It's hard not to feel violated by something like this happening. We didn't even see this person—or these people—snapping photos. All these moments that we thought were just between us are now on full display for the whole world to see, being overanalyzed and misconstrued. My mind goes back to the photos from leaving his apartment...

*What would my friends and family think? I know nothing happened, but they won't think that.*

On top of that, people across the internet call me despicable names and wonder how on earth I'm "good enough" for Tyler Axel.

I knew Tyler was famous, but this is the next level. I never expected a response like this from the world just because I'm falling for someone who is forced to live his life in the spotlight. Tears well up in my bloodshot eyes.

# EIGHTEEN

Y ou're all over the internet. But it seems like no one knows who you are," Mick says with a bit of hope until her face falls, and she finishes by saying, "...yet."

"I don't even know what to say." I'm looking at Mick on the phone and then gaze at Tyler. I've been so preoccupied with the video and my own emotions that I haven't glanced at him. And boy, does he look angry. His face is bright red as he stares at something across the room. I've never seen him like this.

"Hey," I say, tugging on his sleeve. "Are you okay?" My question seems to have pulled him from his trance. He looks at me, and a somberness floods his expression.

"I'm so sorry."

I look back at my phone and say, "Hey, Mick, I'm going to let you go. Thanks for letting me know about this."

"You got it. And feel better, Sunday."

"Thanks, girl. Love you."

"Love you too," she replies, and we close the call.

I turn my gaze to Tyler, who is back to being deep in thought, and say, "You don't need to apologize. This isn't your fault at all."

"I get that," he says, "but because of me, people are judging you and creating videos that advertise our moments together just to gain followers. It's ridiculous." He has a disoriented look, as though he doesn't understand why people would go through all this trouble for someone like him.

"I'm okay," I say, taking his head in my hands so his wavering gaze fixes on me. "I know who I am, and whatever a random girl says on the internet about me won't shake that, so don't worry. Let's just try to forget about it and enjoy today."

I then turn my face away from him and sneeze five times into a tissue.

"God bless you," he says with a laugh once the sneezes have ceased. The sneezing fit seemed to temporarily shake him out of the funk he was in because he draws me into his arms and says quietly, "Okay, let's enjoy today. What should we watch next?"

"How about…" I start listing all his movies, and he rolls his eyes, saying, "Nope," after each one.

Instead, we decide to start a Harry Potter movie marathon and get as far into the films as possible before Tyler has to leave for his show tonight. I only make it twenty minutes into *The Sorcerer's Stone* before falling asleep in his arms.

A week later, I'm on the mend—able to breathe through my nose but still have a lingering cough. Tyler hasn't gotten sick, thank goodness. He must have an immune system of a superhero with all the people he greets after shows and with all the actors that sing so close to him on stage they are practically spitting on him.

*And with all the women he kisses on stage too.*

I'm still not used to having a boyfriend kissing other women— usually, that's a red flag for me, but obviously, this situation is a bit different. If I think about it too long, some jealousy or something like it stirs inside of me. Best to push those thoughts down just like the boys sing about in *The Book of Mormon.* Turn them off like a light switch.

*So, anyway.* Yesterday, I had another ludicrous audition. I went out for the role of Vanessa in the show *In the Heights,* which will be playing in a small theater in Brooklyn. During the dance portion, I accidentally tripped the girl next to me, and we both lost our place in the routine. However, she did *not* think it was an accident. I have never seen a dirtier look come from someone I'd just met. She even scoffed at me. I apologized quickly and went to the back of the room—away from her—to finish the combination. The singing portion went just as terribly. I chose to sing a faster-paced song from *Newsies,* and the accompanist looked at me angrily while I handed him my sheet music.

It wasn't until the end of the song that I knew why he gave me that look—this song was *insanely difficult* to play on the piano, and he finished by hitting a sour note while my voice faltered trying to find a melody for the new key he had put us in. It was not pretty. Safe to say, I won't be getting a callback for that one. And also, whether it's because I'm in New York City or not, people just need to be kinder. Enough with the rude looks.

In other news, the world has figured out my name. A celebrity gossip site tracked down the photos of Tyler and me, somehow tying my face back to an old YouTube channel where I'd posted videos of me singing show tunes. People called me a "Clout Chaser," insinuating I was only going out with Tyler for the fame. It felt like I was back in high school again, where people would say anything to boost themselves up or to justify what they don't understand.

But on the flip side of people saying awful things about me, old acquaintances I haven't talked to in years started reaching out to me on social media asking me how I was doing—as though associating themselves back with me would make them cooler because I'm dating Tyler.

*Hate to break it to ya, folks, but that's not how this works.*

We deactivated some of my accounts because of the sudden influx of messages and friend requests from people I'd never met. Tyler apologized relentlessly for all the adjustments I needed to make to handle this sudden fame-by-association. I continued to tell him it was not a big deal, though I could absolutely see it becoming one. His distaste for fame made a lot more sense to me now. It's quite annoying and time-consuming to fix needless problems. And I'm not even the famous one in this situation!

But we're shaking it off because today is a gorgeous summer day in New York City. Finn had invited Tyler and me to join her and Lucas on a day trip to Rockaway Beach. After being inside our apartment the whole week while I was sick, this outing sounded like an absolute dream. Staying in also made me conclude that we need a bigger apartment—but isn't that always the case in New York?

We meet the boys in the Financial District to grab coffee before taking the ferry. Walking into Gregory's coffee, Finn and I spot Tyler and Lucas chatting in the corner. They see us walk in and flash heart-stopping smiles. They are both incredibly handsome. Finn and I blush as we walk toward them.

"Hey," Tyler says in my ear as we embrace in a quick hug. "I missed you."

We didn't get to spend much time together this week with me being sick and Tyler being busy with some new auditions his agent encouraged him to attend.

"I missed you too."

Finn and Lucas have been seeing each other almost every day since being introduced at the party—I think they make an adorable couple. From what I can tell, his personality fits nicely with Finn's. She is a bit more chill, while he is energetic. He's a bit fiery, while she is gentler. It seems they balance each other out. Also, they're both gorgeous and could make loads of money as a modeling couple, so there's that.

Grabbing our iced drinks, we race to the ferry that is about to leave. Finn and Lucas run hand-in-hand, and the same with Tyler and me. We make it with a few minutes to spare and head to the top section to watch the water and maximize our sunshine intake for the day. It will take just over an hour to get to Rockaway, but it's a much better ride than taking the subway the whole journey, which was the only other option. Lucas insisted the ferry was the way to go.

Tyler and I sit in one row while Finn and Lucas sit in the row in front of us, turning in our direction so we can talk as a group. We start playing Never Have I Ever to pass the time.

"Alright," Lucas starts and rubs his hands together as he comes up with his statement. "Never have I ever...eaten ketchup."

We all look at him like he has forty-five heads.

"Wait, what?" I say louder than I meant to. He looks just as shocked as we are, probably thinking it's a regular practice not to eat ketchup. "You're alone on that one, Lucas, but way to start us off with a mind-blower," I tease. "Also, we're getting you some fries at the beach, and I'll make sure you try ketchup."

"I suppose I can do that," Lucas laughs.

"Okay, me next," Finn says. "Never have I ever gotten a tattoo."

Surprisingly, I'm the only one to put a finger down because I have three.

"Um, excuse me. How do I not know about these?" Tyler says with faux hurt.

"Because they're all hidden," I reply with a wry smile.

Tyler leans over to me, bringing his hand to my ear, and whispers, "Are they on your butt?"

"NO!" My face turns the shade of a gnarly sunburn, and I cover it with my hands.

"He just asked you if they're on your butt, didn't he?" Lucas asks with a laugh. "We were all thinking it!"

"No, they're not on my butt," I say, rolling my eyes. "I have one on my rib, one on my ankle, and the other behind my ear." I bend my right ear back, showing them the tattoo of a small carnation flower.

"Very nice," Lucas says. "Alright, Tyler, you're up."

"Hmmm, okay." He puts his arm around me and then ponders for a moment. I notice his button-down shirt blowing in the wind, revealing his slightly hairy chest. I smile to myself.

"Never have I ever been on a dating app."

All three of us put a finger down.

"Really? I'm the only one who hasn't?" His face is full of surprise.

"Yeah, mate," Lucas says. "You probably never will either, with all the girls flocking to you."

Finn elbows Lucas in the ribs while he looks at her with confusion until he understands that what he said would not be something any girl dating Tyler would want to hear.

"Sorry, I shouldn't have said that," Lucas quickly remarks while looking at me.

"It's fine, don't worry about it," I say back with a plastered smile, though my heart is aching at the thought of women continually throwing themselves at Tyler, no matter his relationship status.

"Okay, I'll go next," I say, trying to blow past the awkwardness. "Never have I ever…signed up for a reality television show."

Both Tyler and Lucas put their fingers down.

"Bachelor?" Lucas asks Tyler.

"Yep."

"What!" Finn and I say at the same time. Tyler smiles and flicks his head to Lucas so he can explain first.

"I auditioned when they had a casting call in the city," Lucas says. "But didn't get a callback."

I'm honestly surprised because Lucas is attractive, charming, and has a great job at a marketing firm. I'm not sure what else they'd be looking for.

We all look at Tyler for his reasoning. "Yeah," he begins and shifts in his seat. "I auditioned as well."

A few beats go by before Finn says, "And?"

"They asked me to be the Bachelor..."

Finn and I drop our jaws.

"You're joking," Lucas says with a deadpan expression.

"No," he lets out an uncomfortable laugh. "But right before they offered it, I started dating someone, so I declined."

"Wow," Lucas says, wearing a face that says he probably would not have made the same decision.

We attempt to do a few more Never Have I Evers, but the game quickly dies out. Finn and Lucas turn back in their seats to face forward, talking and enjoying the rest of the ride.

Tyler and I sit silently for a moment before he leans over to me and whispers, "Just so you know, you are the only one I want to be dating. No one else." He then leans in and gives me an unhurried kiss on the cheek.

With my eyes closed, I smile, but it doesn't stop my brain from racing with the information it has just received.

Once the ferry docks, we grab acai bowls from a local cafe and head to the beach. The rest of New York had the same idea because the sand is crawling with people. You'd think by now I'd be used to having every moment of my day shared with thousands of people. Still, my introverted interior shows as I shudder from seeing hundreds of swimsuit-wearing bodies sprawled before me.

For being a beach that's only an hour's ferry ride from Manhattan, it's gorgeous. The sand is squishy and white, and the water looks clear. Surfers ride the waves in their wetsuits while little kids create sandcastles on the shore.

We find a small area between two groups of people around the same age as us, drinking brown paper-covered bottles of who knows what. Throwing our towels and bags down, Finn and I strip off our shorts and tees, revealing our bikinis. Mine is a lilac shade, and hers is a neon orange. Tyler and Lucas take their shirts off, and as always, I try my best not to stare at Tyler's abs. Luckily, my dark sunglasses save me this time. I can take in his shirtless form in my peripheral vision while my body faces the ocean as though that's what I'm genuinely admiring.

We all spread out our towels in an orderly fashion and lie down. Tyler and Lucas are on the edges while Finn and I settle in the middle beside our respective men. Hearing the waves crash as we soak up the sun is soothing. It's something I didn't know I needed. I don't think you realize the pace of New York City until you step out and slow down. It's necessary to take time like this and decompress from the whirlwind that is our beloved city.

Circling the sand with one of my fingers on the side of our towels, I lean on my elbows next to Tyler. He is on his stomach with closed eyes, and behind my newly treasured sunglasses, I can admire his back muscles without him noticing. They glisten from the suntan oil he had me apply, and as he moves slightly, I can see the muscles twitch and flex. Goosebumps form on my arms and legs.

"Whatcha looking at?" he says coyly.

"Oh, nothing." I turn my head toward the ocean. "Just thought I saw a dolphin out there." I raise my hand to my forehead like a sailor scoping out the formidable seas.

He laughs at me and turns to sit up, grabbing my hand that rests between us.

"Ready to go in?" he asks.

"I was ready the second we stepped foot on the beach," I say sincerely. I'm not a lay-down-and-tan-while-reading-a-romance-book type of gal. I'm more of a get-in-the-water-ASAP-and-bodysurf-until-you-can't-move-anymore kind of gal.

He stands up, hoisting me with him, and we run to the water, leaving Finn and Lucas to continue soaking in the sun. Tyler leaps through the surf and then dives into a wave once he's far enough out.

I take my time, tiptoeing through the shore. Each section of my body that gradually slips under the water's surface recoils from the sudden temperature drop. I'm waist-deep in the ocean before a large wave comes and it smashes into me; my whole body becomes drenched. Tyler doesn't notice, thank goodness.

But the sequence reminds me of falling in love. You can dive in headfirst, letting the ebbs and flows naturally take you. Or you can walk in with timidity. Denying, hesitant, doubtful. Until that unexpected wave crashes over you one moment, and you're swimming in it the next.

After ensuring my swimsuit is still in its proper place, I wade through the water and catch up to Tyler, who drifts past the crashing zone.

"Doesn't it feel amazing?" he asks, running his hands through his hair. I wish I had a camera to capture and treasure this imagery forever.

"It does," I turn my body horizontally and float as the waves gently bob my body higher and lower. Tyler swims up to my side, I turn my head toward him, and then he kisses me. I smile at his kiss and the taste of saltwater on his lips.

"Okay," he says after our lips part. "Time to bodysurf."

"That is literally all I want to do. No more tanning nonsense." We swim back to where the waves are crashing. He surfs the first wave that's big enough, while it takes a few tries for me. I wonder if he ever was on a swim team because—*dang*. He knows what he's doing, *and* he looks good doing it.

Eventually, we catch a wave side-by-side and beam at one another with the happiest expressions. We ride until our bodies are thrown onto the sand. As we slowly get up, groans escaping our lips, we laugh at how disheveled we look. Seaweed is sporadically attached to both of our bodies. Tyler's hair covers half of his face, mine is partially in my mouth, and my bathing suit top is borderline on the fritz. Thankfully, it's still covering all the critical areas.

Once we're situated, and back to looking semi-normal, he looks into my eyes and says, "You never told me you were a professional bodysurfer."

"Ah, yes. One of my hidden talents. That and talking like Donald Duck."

"No way."

"Yes, way," I say in the voice of Donald, squeaking through the side of my mouth.

He laughs with one big "HA!" That turns into a full-blown cackle. I watch in joy.

My face becomes serious. With one eyebrow raised, I say, "Wanna go again?" He looks at me as though I've asked whether the ocean is made of water.

"Uh, yeah," he replies.

Grabbing my hand, he takes me from the shore, and we race back into the tide.

While chasing the waves, I feel like a kid again with my best friend. These moments are so nostalgic, and I am in awe that I can experience them with Tyler. He is everything I could have hoped for and more.

After a few more rides, my older age is starting to show. It's becoming more and more difficult not to let myself get battered by the waves. At one point, I do a complete 360-degree flip under the water and decide to quit while I'm ahead. Drowning would not be the best way to end this lovely day.

We breathlessly walk back to our towels while Finn and Lucas squint at us with amazement at how long we spent in the water.

"Did you two have fun?" Finn asks, stifling a yawn. She looks like she's been napping.

"Yes," we both say, laughing. Tyler wraps my towel around me and gives me a peck on the lips. We lay down next to one another and let the sun dry our skin, eventually falling asleep in the sand. After a short nap, I wake up and look at Tyler. He's staring back at me with a sweet smile.

"Hi," he says with a groggy voice.

"Hey." I turn my body to lie toward him—our faces inches apart. I kiss him quickly and brush some sand off his cheek.

While running my fingers through his crispy, salty hair, he whispers, "I feel like I got hit by a truck."

I laugh because I feel the same way from all the bodysurfing we did.

"Me too." I stare back into his ocean-blue eyes that circle my face. "We're not kids anymore, unfortunately."

"You make me feel like I am," he says, and a smile plays on his lips. "I love it."

"I feel the same way," I reply with watery eyes.

He leans in and gives me a passionate kiss that makes the butterflies in my stomach feel like they're in a tornado. That is until Lucas clears his throat.

*Who invited you anyway, Lucas?*

Tyler and I both look at him. He's pointing off into the distance. A person wearing all black is snapping photos of Tyler and me lying in the sand.

Paparazzi.

*I can't wait to see the headlines for that one.*

# NINETEEN

It's a big afternoon for Tyler and me. He mentioned a few days ago that his family had decided to take the trip out and visit him. They're all spending the morning doing fun touristy things in Manhattan before having a nice Lupper (lunch-supper) with me at Tyler's apartment. I had a shift at the coffee shop this morning that I tried to swap with another barista, but no one could swing it. So now, after finishing work, I make my way out to his place, where he and his family await.

Before hopping on the train, I pick up a loaf of decadent-looking sourdough from the local bakery down my street. I also grab a semi-expensive bottle of wine from the liquor store. I'm not a wine connoisseur by any means, but the worker who helped me said they'd love it. Perhaps he just pointed me to a higher price tag. Oh, well. Too late now.

After a forty-five-minute commute from Brooklyn, I walk up the subway station steps in the Upper West Side and notice that the floor is significantly wet.

*What on earth?*

Climbing the stairs further, I find that it's torrentially downpouring outside.

*No, no, no, no, no!*

It wasn't supposed to rain today, so I left my compact umbrella at home. Panic pulses through me while I linger on the grimy steps with the dozen or so other people who have also just come off the train. We all consider what to do internally. If I don't start walking soon, I will be late to Lupper, but if I go now, I will be drenched by the time I get there. As I weigh the options, my honor for timeliness gets the better of me, and I run into the sideways rain that is covering the streets.

Five minutes later, I burst through the doors of Tyler's apartment building. I am thoroughly soaked through. My clothes don't have a dry spot on them. I pull out my phone and open the camera app to see my appearance. My face comes into view, and I wince. The mascara I so meticulously applied is now bleeding down my cheeks, and my previously flat-ironed hair is now plastered to my temples. I look like a drowned rat that should be resting on the corner of 57th avenue rather than standing in sopping socks in this high-end apartment building.

Placing my phone back in my purse, I squeak my way through the lobby. The doorman, Barry, whom I have become familiar with over the past few weeks visiting Tyler, gives me a sorry smile and asks, "Would you like me to get you a napkin?"

Glancing down at my clothes, it's evident that wiping myself with a napkin would be as effective as trying to drain out a lake with a Dixie cup.

"I'm okay, thank you," I say politely.

Making my way to the elevator, I leave a trail of rainwater behind me. My heart thumps like a jackhammer as I press the "up" button, uncertain of what's ahead of me just a few floors above. When I step into the elevator, I lightly nod and blow a long breath out the side of my mouth, ready to accept my fate.

*They're going to think I'm an idiot.*

Before any more last-minute doubts or worries can flash through my mind, I'm quickly sent up to the sixteenth floor, and the elevator doors slide open. I walk down the hall to Tyler's apartment, and with a deep inhale, knock on the large black frame. Water marks from my knuckles drip down as I take my hand away. From the other side, I can hear a woman say, "She's here!"

As the door swings open, Tyler's joyful face comes into view until he takes one good look at me, and his eyes bulge with a crinkled brow. A goofy smile forms on his lips.

"What happened to you?"

"I got caught in the storm," I say with a sorrowful pout before handing him the bottle of wine and the soggy package of bread.

He somehow restrains his laughter—being the stellar actor he is—and composes himself before leaning down to kiss me on the cheek without saying another word.

"Ewww, gross!" his sister Haley remarks. I can see her peeking at us from across the room. Unsure whether her remark is from our quick kiss or my dampened state, I shake it off and laugh because, at this point, there's nothing else I can do. Tyler takes my waterlogged, wrinkled hand and leads me in to officially meet his family as his girlfriend.

"Hi, everyone," I say with a bright, embarrassed smile. His mom is at the stove, stirring something in a pot that smells magnificent. She turns in my direction, looking me up and down, before giving me a funny face and setting her spatula next to the pot.

"Oh, you poor thing," she says. Even though I'm still visibly sopping, she disregards my messy exterior and wraps me into the warmest hug.

"Sorry about all this, Mrs. Axel," I say as we embrace.

"Oh, please. Call me Brenda! Ted, get over here," she calls to her husband, who is watching baseball on the sofa. Ted approaches me, gives me a cautious side-hug, and says, "It's nice to see you again." His laughter lines decorate his face just like Tyler's when he smiles. I look between the two of them and notice other similarities like their stature and thick head of hair. Tyler's blue eyes, however, neither come from his mom or dad, as theirs are varying shades of green.

"And this is Haley," Tyler says to me with a hand on the small of my back, leading me into the large living room. She's snuggled up on the sofa near where her dad was just sitting.

"Tyler, honey, get Sunday some fresh clothes, please," Brenda tells her son. While he moves to his room and Brenda walks back over to the stove, I squeak my way to the arm of the couch and introduce myself to Haley.

"Hi, Haley. It's so nice to meet you in real life."

She smiles shyly, staring at my moistened shoes, and says, "Hi," back. Knowing it might take a bit for her to warm up to me, I don't press further, though I add, "I love your headband." She brings her hand to the large red bow in the middle of the band and grins sweetly.

"Sunday," Brenda calls. "Tyler told me you're vegan. I'm whipping up a traditional English meal—bangers and mash—also known as sausage and mashed potatoes," she teases with an American accent. "We found some vegan sausage for you and Tyler to eat. Also, I'm using non-dairy milk and vegan butter for the mash."

"That sounds amazing, thank you." I look at Tyler, who walks back from the hallway with fresh clothes, and give him a kind *you shouldn't have* look. A wise vegan always knows to bring bread to a party in case the host makes nothing they can eat, but because of Tyler's intentionality, I won't be gnawing on a loaf of soggy bread that's likely sprouting mold as we speak.

"It's about ready," Brenda says to everyone. I go to the bathroom to change into the T-shirt and joggers Tyler has provided. Looking in the mirror, I wipe the misplaced makeup off my cheeks and draw my hair into a messy topknot. This is not at all how I would have wanted to present myself to Tyler's family, but it will have to do.

Leaving the bathroom, we all settle at the solid oak dining table. Beside me are Tyler and Haley. After a quick prayer led by Tyler's dad, we dig in.

The vegan bangers and mash are spectacular.

I find that I've already begun speaking with a British accent in my head after being around them for such a short amount of time and I'm doing my best not to slip up.

"This is so good," I say with the most American accent possible that I almost sound like a Valley Girl.

"Thank you, dear. I'm glad you like it," Brenda responds with a hint of confusion in her tone.

I notice a jar of pickles on the table near Tyler's mom. He sees me looking at them and leans to me, whispering through the side of his mouth, "Told you she loves her pickles." I hold back a giggle.

Turning to the rest of the table, I ask the family, "How was your morning? What did you guys end up doing?"

"Tell her, Haley," Brenda prompts while scooping more mashed potatoes onto her plate.

Haley hesitantly looks down at her plate before quietly saying, "We went to the American Girl Doll store, and I made a new doll."

"No way," I say. "I've always wanted to do that. Was it fun?"

"Yeah," she smiles. "Want to see her?"

"After lunch, sweetie," Brenda says.

"It was fun," Tyler adds while placing his arm around the back of my chair. "Then we went to Times Square—one of Mum's favorite spots." He rolls his eyes at her.

"Don't make fun of me. I just love all the lights!" she says defensively.

"I love it too," I admit, and Tyler quickly looks at me with one of his eyes twitching slightly. "I know, I know. New Yorkers are supposed to avoid Times Square at all costs, but I think it's unique and fun."

Brenda and I laugh together because Tyler is beside himself, trying to understand how we could possibly like a place so touristy and horrific to him. It makes me happy to have something in common with his mom so quickly, besides our adoration for Tyler himself.

"I love all those people they have dressed up around every corner," she says.

"You mean the people dressed as cartoons who only want your money or the Naked Cowboy?" Tyler asks and I almost choke on my drink.

We continue laughing and discussing the wildness of New York City, and I notice that Tyler's dad is a man of few words, but his laughter fills the room. He has a kindness to his voice when he does share that makes you feel like you could tell him anything, and he would never judge you for it.

Once Lupper is over, I help Tyler clear away the plates, bringing them to the sink to be washed. Tyler does most of the work while I stand there chatting with his mom about silly stories of his childhood.

"He always had a knack for getting in trouble, this one," she begins.

"I was an easily bored kid," Tyler explains.

"Yeah, and he was awfully good at lying about what he was really up to in his room each time I suspected he was up to no good." She wags a finger at him, and he laughs.

"I was practicing for the days ahead of being an actor." He emphasizes the syllables of ac-tor.

"Uh-huh," she rolls her eyes. I'm leaning against the counter, enjoying their interaction, when Ted calls me to the living room.

As I approach them, he says, "Haley wanted to show you her doll." She's sitting on the ground in front of the sofa holding a little doll that looks *exactly* like her. Brown bangs, purple glasses, and a sweet smile.

"Oh, my goodness, I love her!" I say while I squat down next to her on the floor to get a better look. "Did you name her after yourself?"

"No, I named her Bailey," she says while brushing through the doll's hair with a tiny plastic comb.

"That's a perfect name for someone who looks just like you." I sit down next to her. "May I hold her?"

She looks slightly uncertain but then passes the doll to me.

"She's beautiful," I say while holding her as if she is made of pure porcelain. No way I'm dropping this girly.

"I even gave her freckles like me," Haley says, pointing at the doll's cheek.

"I see that. They're adorable." I pass back the doll gently.

"Do you want to see what else I got?" she asks, visibly becoming more comfortable with me.

"Yes, please."

She takes me into one of the guest bedrooms and unloads a shopping bag full of various outfit options, grooming tools, and little trinkets like a stethoscope and a magnifying glass to play with.

"Woah! That's a lot of stuff," I say as she reaches into the bag, grabbing more items. "I love this outfit you chose." I lift up a little green dress with white polka dots.

"Tyler picked that one out," she tells me.

"Oh, well, he has good taste. But so do you, Haley. All this stuff is so fun and perfect for caring for Bailey."

"Yeah," she smiles while putting some barrettes in the doll's hair.

"How's it going in here?" Tyler chimes in before walking through the door. He flops onto the bed while Haley and I sit on the ground, marveling at her new dolly gear.

"Good," Haley says while adding different clips and ribbons to Bailey's hair. "Sunday liked the dress you picked out."

"Oh, did she?" Tyler looks at me with raised eyebrows. "I think that dress would look very cute on Sunday. Don't you, Haley?"

"It wouldn't fit her, Ty." She rolls her eyes. Tyler and I both stifle our laughs.

"I didn't mean that exact dress, silly. I mean, one like it. In Sunday's size, of course." He winks at me.

"Yeah, that would be very pretty," Haley says unemphatically, too focused on her new doll to care.

"Do you want us to leave you alone to play with your new things?" he asks her.

"That sounds good." I let out a little giggle at her straightforwardness, and we leave her in peace to continue to play.

Tyler takes my hand and sneakily leads us into his bedroom. He closes the door behind us and turns to me, asking, "How are you holding up?" He then pulls me in close, wrapping his arms around my back.

"I'm really good," I say as my face nuzzles into his chest. "Your family is so sweet. I like them a lot."

"Yeah?" he says. I can feel his breath on my ear.

I lean back to look at him and nod with a happy grin. He reciprocates and leans in for a passionate—*but not too passionate because his parents are on the other side of the wall*—kiss. I feel light from my head to my toes.

"That was nice," I say with my eyes closed. He laughs quietly and brushes a piece of my wavy hair that has fallen out of my bun back behind my ear. Even this simple gesture from him sends chills down my spine.

Before we're gone too long, we wrap up our kissing excursion and head back into the living room. Everyone is sprawled out on the sofa while Tyler and his dad fixate on the baseball game happening on the television.

His mom asks me questions about general things like my job and hometown. She tells me how she grew up in a small town in England outside London. Then after she met and married Ted and had her babies, they moved to the U.S. while Tyler pursued acting so they could go to his shows.

It's fun to watch her talk and interact with her family—she has a similar humor to Tyler, and it seems we'll get along very well. I'm grateful his family has welcomed me in like their own.

At about 5 p.m., Tyler has to leave for his show. I say my goodbyes to his parents and Haley, thanking them again for the meal. They all hug me goodbye—even Haley. She runs over to me before I walk out the door and tells me she enjoyed meeting me.

Tyler and I walk a short way to the subway station, with the setting sun glistening at our backs. There's a beautiful little garden with oscillating golden hues shining upon it—we stop and take a photo together in its light, with coy, closed-lip smiles.

Moments later, we step onto the train, and it is jam-packed. There are no seats available, only a small bit of area to stand near the closing doors. We're all practically a tin can of sardines hurtling through the underbelly of New York City.

Holding onto one of the poles, Tyler looks at me in a new way I haven't seen before. It's full of delight and—maybe, just maybe—*love*.

We're gazing at one another amid the hundreds of people in this subway car. He wraps his arm around my back, drawing me into his chest, and kisses me as though the train were completely empty. Initially, I'm taken aback by the PDA, but that all falls away within seconds. I soften at his touch, threading my arms around his neck and running my fingers through his flaxen hair. The subway train comes to a stop, and we stumble forward slightly, but Tyler catches us before we can do any real damage to the people around us. He smiles at me and then rests his chin atop my head. I close my eyes and stay there until we arrive at his stop. He gives me one last kiss goodbye, then exits the train and disappears into the crowd. I find myself standing among the commuters with a lingering grin that I don't think will ever fade.

I can see a future with him. I *want* a future with him. All of his dreams, and endeavors—I want to be a part of them and do anything I can to bring them to fruition. I want to help him become all that he can be. I can see myself waking up in the morning and reminding him how incredible he is. Then going to sleep and reflecting on how he grew that day. In the brokenness and in the dark times, I want to be by his side, showing and digging out for him even an ounce of light.

And it's at this moment I know.

*I'm in love with Tyler Axel.*

# TWENTY

Tonight is Tyler's 54 Below show. Finn, Lucas, and I are all attending to watch and support him. Since it's a nicer venue, and I want to look *good* for Tyler, I put on a satin, hunter-green, spaghetti-strap dress that ends right at my calves. My hair is half-up and half-down with wavy curls, and my eyeshadow is varying shades of green. Finn taught me her makeup methods on one of our girl's nights, and I've been doing my makeup like it ever since. I glance in the full-length mirror in our hallway and do a little happy dance because it all came together quite nicely.

"You look so good," Finn says as she sees me admiring myself.

Embarrassed, I say, "Thank you." I look at her outfit of choice, and she looks stunning. She wears a linen black dress that splits at her hip. I remember her picking it out from one of our recent Zara trips. On her lips is a bright-red stain, making her look like a modern-day Marilyn Monroe. Lucas is going to be beside himself.

Tyler sends a driver to pick Finn and me up, while Lucas plans to meet us at the venue. Walking out of our apartment—looking chic as ever—we see the SUV awaiting us in the street. It's my dear friend Bob from the last time I drove with Tyler. I make friendly conversation with him as Finn and I slide in and then buckle up *immediately.*

With a clenched jaw and one of my eyes squinting, I quietly say to Finn, "*Put. Your seatbelt. On.*" She gives me a nervous look before understanding the memo. Buckling herself in, she tugs on the strap to ensure it's secure and then flashes an inconspicuous thumbs up.

In record timing (*not surprisingly*), we make it to the restaurant— in one piece, might I add. Clusters of people are already huddled outside the front door, likely awaiting a sighting of Tyler.

The day prior, Tyler had given me three VIP passes so that we wouldn't have to wait in this queue of fans. Bob brings the car as close to the venue as he can without running anyone over, parks, and then escorts Finn and me inside.

Walking past the crowd is utter chaos. Flashes are going off like crazy. People are yelling and pushing one another to get a closer look at us. While I try to keep my head down and continue walking, "Axel-ents" (the self-imposed fan name for Tyler's followers) still scream my name. I look up to meet their gazes, lingering on those smiling at me, giving them a big grin back. Unfortunately, those kinds of looks are few and far between. Happy faces are sprinkled amongst a myriad of utterly disgusted or irritated expressions. I do my best to disregard them, smiling for the photos and moving along to get past this as soon as possible.

Once we're at the door, we show the representative for 54 Below our passes, and she swiftly lets us in the building. Finn and I sigh in relief once the doors close behind us.

I see Tyler on the stage out of the corner of my eye. He's sound checking and makes eye contact with me. Giving me a sweet grin and wink, he continues to check his mic. The representative introduces herself as Claire and offers to take our coats, letting us know we can wait at the bar and order drinks before the show begins.

Finn asks the bartender for a glass of cabernet sauvignon that I try a sip of, and my face contorts. I let out a "blegh" because it is so dry. I stick to a Moscato—looking classy but essentially drinking sweet grape juice. While enjoying our on-the-house drinks, Tyler walks over to us and gives me a once-over with his eyes.

"What brings you, beautiful ladies, here tonight?" he asks while attempting to lean on our table with his forearm, but he slips instead, banging his elbow on the counter while letting out an "oomph" sound. Recovering, he settles back into a charming stance and leans against our table with a goofy smile. Finn and I laugh at his antics.

Continuing with the charade, I swirl my wine in my cup before taking a delicate sip. Leaning back in my seat, I say, "Some guy invited us to watch him sing. I'm not sure he's any good, but the free drinks are pretty great." I raise my glass toward him with a sultry wink.

He shakes his head while keeping his eyes on me and laughs before lifting me up from my chair and kissing me softly. He turns his mouth to the edge of my ear lobe and whispers, "You look gorgeous." If you cracked an egg on my face right now, I'm pretty sure you'd be able to make an excellent breakfast because my cheeks are *burning*.

He turns to Finn, "Finn, great to see you again."

"You too," she says while lifting her drink in a 'cheers' motion. "And thanks for the free drinks, guy." She smirks. Tyler chuckles while putting his arm around me.

"Anytime." He tilts his head toward my drink and says, "May I?" I nod.

As the liquid touches his lips, he grins into the glass. Although my favorite crow's feet have come out to dance for me around his eyes, I know he's about to make fun of me for my wine choice.

"Don't say it," I say with raised eyebrows and a finger lifted.

"I—"

"Tyler," I draw out like I'm his mother.

He laughs and hands me back my drink.

"It's delicious," he concedes.

"Thank y—"

"…if you were four years old." He opens his mouth in an O shape, leaning away he knows I'm about to hit him for teasing me. I do attempt to smack him but miss.

"Dodged it!" he yells triumphantly while I roll my eyes at him.

"If you ladies would excuse me," he says. "I'm going to order a real alcoholic beverage from the bar." He looks at Finn and whispers loud enough so I can hear with his hand near his mouth, "Did she bring that juice from home?"

I playfully push his body toward the bartender and say, "Go get your 'adult' drink, ya big weirdo."

Finn is still laughing as I sit back down. "Is he always like that?"

"Not always—thank goodness," I say with a laugh.

Her expression becomes serious. Looking at Tyler to ensure he's out of earshot, she asks quietly, "Have you still not mentioned the moment you two had in the theater before you met in the park?"

"No," I say, and it seems silly not to have brought it up at this point. I mean, we *are* in a relationship. I was just hoping Tyler would've said something about it by now if it meant as much to him as it did to me.

"You really should say something. Maybe he's waiting for you to do it," Finn encourages.

"Yeah, maybe," I say, glancing at him as he leans on the bar counter, talking with the bartender. He looks back at me with a smile that makes my heart thunder.

The first interaction between Tyler and I at the theater was a moment I would never forget. It was so precious and sacred. And the true reason I haven't brought it up to him is because I'm afraid he doesn't even remember it happened.

Backstage with Tyler, we sit in his dressing room while the rest of the crowd filters into their seats before the show starts. Lucas arrived half an hour ago and joined Finn at the bar.

Tyler has just performed his beloved—semi-psychotic—ritual in the mirror. This time, I didn't hold back my laughs as he affirmed himself, but instead added, "Yeah you are!" to the different positive statements.

"I should get back to my seat," I say, looking at the time.

"We still have a few minutes." He walks over to me and lifts me from my chair before kissing me slowly.

"This might have to be my new ritual," he says as he brushes a piece of hair from my face while we lean together against the closed door.

"Yeah?" I say with eyebrows raised. "I think I could manage that." He leans in and kisses me again until there's a knock coming from behind us. Pulling his head away from mine, he continues to stay close.

"Yes?" Tyler calls out.

The person tries to get in, which shakes us slightly, but the weight of our bodies prevents them from opening the door. Giving up, they shout through the crack, "You're on in ten!"

"Sounds good," Tyler says back, stifling a laugh.

We hear the manager walk away, and Tyler gives me one last kiss before saying he has to change into his stage clothes.

"I'll go get in my seat. See you out there," I say and then kiss his cheek softly and slowly. "Good luck." His eyes are closed, and the corners of his mouth turn up, cheeks pink. I slip away from him and begin to open the door to leave, but he yanks my hand and twirls me toward his chest.

"One last thing," he says with his blue eyes glimmering. "Would you maybe want to sing a duet with me tonight?"

My pulse immediately starts to rise, and I close my eyes, but I can't help the smile cracking on my lips. "Tyler Pickles Axel, why the *heck* wouldn't you have asked me this sooner?"

"I didn't want you to think about it too much and then say no." His eyebrows crinkle as if he's saying, *pretty please?*

"What song?"

"Only my favorite song currently," he teases, and I know exactly what song he's talking about.

"Okay, fine." I bite my lip as my excitement ramps up. Not only will I be *seeing* a show at 54 Below tonight—checking that off my bucket list—I'll also be *singing* at 54 Below.

"Thank you," he says to me, and I shake my head with a laugh, exiting the room. I follow the hallway to the back entrance, where the audience is seated. Walking over to our table, I take a seat next to Finn. Lucas is holding her hand in his lap, and my insides feel all warm and fuzzy for them.

"Hi, Lucas," I say.

"Hey, Sunday! Good to see you," he says with much enthusiasm. I'm wondering if he's trying to make up for the many beach interactions I had with him, but I've already moved on and resolved that I really do like him. He's fiery and silly—an excellent match for Finn.

"You too. How was dinner?" I ask.

"It was amazing," Finn says and passes me the basket of bread to snack on. "Sorry, they didn't have anything else for you."

"No worries, I can always grab something after."

Lucas starts chatting with Finn about something I can't quite make out, so I use this time as an opportunity to look around at the crowd settling in their seats. It's primarily women—which isn't surprising—some younger, but a lot look to be in their mid-50s.

Days ago, Tyler had shown me some of the fan mail he gets sent to his stage door, and while most of it is charming, some of it is quite scary. Like a lock of their hair, or a poem that seems as though it should have been written by a 10-year-old but has a 45-year-old woman's photo attached to it. As an outsider looking in, I was slightly creeped out by many of the items sent, but Tyler was so gracious—opening every single item delivered to him at the theater.

An announcer comes up on the stage as the tasteful jazz music lowers, and the audience quiets to listen.

"Good evening, everyone," he says as the spotlight approaches him. The bright light causes him to squint and lift a hand in front of his face. "Thank you all for coming out to this special night. We are thrilled to have one of today's biggest Broadway stars gracing this stage tonight. Tyler Axe—," he starts, and the crowd screams.

"Oh—I guess I should've waited to say his name. He's not coming out quite yet." The announcer gives an embarrassed chuckle that's endearing. It seems like this might be his first time doing this. When he makes eye contact with me, I give him an encouraging smile, hoping he gets the message that he's doing a great job.

He goes on. "The man you're about to see is a graduate of Carnegie Mellon University. He made his Broadway debut as the role of Fiyero in *Wicked*. He originated the role of Samuel in *Belle Époque* on Broadway. He is a two-time Tony Nominee for his roles in *Cherry On Top* and *Belle Époque* and a Tony award winner for his role in *Cherry On Top*." My eyebrows perk up when he says that. I vaguely remember watching the Tony Awards that year and seeing Tyler hold up his award, giving his thanks. I make a mental note to watch it later tonight on YouTube.

The announcer continues. "He has starred in movies like *What You Will*, *Hunting Eternity*, and *Man of the Night*. And he is currently starring in the musical *Belle Époque* on Broadway." For a moment, he departs from "announcer mode" and lets us in on his giddy side, saying, "If you haven't had the pleasure of seeing it yet, you don't want to miss out." A small squeal escapes his lips because he is enamored by the wonder of Broadway, just as so many of us who are nestled into these seats.

"Now, without further ado, here is TYLER AXEL!"

# TWENTY-ONE

Tyler walks out on the stage, and roaring applause fills the room. He's dressed up for the occasion in a form-fitting gray suit, white button-down shirt, and shiny black dress shoes. His sandy hair is perfectly coiffed, not a strand out of line. This is by far the most handsome I've ever seen him look. I could pass out right into the breadbasket in front of me. And I'm not the only one who feels this way; I hear multiple women gasp around me.

*I'm with ya, ladies!*

As he makes his way to the microphone, I feel his eyes move to me. He gives me a stealthy wink, and I can sense my body reddening.

My eyes glance toward Finn, and she is beaming with delight at our interactions.

"Hi, everybody!" Tyler says enthusiastically into the microphone with a joyful grin.

People wave and say "Hi" back. If I were in the audience as someone who didn't know Tyler, I'd want to get his attention—so I don't judge those hooting and hollering.

Typically shows like this are a free-for-all where the artist can plan to sing whatever their heart desires. I asked him not to tell me the finalized set list because I knew it would be more fun as a surprise, but I may have thrown some of my suggestions in as he was prepping. We sat on his sofa as he held a pen and paper in his lap that I avoided looking at. With my legs dangling over the arm of the couch, I suggested emphatically, "'Waving Through a Window' from *Dear Evan Hansen*! Your voice would be perfect for that."

"Oh, that's a great one." I see him jot it down from the corner of my eye, and I smile.

"Or maybe something from *Les Mis*—those are always a classic."

"True, true."

"Or even something shocking—like a Miley Cyrus song people wouldn't expect."

At this, he busted into the chorus of "Wrecking Ball," and it startled me. All I could picture was him in his underwear swinging on stage.

"Okay, maybe no Miley," I teased.

To my surprise and delight, he starts off the show by singing "Waving Through a Window." I knew his voice would sound marvelous, but it's even better than I could have imagined. He absolutely smashes it. The crowd goes wild once as he holds the last line and the pianist's notes ring out.

He tells silly stories in between each number, and I'm grateful to learn more about him with the other lucky people in this audience. One that surprises me the most is when he tells the journey of the neck and neck process he experienced with Ryan Gosling for the leading role of Sebastian in the movie *La La Land*. In the end, the producers cast Ryan, but with it being one of my favorite films, my brain quickly replaced Ryan with Tyler as each epic scene streamed through my mind's eye.

The need to ask him after the concert if he learned any of the tap-dancing scenes quickly goes on my mental to-do list. And I also must ask if he learned how to play the movie's theme song on the piano because if so, I will have him play it to me as a lullaby to me each night as I fall asleep.

He whistles and sings "City of Stars," this beautiful song that Ryan Gosling sing and dances to on the Los Angeles pier in the movie, and I just about become a puddle of tears and admiration.

After a few more show tunes, he breaks out an old Billy Joel song. I now remember hearing him hum this melody at different moments throughout the past few days. He sits on the stool provided and soaks in the slow song. It's beautiful and moving as he sways to the music, feeling every note reverberating through his body.

"For this next number, I'd like to ask a special guest to come up and sing with me."

My stomach turns to one giant knot, knowing this is probably my cue. As I straighten out my dress on my lap, I look up and notice Tyler is not looking at me; rather, he's looking behind the curtain at the edge of the stage.

"Please join me in welcoming...Brittany Oliver!"

My hands find their way into a clap, but a slew of emotions comes over me. I'm not sure what's going on inside my heart. Maybe I'm surprised that Brittany is here because he never told me she'd be joining him in singing. Or perhaps I'm jealous, wishing it were me up there at this moment. It could also be that Brittany hasn't been particularly interested in getting to know me the few times I've met her. Or all the above. I sit silently in my seat, forcing my lips into a smile.

She waltzes out onstage in a gorgeous blue cocktail dress that shows off her long, tan legs. After embracing Tyler in a lingering hug, he asks the crowd, "So, how many of you have seen *Belle Époque*?"

He lifts a hand to his forehead so he can see the audience members who raise their hands and cheer. About a quarter of the crowd, including myself and Finn, lift our arms high.

"Amazing. Well, for those of you who don't know, this is my costar, Brittany Oliver. She's an incredible actress and singer, and I asked her to join me tonight in singing our love song from our show." The crowd cheers the loudest they have thus far. I try my best not to glare at Brittany while I clap along with the rest of the audience.

They begin singing to one another, and Finn grabs my hand under the table as if she knows something is off. I look into her eyes, and she stares back with an expression that asks, *are you okay?* I nod back, smothering my emotions.

There's a moment before the final note where Brittany is all over Tyler. She grabs the front of his jacket, forcing him toward her so they're face-to-face. This is the moment in the show when their characters kiss for the first time. My body trembles with fear as I watch her lean in, about to lay one on him. But he turns his face toward the crowd with a big smile as they continue singing, and she kisses him on the cheek. She makes the missed opportunity seem intentional with bobbing eyebrows and a silly smile.

Once they finish, the audience goes ballistic. I clap slowly, trying to hide any feelings besides joy from my face. She embraces him in one last hug as her foot pops like freaking Mia Thermopolis. Tyler slides out of her grip quickly, allowing her a chance to bow for the audience. Brittany curtsies and then exits the stage while the crowd is still applauding. My heart rate finally settles once she's back behind the curtain.

*Good riddance.*

I'm focused on a little lint ball at the edge of the stage while processing what has just happened. Finn taps me aggressively on the shoulder. Lifting my gaze to her, I notice she's pointing to Tyler, who is staring at me with his hand held out to lift me onto the stage.

"Go!" Finn whispers, and I shoot up from my chair. Apparently, I missed some introduction of him calling me to the stage. I adjust my dress and walk toward him. He walks down the little stairs at the front of the stage, meeting me at the bottom step.

"You alright?" he whispers in my ear.

"Yeah, I'm fine," I say, giving him my best convincing smile while he takes my hand and leads me up to the stage. While walking, he begins to speak to the audience. "Everyone, please give a warm welcome to Sunday Truelove."

To my surprise, they applaud just as loudly as when Brittany walked out. Finn and Lucas cheer the loudest, and I half-smile in their direction as a thank-you for being my biggest fans in this room.

Tyler continues speaking as I stand awkwardly on stage, unsure of what to do with myself. He grabs onto the mic stand and says, "If you don't have the pleasure of knowing Sunday, you're missing out. She is like sunshine in bodily form, filling the world with light and warmth." My face flushes, and I hold back a smile as he looks at me. His unexpected words settle over me like a warm blanket.

"Her heart is tender," he continues, "and she is wholly kind. She can make the grumpiest person laugh, and the saddest person smile."

I glance toward the front row and see women starting to tear up. Whether it's from the sweetness of his statements or jealousy that he's articulating them to me, I'm not sure.

Tyler continues speaking as he faces the crowd. "And I know from firsthand experience that Sunday can tear the roof off a place with her vocals. So," he turns back to me with a gracious expression. "I would love to have the honor of singing this next song with you if you don't mind." His lips turn up into a grin. I smile back, nodding.

The accompanist begins playing "Seventeen" from *Heathers*. The song Tyler and I sang together before our first kiss. Once again, we enter into the characters of Veronica and J.D., really hamming it up for the crowd. I pretend I'm disgusted with Tyler at the start of the song because of the choices his character has made. I'm finding it so enjoyable to truly act with Tyler. We feed off one another easily, and it's all very playful and fun.

He is so in tune with the character of J.D. that he scares me yet again, which only helps me enhance my character who is supposed to be frightened of her lover. Like Veronica in the story, I visibly show through my posture and facial expressions that I'm torn with this man before me. Unsure of whether or not I should trust him, but still feeling this pull to shower my love and affection on him. As I act this out, I realize that I don't feel an ounce of worry or fear with Tyler in our real lives. I do trust him and his intentions toward me. He is kind, good, and loving, not just toward me but to everyone.

It's at this moment I'm struck by the truth that Tyler is the one I feel I've been searching for my whole life. He is the one I want to be with all my days. Something significant shifts inside me as we sing this song and pretend to be these messed up characters who fought to the literal death for their love. Somehow, I gain the courage to share my true feelings with Tyler.

*Tonight is the night that I will tell him I love him.*

When we reach the song's climax, Tyler turns me, so my back is resting against his chest, and we face toward the audience. Singing the final notes, he spins me around like we did that night in the karaoke room, and we finish the last lines together as a whisper in the same microphone.

As the song ends, the audience's cheers fill our ears. We continue to look at one another for a few seconds before Tyler kisses my forehead and turns us toward the crowd. We hold hands and bow together, and then Tyler gently pushes me to the front of the stage, allowing me to take my first official bow in New York City as a rising star on Broadway. The crowd stands and cheers and it is utterly overwhelming.

I've never experienced anything like this feeling.

Once the noise simmers, I smile one last time and start to return to my seat, but Tyler grasps my hand and keeps me with him. He lets go only to walk to the side of the stage and bring over the stool he sat on a few songs before. His hand motions for me to take a seat. My eyebrow perks up, wondering what he's planning on doing now, but I oblige.

Turning toward me, he says, "Sunday, though we only met months ago, I feel like I've known you my whole life. You are truly a wonder," he takes a beat before saying, "and this song is for you."

The pianist starts playing the introduction of a song, and my ears remember the tune even before a note escapes Tyler's lips. It's the last song played in his show, *Belle Époque*.

The same song Tyler sang to me only months prior.

As he sings, I'm brought back to that night at the theater. It feels like we're in the part of romantic movies where the chatter around us dies out, ambient music fills the room, and it's only us in this place. Everything else is blurred while Tyler and I are, once again, floating above the clouds.

Twinkling stars shoot across the sky while the moonlight shimmers on our bodies. Hues of purple and pink fill our eyesight. We're high above all the confusion and difficulties this world brings—nothing can touch us. Not at this moment. Not from the sky.

Tyler's orb-like eyes stare into mine, different shades of blue dance with one another in each iris, and it feels like we could stay in this moment forever as he sings the lyrics of this glorious song to me.

*Our song.*

My heart flutters as I keep my sights fixed on him. His eyes stay set on mine, and I feel so dearly loved and cherished by him, so much so that it sends a chill through my body. Goosebumps appear on my skin. Warmth fills my belly. He has accepted all of my quirks, oddities, and emotions, coming to know me better than anyone else. And he has completely won me.

Tears blur my vision. I blink them away quickly so I don't miss this moment. Every word he says is flooded with intentionality and love. Though he has walked around the stage for some of the song, right before the last notes, he takes a place kneeling in front of me. We're eye-to-eye as he holds my hand in his.

When the last line leaves his lips—those wonderful, precious words I will treasure for all my life—I know without a shadow of a doubt.

*"My life is full of wonder, all because of you."*

He remembers.

# TWENTY-TWO

**W**alking off the stage after Tyler has serenaded me again, it feels like my body has been placed in an anti-gravity machine. I float back to my seat. Nothing could possibly break this high I feel.

The rest of the night flows by in a warm and fuzzy haze. When Finn and Lucas decide to head back to Brooklyn together, I walk backstage and wait for Tyler in his dressing room as the promise of a late-night dinner at a nearby vegan cafe looms in our near future. He's gone with his security guards to greet fans outside the theater, so I slip my phone out of my pocket and tap at the screen.

While scrolling through social media, I notice I'm tagged in a photo from a popular celebrity sighting page. It's of Tyler and me from our day at the beach with the caption: "Tyler Axel's new lover looks like she could lose a few pounds." My stomach drops as I swipe through the photos. The editor has zoomed in on my thighs and belly—showcasing the most unflattering angles that could have been captured. My hand rises to my agape mouth, but I quickly exit the app and close my eyes—I don't want any negativity infiltrating these moments. Shaking off the feelings, I instead try to wrap my mind around how I will tell Tyler I love him in just a few moments. I want the world to shrink down to just him and me, with nothing but those three words between us.

*Do I just come out and say it? I should probably say something before I just blurt it out.*

*"Hey Tyler, your show was great. And ALSO, I love you."*

My concocting is short-lived because someone knocks, and my eyes fly open. Assuming it's Tyler, I walk up to the door, singing, "Yes?"

A female voice responds back. "Can I come in?"

Confusion furrows my brow. I crack open the door, and to my surprise, Brittany Oliver stands on the other side.

"Oh, hi!" I say, propping the door open against my hip. "Tyler isn't here. He's with some fans but should be back soon."

"I was looking for you, actually," she says with a dry smile. Though her lips curl upward, her eyes remain steely, and a wariness creeps up my spine.

"You were?" I open the door further so she can enter. "Come on in."

She sits in the only chair in the room—the one I was just sitting in—while I lean against the vanity table with my arms crossed over my chest, trying to keep my face neutral. Inwardly, I feel my skepticism giving way to utter chaos. My thumping heart picks up speed.

*What on earth could she want to talk to me about?*

Her demeanor doesn't quell my anxiety. She looks poised as she sits up straight with her legs crossed and hands folded in her lap. The corners of her mouth turn up as though she senses I'm uncomfortable and wants to relish in it. A clock ticks away on the wall nearby, and in the silence, it feels deafening. I smile back politely.

"I've been meaning to talk to you for a bit now," she starts. "I know you don't know me, and we've only met a few times, but I feel like I need to warn you about something."

My forehead scrunches together though I don't want it to. I try to relax my face, mirroring Brittany's expressionless stare. "Uh-huh. Go on."

"It's about Tyler. I know you're super infatuated with him right now, but I've seen him do this with multiple women."

I can feel the color draining from my cheeks, while my palms become moist with sweat. A moment passes in silence before I ask, "Do what exactly?"

"You know, he's on from one girl to the next every month. Sweeping them off their feet and dumping them like trash weeks later."

My eyes sweep to the corner of the table, away from her stoic gaze. It takes time before my brain registers what she has just accused Tyler of.

*This can't be true. She's just jealous.*

I don't make a sound or move a muscle, but she continues. "It's his thing. I've seen it happen more times than I can count since I joined the cast." She picks idly at her cuticle and adds, "He sings to every pretty little thing who sits in that seat at the front of the stage."

My eyes shoot up at her. "Wait, what did you just say?"

Though she looks empathetic with her facial expression—even moving toward me to delicately place her hand atop mine as some sort of calming gesture—there's a twinkle in her eye that makes me think she's enjoying this. Like she's just snagged at a loose thread and is taking pleasure in the process of the unraveling.

"I'm sorry to be the one to tell you. But from one girl to another, I feel like I need to inform you that he's just using you. He'll tire of you just like he tired of the girl who came before you."

Every word feels like a slice; stinging heat radiates from my chest.

"The serenading is not as significant as you might have thought," she adds. "It's just another night at the theater for Tyler." Brittany rolls her eyes as if this is just fun girl talk—as if she's just sharing a fun little quirk of her costar and not cutting my heart out.

My eyes dart back and forth between hers, and I slip my hand out of her grip. I can feel my lip quiver, but I bite down on my tongue before she notices. Pain begins to slosh around in my chest.

"I know you thought you were special to him, but the truth is, you aren't." She says the words so softly yet so matter-of-factly, letting them seep into my body like a poison.

"I'd better go," she says. "I wish you the best of luck in life."

Brittany rises from her seat with a detestable spring in her step and brings her hand back to mine, tapping it as though we'll never see one another again, and she walks out of the room without another glance.

Minutes go by as I stare in an utter daze at where she was just seated. I finally close my eyes, hoping to pass off this encounter as a cruel delusion. But as I attempt to wake from this nightmare, the reality of the situation hits me like a tidal wave. It's as though my body has been thrown into the ocean, but the waves are never-ending. *Which way is up? Am I drowning? Will I be okay? Where is the surface so I can get some relief?*

The panic truly sets in now, manifesting in an unsteady haze, and my brain swims amidst the fog that is every memory and thought thrown into question. Every beautiful memory, the joy, the hope...they all begin to blacken and wither to ash like love notes curling under a flame. I try to stop the rising tears in my eyes by chewing on my cheek, but it doesn't help. My body instinctively lets out a long sob for my world that has come crashing down right before me.

While I stand there, shaking from the cries coming out of my belly, I can't help but question Brittany's motives. My mind feels swarmed like a beehive, buzzing unceasingly.

*Do I listen to her words or not? Do I trust her, or should I brush it all off as jealousy and just simply avoid her the next time we come into contact?*

I come close to convincing myself that Brittany's words couldn't possibly be true, but then I'm reminded of her knowledge that Tyler sang to me. I let out another long sob at the thought of our moment—

CASEY TYLER

244

such a pure and undeniable connection—being just another act, a routine scene that may as well have been in the script.

*How would she know that? She was dead in that scene—unmoving and eyes closed—she wouldn't have known...*

*Unless he does this with multiple women, connecting with them in that intimate, romantic moment and then sweeping them off their feet only to move on with someone else shortly after.*

My neck prickles with the first washes of shame that I was so naive to think that moment only belonged to us. When held against Brittany's testimony, that moment belonged to everyone. It was just another farce of intimacy meant to be consumed at large like a paparazzi's photo.

Though I don't trust Brittany Oliver as far as I can throw her, I feel this doubt she has planted in me growing fast. It's one thing when your mind starts to worry on its own, but it's another when someone verifies your secret insecurities with a few blatant statements. Though I want to be skeptical, to brush Brittany's words off like a rude tabloid post, I struggle to do so.

But while I feel branded by her painful words, is it really Brittany I should be angry at here?

My mind flashes like a projector reel of all the questionable and seemingly negative moments from the weeks past with Tyler. Even his own mother said that he's incredibly gifted at lying. Initially a playful memory, it taunts me now, and I instinctively try to swat it away. But perhaps this is all a ruse, and I *am* just another casualty on the list of women that fell for his tricks.

While the memories flash by, they begin to form little cracks into our love story. Like a pottery piece that was once spotless and beautiful but now is becoming chipped and fragile as each moment is scrutinized.

*What if all is a lie? Our love seemed too good to be true, didn't it?* He *seemed too good to be true.*

As my mind runs rampant with no end in sight, there is a light knock on the door before it slowly creaks open, and Tyler walks in. I jump and try to smooth over my fraying emotions as though they were a crumpled page.

"Hey," he says with a small smile. As his eyes meet mine, his soft expression gives way to concern. "Whoa, what's going on?" he asks, drawing me into his arms. I feel stiff against him, unsure whether I should let him try and comfort me.

He leans back to get a better look at my face, wiping the hot tears that fall down my cheeks. I can't even look at him. My sight becomes focused on anything across the room.

"Tell me what's wrong," he whispers, leaning his forehead against mine. Although I can't bring myself to meet his eyes, I can feel his gaze on me like a spotlight.

"I—uh," I try to start but don't know where to begin. He gently pulls my head toward his chest, and I rest it there, letting my sobs loose like a dam that continues to burst. He holds me quietly, allowing it to happen.

After a few minutes, I take a deep breath and clear my throat, saying, "Brittany was just in here." More seconds go by, and I still can't manage to find the words.

"Okay, tell me what happened." His promptings are quiet, gentle, and caring, and I wonder if this, too, is all an act. I rub my face with my tear-soaked hands, trying to make sense of it all.

"Sunday," he pleads. "Please talk to me."

"I'm sorry," I say with my hands still covering my face. As I grasp at the words, I realize there is no pleasing way to explain the interaction between Brittany and me. I begin by simply spilling it out, clearly and bluntly.

"She told me that I'm not the only girl you've done this with and that your trend is to sweep women off their feet and then leave them in the dust." I wipe my nose with a tissue from the vanity and look up at him, trying to find any source of validity to her words by his physical response. This potentially catastrophic statement I've just let loose hovers between us as he pauses to respond.

His face is downcast, and his jaw clenches. The muscles twitch and tighten while he stares down at the space between us. More seconds go by before he shakes his head, letting out a frustrated laugh, and he looks up at me with weeping eyes.

"I'm so sorry," he says, inhaling deeply before letting the breath out. "I don't know what Brittany was trying to accomplish by saying all that."

I look at his face, full of anguish, and continue overanalyzing every little twitch and expression.

"Is it true?" I ask without blinking, waiting for an honest answer.

He looks at me for a beat and drops his head again before answering, "I'm not sure why my past relationships have to taint ours."

I shut my eyes and pause again before saying, "That's not what I'm asking. I want to know if our moments together were just some act—something you do with every girl that intrigues you."

"Is that what you think?" he asks with a new despondency in his eyes that sends a pang through my soul.

"I don't know what to think anymore." My voice begins to rise. "Twenty minutes ago, I was floating with you in the clouds, thinking that nothing could bring us down, and now everything is just a mess, and I feel…" I catch my breath. "I don't know how I feel."

After a few moments of quiet, I say, "It's like these moments where I felt so seen and loved by you have all lost their value now."

My sentence lingers in the air, with the silence surrounding it, before Tyler lets out a guttural sob. He wipes his tears with the back of his hand and tries to regain his composure.

"I don't know what else to say besides the truth." He takes my face in his hands while my lower lip quivers uncontrollably.

"What I feel with you is different than anything I've ever felt." He lets out a long breath before continuing. "You may not see it that way, but our moments are not void in my eyes."

His blue eyes look longingly into mine, and all I want to do is believe him.

I turn my gaze from him, saying, "I just need some time to process all of this."

"Okay," he nods and steps away from me. "I understand."

Grabbing my purse, I wipe my eyes one last time and stop at the door. Without turning my face toward him, I ask quietly, with my heart in my throat, "Do you remember?"

Brittany's words ring in my ear. *He sings to every pretty little thing who sits in that seat at the front of the stage. It's just another night at the theater for Tyler.*

He pauses. "Remember what?" he whispers.

I stifle my imminent cry and choke out, "Nothing."

Without looking back, I leave the room.

When you're floating above the clouds, it's only natural that the skies will eventually clear, and you'll be falling.

Walking to the subway station alone, I weep uncontrollably. I make every attempt to compose myself, but nothing helps. A kind gentleman sitting across from me on the train notices my tears and hands me a tissue from his briefcase.

"Even the darkest night will end, and the sun will rise," he says with a half-smile, empathy pouring from his voice.

"Thank you," I whisper back to him.

The sun will indeed rise again, but this time, without a cloud in the sky to dance upon.

At the very least, there will be no more falling.

# TWENTY-THREE

*A Year and a Half Later*

The day after Brittany came backstage at 54 Below, I called Mick and told her what happened as best as I could in between my fluctuating sobs. She was on the road to my apartment within an hour. We spent the next few days doing things we loved, like visiting new dog parks, checking out local vegan restaurants, and exploring more of Williamsburg. We didn't dare make the trek out to Broadway or Times Square.

Mick and I processed each night as I let it all out on the table—telling her how Tyler had been everything I'd dreamed of and more. That he swept me off my feet. That I was in love with him. But if our story was all a lie, my heart couldn't take that. While I pegged some of my hesitations of moving forward with him on his fame, which caused the horrible judgments slammed on me by thousands of people I didn't even know, I knew the real root of my fear came from the distrust that had been formed. It scared me to think everything we had built together wasn't real. That I wasn't being valued or seen for who I was, but I was just another prop he pursued for a moment and then would toss to the wayside sooner or later.

After many late-night talks with Mick and agonizing days where my relationship with Tyler floating in limbo, I called Tyler to see if we could meet and discuss our future.

While taking the subway to see him, I caved and looked up his name on the internet—something I never dared to do while we were dating. I was so happy to live in ignorant bliss in those days that I never allowed myself to question his sincerity or character.

As the subway stopped at each station, through the spotty Wi-Fi, I came across a thread dedicated to encounters fans had with Tyler. There were multiple alarming comments. While most said he was a pleasant guy at the stage door or while bumping into him on the street, some accused him of being a serial dater based on the various paparazzi photos of him and different women.

There was one comment that especially irked me. A year before we would meet, while he was beginning his run in *Belle Époque*, a woman commented on how he clearly checked her out while she was in the audience. It felt too similar to our story, and I couldn't get it out of my mind. Our moment no longer felt sacred.

When I walked the short distance to the small park in the East Village, I found Tyler standing there, waiting for me, looking somber.

We sat together on a bench, and before I could say anything about where my head was at, he told me he wanted to end things. I was shocked by his change of heart. I thought he would fight for us. I thought he would explain his side of the story further and attempt to ease my doubts. But he didn't. While I was uncertain of my final decision for our future together, Tyler had made it for us. I left the park feeling blindsided and uneasy but tried to find peace in his decision.

Our story reminded me of Orpheus and Eurydice. Walking this fine line of trusting one another while doubts wrestle their way in and wreak havoc. In the end, we turned our gaze toward the cracks that had formed along our path, ultimately sending our relationship to the grave.

It was as though all the pieces to a puzzle had now come together, and it made total sense why our relationship was so wonderful.

It was too good to be true.

I have not seen, talked to, or heard from Tyler since our time in the East Village. A few months ago, I saw his face in an ad for a new show in the West End. I assume he's living in London now, which takes the weight off my shoulders with the fear that I'd bump into him on the streets of New York.

Processing the loss of our relationship was brutal. It was my undoing. My family and friends comforted me to the best of their ability, but I don't think I understood to what degree I hoped our relationship would last the long game. That we would spend our lives together, and our paths would stay aligned without any missteps.

I learned the hard way that this life isn't a fairytale—that only happens on the stage or in the movies.

Regarding my career on the stage, I auditioned for seventy-three theater roles in the six months following Tyler and my breakup. I received three callbacks from the auditions, resulting in three emails telling me they thought another actress was better suited for the part.

After that much rejection, I was ready to pack up my things and leave the city for good. This place I once was so fond of had kicked me to the curb more times than I could count. Yet, something inside of me told me to stay.

I figured out what that was as I lay in bed crying on a wintry evening after returning from another dreadful audition experience. The producers and casting directors didn't even look at me. They only stared at their papers or phones while I, once again, sang my guts out, only to be stopped in the middle of a note. With a dry smile, the main producer said, "Thanks," and I was ushered out. It was humiliating, and it also was the last straw.

That night, as the tears flowed from my eyes, something stirred in me to take matters into my own hands. Instead of waiting on the decisions of others to project my career forward, I could begin to create something for myself.

I began the process of writing—knocking out an opening song that same night. I'd written in the past with different musically inclined friends and always loved it, but I stowed the practice away as I pursued different singing and acting routes over the years. But that night, as I penned the lyrics of the opening number, I felt like

Alexander Hamilton with a quill, Elphaba with her broom, and even Sweeney Todd with his razor—dark, but true.

Writing was something I was made for—it made me come alive. The song set the trajectory for my entire project. From the depths of frustration, misunderstanding, and bitterness, I found beauty even there. It took a bit of time, but I learned during the months of writing that I first needed to see and appreciate my own value before others ever would. I had been waiting for someone to tell me, "Great job!" or "You're so talented," but why stay idle and wait for that affirmation? I didn't need anyone else to see me or tell me who I was. I could find my identity in nothing else apart from whom I was created to be—Sunday Truelove. A dreamer. A writer. A creative.

My story unfolded as I whipped out my notebook and jotted down more lyrics. They say to write about what you know, and that's exactly what I did.

In theater, there is a term called "the fourth wall." It refers to this invisible barrier between actors and the audience that separates reality (the theater) from fiction (the story occurring on the stage). When the fourth wall is broken, the audience becomes an even more significant part of the production because the actors not only acknowledge their own fictionality but also, they acknowledge the presence of the audience.

The show I began to write leverages that idea. Not only are the actors aware of the audience, but the male lead on stage begins to fall in love with the woman situated amongst the audience in the front row. Our leading lady.

Act one begins at the climax of the fictitious show happening on stage. Our opening number is told from the leading lady's perspective when she notices the male star on stage staring into her eyes during his final number. He becomes enamored by her, and that's where the story of our production begins. As she rises from the audience, singing to her new lover, she is lifted onto the stage and enveloped in the 1900s Parisian world.

If I wasn't working at the coffee shop, walking dogs for extra cash, eating, or sleeping—I was writing. Luckily, my friendships didn't suffer much from this new lifestyle change because many of my budding relationships were a part of the project's genesis.

The first person I showed my work to was Gavin. This incredible human who had become one of my closest friends turned into my confidant. It was terrifying to finally reveal what I'd been spending sleepless nights working on, but I knew the value of my creation. They would not just be silly songs for a rinky-dink musical. The music and lyrics were worthy of being sung worldwide.

The day I sang the opening number to Gavin, he looked into my eyes, and I knew right then that he saw it too. He came alongside me, mapping out the script and flow of the show while I continued to pluck away at the story through song. We spent many late nights wrestling with the material, tweaking and rewriting it to become exactly what we had envisioned and hoped.

Once we had the final script, Jacob and Rachel began crafting the various dance numbers throughout the scenes. Finn sketched out and created every costume, while Lucas used his marketing background to promote the show in any way he knew.

After much hard work, we raised funds and rented a small theater in Brooklyn for a weekend slot. Gavin played the male lead, while I played the leading lady. Rachel, Jacob, and Shelly all joined as dancers, and we held a casting call for the other necessary parts.

On opening night, the Brooklyn theater was packed. Lucas created a lot of buzz about a show that would leave you feeling like falling in love was possible in every situation—even as a member of the audience.

We stood backstage and gathered in a big circle as we held hands to pray. It was such a sweet moment between friends who have become my family. With Gavin standing by my side, he squeezed my hand and looked me in the eye with a silly grin. We had each other's backs no matter what.

Nerves ran through me as I sat in the audience with the rest of the crowd, making my initial debut. Sitting next to me was Mick, who held my hand before my cue. A silent awe went through the seats as I stood up and began to sing the opening number from the front row amongst the other theatergoers.

Once the production concluded that night, I took my first bow as an actress in my beloved city with all my friends and family surrounding me. It felt even better than I could have imagined. As we stood there with roaring applause, I thanked God that I didn't let the criticism or rejection stop me from pursuing this dream because if I had, then we wouldn't have this beautiful show.

And as we were just about to walk off stage, Lucas's voice boomed through the theater for an announcement. He pulled Finn out of the audience, telling her how much he loved her, and then proceeded to get down on one knee, asking her to marry him. It was the perfect ending to our story of love defying all obstacles.

None of us knew that night, but a well-known Broadway producer was sitting in the seats. And this morning, Gavin and I met with that producer to consider whether our show could have a run on Broadway.

As I walk with a smile down Madison Avenue, I glance down at my whooshing pleated skirt that sways over my knee-high, heeled boots. While my Connecticut style has long since faded and in its place has grown a city-appropriate wardrobe, I realize now, it's all just become more *me*. New York has shaped me. Though my Connecticut roots will remain no matter where I live, I see now that New York City has adopted me as its own daughter.

These streets that pulse with millions of glorious stories have become my hiking trails. The skyscrapers have become my mountains. This place holds my heart now and forever. I thought I knew the extent of my love for the city years ago, but it is now even more treasured than ever before.

I walk with newfound confidence, knowing it was my path not to abandon this place but instead to trust in my worth, remaining through the dark times.

I endured. I fought. And most important of all, I created.

And in six months from now, our show, *He Sang to Me,* will have its first opening night on Broadway.

# TWENTY-FOUR

Gavin and I sat with our hands interlaced under the Broadway producer's glossy black desk as we listened to him pick apart our show for fifteen minutes straight.

*This is going well.*

I started to wonder why on earth he even arranged this meeting if he disliked so many aspects of the production. Was this just some sort of cruel joke? But once he finished listing the changes, he said the following sentence I will forever remember:

"After all of that is squared away, I think we have ourselves a Broadway show."

Gavin and I looked at him slack-jawed and then turned toward one another. Disbelief ran down both our faces. But as his conclusion registered, we were both swarmed with celebration and joy.

*We did it. We were going to Broadway.*

After letting us revel in a small moment of jubilation, our producer, Jamie, told us of the next steps. We would have a professional writer tweak the script. A music producer would come in to make minor changes to the songs. As that happened, he would simultaneously send out a casting call. His team would do the behind-the-scenes work to get that started, but Gavin and I could be a part of the casting team if we so desired since the characters came from our own imaginations. We both nodded emphatically showing our willingness to participate.

He then discussed the financial aspects of creating a show like this, which I barely paid any attention to because my mind was already thinking of my Tony Awards attire.

After we both shook Jamie's hand—Gavin wrapped him in an awkward hug that I don't think Jamie particularly loved—we left his office and stepped back onto 9th Avenue. Gavin and I remained quiet, keeping it cool around the crowd walking in and out of the building we had just exited, which hosts Broadway producers and stars alike. We relaxed until we reached the street corner, and then both let loose high-pitched shrieks.

While jumping up and down, Gavin and I embraced in a tight hug and continued hopping, yelling words of excitement and gratitude in each other's ears.

"OH MY GOSH!" I screamed. "Did that really just happen?"

"Have I actually understood?" he sang back to me with a smirk. "It happened. And I'm surprised that I didn't poop my pants or something."

"That would not have been ideal," I laughed. "Gavin, we're going to *Broadway*."

"I know," he squeezed my arms, then with a sarcastic sigh, he said, "and it only took us creating our own show to get there."

I laughed. "Who cares! We made it! We need to throw a soirée or something this weekend to celebrate and tell everyone who ever had anything to do with the show."

Quickly the thought flew through my mind to reach out to Tyler and tell him our news. He would have been thrilled and so proud of our work. But I tossed the idea aside because I wasn't ready to open that can of heart-wrenching worms.

"I love that idea. We can do it at my place, and we won't tell anyone until that night," Gavin suggested with a pinky lifted.

I pinky-promised him back. "Deal."

Keeping the secret from everyone for two full days was excruciating. I almost spilled the beans a handful of times, but Gavin and I agreed we would tell everyone together, so I kept my mouth quiet, changing the subject quickly anytime our production came up in different conversations.

After picking up various snacks and drinks from Trader Joe's, I head to Gavin's apartment—a place now so familiar to me from the many nights spent covering his hardwood floor with drafts of songs and scripts.

"Hi, friends!" I call after letting myself in with the hidden key above their light fixture. Once I drop the groceries on the counter, Eric emerges from the living room.

"Hey, Sunday. Good to see you."

I pull him in for a hug, saying hello. From the bedroom, I hear Gavin call, "Hi! Be out in a minute."

Eric has a giddy smile and continues looking at me as though he's about to explode. This persona is unusual for him. He's typically stoic, while Gavin is the flamboyant one.

I look back at him with a funny face before he whispers, "Gavin told me the big secret." He giggles.

"What! Gavin! We pinky promised." I yell through the house.

"Whoopsies!" he calls back. "I couldn't help it," he says before coming out of the bedroom and adjusting his vibrant red bow tie. He's wearing a white button-down shirt with black suspenders and pants that hit above his belly button. I've told him in the past that they make him look like a grandpa, but he assured me that the look is "in style" right now.

"He's my husband," he replies with a whimpering face and kisses Eric on the cheek. "I tell him everything."

"Okay, fine." I concede with a sigh before swiftly turning back to excitement mode. "Isn't it wild?" I say to Eric.

"You deserve it. You both worked so hard. It was only natural that thousands should see the show," Eric says.

"Thanks, Eric. You're so sweet," I say.

Gavin rolls his eyes. "Alright, enough with the sentimental *crapola*—let's cut cheese and decorate!"

"You want m—" Eric stops his sentence as Gavin raises a finger to shush him, looking at him with squinted eyes.

"I mean the *store-bought* cheese."

It takes about an hour to get the place "soirée" ready. We create a table-long charcuterie board, filling it with crackers, fruits, and various kinds of cheese. Gavin says over five times, "I've never met a charcuterie board I didn't like." At first, it was funny, but after the fourth time of him saying it, Eric and I graciously ask him to shut his cheese hole.

Once everyone arrives, we encourage them to mingle for a bit. They all enjoy the charcuterie table that Gavin, of course, loves. My insides feel like a volcano, ready to burst at a moment's notice as I make small talk with my friends. All I want to do is tell them the news.

About fifteen minutes into the party, I grab Gavin by the arm and ask with big puppy dog eyes, "Can we tell them now?"

"Yes, please," he says with relief. "Before I have a heart attack. I can't manage all this small talk without divulging how awesome we are now that we'll be on Broadway," he snickers, and I giggle back. We make our way to the living room, and I quickly FaceTime Mick, propping my phone on the table. Gavin and I clink knives on our wine glasses to get the party's attention.

"Everyone," Gavin yells. "Sunday and I have some important news to tell you."

The room goes quiet, and I hear one of the ensemble members whisper to his friend, "Is she carrying his baby?"

Gavin also hears him because he flashes a look of disgust toward the two before saying, "What?! No! She is not pregnant." He points to my belly and then says, under his breath, "You sickos." I choke out a laugh.

Gavin shakes his head, composes himself, and starts again. "Anyway, like I said, Sunday and I have some big news. Most of you don't know this, but on the opening night of *He Sang to Me*, we had a special guest in attendance—"

"Tyler Axel?" one guy asks from the back of the room, and my stomach drops. I haven't heard his name in months because my friends know what a sore subject he is. For a moment, I'm flooded with fear thinking he's in this room. My eyes scour for him, but quickly resolve he's not here.

"No, not Tyler Axel," Gavin says, getting visibly annoyed now. He glances at me with a dirty look, saying, "Thespians. Can't get a word in edgewise."

I take the reins and shout over the growing conversations amongst the crowd. "Gavin is trying to tell you all that a few days ago, we met with a well-known producer. And in six months..."

"OUR SHOW IS GOING TO BROADWAY!" we both yell.

For a few seconds, the twenty-five or so people in the room stare blankly at us. Then it's like a low-budget fireworks show, where the clapping and cheering happen sporadically until the big finale, and everyone is freaking out—finally understanding what's going on.

The cast members hug one another while some come up to Gavin and me to give their congratulations. While the show is going to Broadway, it will likely leave many of these people behind, which sends a sting through my heart. Most partygoers are excited for us, but some have already accepted that reality and quickly moved on from the enthusiasm.

"Who wants champagne?" Gavin yells over the crowd.

While sipping my drink, Finn and Lucas find me talking with one of the lighting techs, but I leave my conversation with him to finally relish in the news with two of my closest friends.

They pull me into a group hug, and Finn says, "I'm so proud of you, Sunday. It wasn't an easy road, but your persistence paid off. This is so exciting."

"Thank you," I say while covering my joyful smile.

Lucas bumps me on the shoulder. "You're really impressive, you know that?"

"Aw, thanks, Lucas. And thank you both for all of your hard work. The show wouldn't be what it is without you guys."

Glancing around the room at the creatives and storytellers gracing this space—dancers, production people, actors, costume designers, dressers, and so many more—they all believed and fought for the vision Gavin and I had. I feel hot tears prick in my eyes while gratefulness rises like a glorious stream within me.

The following week, Jamie's team has set up our first casting call. Gavin and I sit together in a large, sterile room in Midtown, joining a table's worth of producers and casting directors for our show. After getting introduced to each of them, I quickly Googled their names and found that most have been involved with my favorite shows on and off Broadway. I smile to myself, knowing that I'm sitting in the company of the Greats.

A long list of Equity members are coming in today, along with some prominent Broadway actors and actresses who have been directly asked to audition. We sit through about thirty auditions before lunch. While Gavin and I are grabbing sandwiches from the provided platters, he whispers in my ear, "I didn't care for a single one of those people."

"I know. I felt the same," I whisper back through the side of my mouth, looking around to see if anyone is within earshot to hear us.

"They're all missing something," he says.

I plop some salad on my plate and respond. "I agree. All of the women auditioning for Lila were almost *too* confident. I don't think they realize that her whole character arc starts with her believing no one sees or understands her."

"Yeah. And the guys for William were all attractive—don't get me wrong—I mean, whew!" He dramatically starts fanning himself with his hand and I laugh. "But they had subpar vocals. We need a powerhouse to sing all those parts."

While we never talked about it directly, I assume by now that Gavin knows Tyler inspired the role of William. He understands that whoever plays William has to stand up to what I experienced from Tyler the night he serenaded me.

"Totally. We'll find them, though. They're out there somewhere."

When we finish our lunches and move back into the audition room, one of the assistants hands out the next headshot and resume for us to review. Before I flip it around to see who it is, I notice Gavin's eyes bulge, and the color drains from his face while he stares at the photo.

"What?" I ask while turning my papers over, looking to see what horrifies him so.

My jaw drops and my body recoils.

The beautiful, airbrushed face of Brittany Oliver stares up at me from the glossy photo held in my hand.

# TWENTY-FIVE

**Y**ou've got to be kidding me.

This cannot be happening. My eyes shift to the open door, and I see Brittany Oliver waltz in like she owns the place. She makes eye contact with me and smiles sweetly.

I do not reciprocate the gesture.

After my last encounter with her at Tyler's 54 Below show, I thought that if I never saw her again on a stage or screen, that would be just dandy. And now she's here. Auditioning for the lead role in a show I created.

*Oh, how the pendulum has swung.*

The rest of the people at our table perk up after she enters. They have no idea I'm practically crawling out of my skin. Gavin and I take a glance at one another with dread.

Brittany stands on the mark in the center of the room, confidently announcing, "My name is Brittany Oliver, and I will be auditioning for the role of Lila."

A scowl comes across my face that I don't even attempt to hide. One of the casting directors says, "Thanks so much for coming in today, Brittany. We appreciate your time."

It makes it sound like she was one of the actresses the producers specifically asked to come in for an audition. While I didn't get a chance to look at that finalized list of people, I would have had a grand old time with a bottle of Wite-Out if I'd seen it. This situation couldn't be more opposite from what I would have hoped. She's not only here in the flesh of her own volition, but she was *sought out* to be here. If only these folks knew what lies underneath her tender smile and airbrushed exterior.

The accompanist in the corner of the room begins to play the song "Roar" by Katy Perry. The song choice annoys me even further because the lyrics fit incredibly well with the character of Lila and her progression toward the end of our show.

*She must have done her research. Or, more likely, her reps did. Either way, I'm still ticked.*

I'm playing the part of an unfazed judge of her performance quite exceptionally, but my eye still twitches slightly because she is *nailing* the song. I look down the row to see the expressions forming, and besides Gavin who sulks in solidarity with me, the rest are gobbling

Brittany right up. They're on the edge of their seats with goofy smiles plastered on their faces.

When she finishes her song, one of the casting directors even applauds. If my eyes were laser beams, that casting director would be dead.

Brittany smiles, says, "Thank you," and curtsies.

*What is this, the royal court? Get out of here!*

Jamie thanks her for her time and asks her to wait in the other room for the next portion of the audition. I can't tell if my blood is boiling because Brittany Oliver just dared to audition for a show made from my own imagination or because I've never had an audition go as well as hers just did. Anger rages in my bones.

It makes me want to throw up in my mouth when I picture her on the stage, stepping into the role of Lila. The character couldn't be further from the person I know Brittany to be, but lucky for her, she's a phenomenal actress who can use her talents to make you believe anything—even that she's a good, kind, and loving person.

I rub my face with my hands and, while pulling my cheeks down, I gaze at Gavin. He seems a bit less miserable than me now. He might even be smiling. Indignation rises in me. Placing my hand near my mouth, I hiss, "Why are you smiling?"

He jumps and looks back at me, defensively whispering back, "I was not!"

"Yes, you were! I just saw you."

"Okay, *fine*. I was smiling. But it's not for any other reason than..." He waits a moment, then draws my hands into his, saying, "Sunday, our show is going to be a hit. The most influential and prominent Broadway actress just auditioned to play a role that *you* created." He points to my chest. "That is remarkable. I know you two have a rough history together, and I'm sure you're feeling loads of emotions right now, but just look at the silver lining. She is going out for a role that's under our jurisdiction. This is incredible!"

It takes me a minute to comprehend, but I let out a white-flag sigh. "I guess you're right. I just *really* don't want her to play the role."

"I know," he says and brings a hand to my cheek. "I'm sorry. I know it's not what you imagined. Let's just see what happens."

We turn in our seats and divert our attention to the casting director.

"What did you two think?" she asks Gavin and me.

"She was great," I say with a bit of reluctance on my tongue.

"Agreed," Gavin adds.

The casting director continues. "We have a few more auditions to go through before the day is up, and then we'll ask our top choices to come back in and do a monologue." We nod.

Thirty minutes later, we get a break to stretch our legs and grab coffee. I make my way to the ladies' room and bump into Brittany as she's walking out.

"Oh, hi," I say. My first instinct is to run past her, close myself in one of the stalls, then block my ears with my pointer fingers, and sing loudly, "LALALALA." But I can't because we're playing Chicken, both trying to get around one another awkwardly. Once we establish our paths and move in our desired direction, I quickly call back, saying, "Great job in there."

I notice she doesn't leave the lounge area of the restroom but stands unmoving after I've brushed past her. She turns to me and says, "Thanks."

I'm walking slowly toward the stalls while nodding because it seems like she wants to say something else.

*Just spit it out, lady. Do you want to tell me that my story sucks? Or that William is just going to dump Lila and run?*

"I read the script," she says quietly. "You guys did an incredible job with the whole show." I stop in my tracks. She's coming off warmly, and I'm surprised by the change in demeanor since I last saw her. However, she is an actress capable of making me believe anything she wants, so I keep my guard up.

"Thank you. That means a lot."

"Hey," she walks toward me, grabbing my arm. "I've wanted to talk with you for a while now, but I honestly didn't think I'd ever have the chance."

*Oh great, another talk.*

A knot situates itself in the center of my belly.

"It's about the last time we interacted," her face goes solemn. "I want to apologize for that—"

*Abort. Abort.*

"Oh, it's no big deal," I interject, trying to tear myself away from the horrible memory.

"No, it is a big deal," she adds. "I said some things I shouldn't have because," she lets out a strained laugh of embarrassment and continues, "I was jealous. I had developed feelings for Tyler throughout our run together in the show, and he told me he didn't feel the same. He only wanted a friendship with me."

My eyes sway back and forth between hers. Unless she is the most Oscar-worthy actress on planet Earth, this just might be sincere.

*She's telling the truth.*

"And one day before our show, he told me about this wonderful moment he had with a girl in the audience. How there was this electric connection he felt—"

I stare at her blankly while my mind churns all this new information.

"When he brought you to the theater to show you backstage, I couldn't take it. It was so clear he was falling for you, and I wanted that to be me." Her eyes become glossy with tears. "I wanted to be the one he chose. So, I went into his dressing room that night at 54 Below, knowing you'd be in there waiting for him. I told you that he had this moment with every girl in the front row, but the truth is, it was only for you. He told me himself."

"Okay," is all I manage to get out, and she drops her grasp down to my hand, looking at me with what seems like genuine empathy.

"And yes, he went out with a few ladies before he met you, but I've never seen him quite so smitten until the night he sang to you. He fell for you hard, Sunday," she says with a crooked smile before it shifts to a sorrowful frown. "And I am so sorry that I ruined that for you."

She takes a beat before saying, "I've learned a lot since then—I'm in a healthy relationship, and I know that if something like what I did to you ever happened to me, I'd be devastated. I truly am so sorry." Tears slide down her cheeks.

I take a breath, blood pulses in my ears. "Thank you for telling me the truth."

She wipes her nose with her sleeve and nods her head.

Internally, I feel torn. The night she cornered me in that dressing room was one of the worst nights of my life. But it seems like she genuinely regrets everything that happened. As I process whether she would be doing any of this repentance for her own gain, a thought goes through my mind that she's just saying this to get on my good side. Now that I'm in the driver's seat, being a part of the casting crew for our show, she could simply be saying all of this to sway my vote. But even so, I would never put myself through humiliation like this to attain a role. Being a Tony winner, she could easily audition for whatever she wants and have a fair shot at it. It seems as though what she has said is the truth.

Although everything in me in screaming not to, I know that forgiving her is the best road to take.

"Hey," I say, and she looks up at me with shimmering eyes. "What happened that night is something I would never want anyone to go through, but it's one of the reasons this show was created. I leveraged the experience and created the character that *you* just auditioned for. Though it doesn't make what you did okay, I can confidently say that beauty came from the ashes. We wouldn't be standing here now if not for all that's happened."

"Really?" she whimpers.

I pull her into a hug to comfort her, not comprehending the level of anguish she's experiencing after just admitting the lies she told. After we let go, she nods and leaves me to be in the restroom alone. I make my way into one of the stalls, shutting the door. With my head in my hands, I take a deep breath and begin to weep.

Brittany fabricated the story of Tyler singing to other women every night. All the lies I believed for so long were never true. He only sang to me. Our moment was not tarnished or void. It was still sacred and pure—utterly magical after all this time. This blanket of sorrow and sadness laid over the memories of Tyler and me feels like it's suddenly lifting.

While I can't change what happened, nor do I know if I'll ever see him again to have the chance to reconcile what was lost, as I stand in this bathroom stall, it's not Brittany's words of regret that settle into my mind. It's Tyler Axel's words from the night we were together in Domino Park.

*Don't give up on your dreams.*

I let out a sob as the dream of a future with him is likely lost. But then I compose myself because there is one dream I have an opportunity to achieve *right now*. And I know more than anything that Tyler would want me to chase it.

Wiping my eyes and fixing my makeup in the mirror, I leave the bathroom stall and walk into the audition room. Taking Gavin aside, I lead him to a secluded hallway.

"Gavin," I whisper. "I know we both agree that Brittany was magnificent. But I still feel like she was missing something. And I think it's the same thing all the actresses we've seen are missing." He looks back at me, befuddled. I explain more. "The character of Lila is not in their bones yet. They don't know what she's walked through or fought for. But I think I know someone who does."

He squints an eye, still not understanding my suggestion. I physically point to myself.

"I can do this," I say with confidence. "There's something deeper when the lyricist sings the words versus another person who comes along and belts them with a stellar voice. They haven't wrestled with the lyrics. They might not even understand what they mean! But these words—this show we created—it's all inside of me. And I think," I cross my fingers, "that the table will see that."

His eyes are slightly closed, still unsure, but then a slow smile creeps at his lips.

"Yes," he says with such assurance. "You want to pull a Lin-Manuel Miranda, writing and starring in your own show."

I grin. "That's exactly what I want to do."

I race to Jamie's office and print out my resume and headshots before slipping them into the queue right after the papers from the actress up next. I pray the rest of the panel doesn't mind I'm going behind their backs, but it's worth the risk. Now is my time to shine.

We all sit and wait for the current actress to finish her song portion. While her voice is stunning, it's the same thing we've seen all day. When she leaves the room, I rise from my seat and, as confidently as I can—straight back, broad shoulders—move to where she just stood. Everyone at the table is looking at me funny, besides Gavin, who has the widest grin on his face.

Before they can ask any questions or object, I say, "My name is Sunday Truelove, and I'll be auditioning for the role of Lila."

Jamie leans back in his chair, while a smirk forms on his face. The rest of the crew looks stunned—and not in a good way. My eyes remain fixed between Jamie and Gavin, whose looks of joy and confidence in me give me the courage to go on.

I've learned repeatedly that it's not acceptable etiquette to audition with a song from the show you're auditioning for, but I toss that all to the side, knowing full well it may be my last chance to bring this dream into fruition. I hand the accompanist my sheet music and prepare to sing the lyrics that have been bubbling in my bones since I wrote them by myself in my small, Brooklyn bedroom.

Closing my eyes briefly, I settle into the character of Lila. It's not difficult to channel her because, well, Lila is essentially *me*. Her desires, issues, and frustrations were all based on things I've dealt with or was dealing with when I wrote the songs.

The accompanist begins, and I take a deep breath. With shaky hands and passion vibrating in my soul, I begin the climax of our opening number.

*As the final verse leaves your breath,*
*head lifts, gaze moving to me*
*Those blue eyes stare into my soul,*
*and you sing so sweetly*

*This night will be magic*
*All I dreamed of*
*And though the story is tragic*
*I'm leaving here in love*
*By this wonder I've met*
*I'll never forget*
*Oh, this night will be magic for me*

# TWENTY-SIX

The room is silent as my last notes reverberate off the walls and dissipate. My eyes open to an emotionless crowd. As I sweep from the right to the left of the table, no one is moving a muscle.

Slowly, Gavin leans his body forward, his chair squeaking as he turns to look at the rest of the line. I focus on Jamie, whose stoic face suddenly transitions. He lets out a surprised laugh that sounds like one loud "HA!" It reminds me of Tyler, but I brush off the thought as he rises and starts applauding. The rest of the table follows suit and gradually applauds with him while rising to their feet.

After everything I've been through—the vocal lessons, the acting lessons, the practicing, the waiting in lines, the rejection—*this* is the audition experience I've been waiting for. My hands cover my mouth, hiding my ear-to-ear grin.

My gaze shifts to Gavin, who looks happier than when we found out the show was going to Broadway. He does a little dance for me, and I put my hands together and bow, offering my gratitude to the whole table.

Days later, I'm sitting on the floor at Gavin's, reviewing some of the music producer's suggestions. Gavin lounges next to me, leaning against his green velvet couch. As we're in the middle of reading a lyric change, I notice a call come in on my phone from the casting director.

I look toward Gavin with wide eyes, and he releases a high-pitched scream, knowing exactly what's happening. I pick up my phone to answer and tap it to speakerphone.

"Hello?" I say.

"Hi, Sunday. This is Lynn. We met last week."

"Hi, yes!" My stomach situates itself in my throat. "How are you?"

"I'm well," she says kindly, keeping her voice steady, and giving me no inclination whether or not the part is mine.

"I'm calling because, as you know, since you auditioned, you were no longer a part of the final casting decisions." Gavin takes my hand from the floor, holding it in his lap as my throat goes dry. It hits me now that being rejected for this role would be the worst form of rejection because I *literally* created this character after myself. Lila *is* me. But even as these thoughts enter my mind, peace washes over me. I know who I am. I know my value and my worth. If they can't see that, it's on them. I shift my focus and trust their decision no matter what the outcome.

Lynn continues. "We were all astonished when you stepped up to the plate and decided to audition for the role," she laughs lightly. "And as the few of us weighed the options for the character of Lila," she takes a beat, and all I can hear is my ragged breath and heart pounding before she adds, "we couldn't imagine a better fit than you. We'd like to offer you the role."

*Oh. My. Gosh.*

My body physically doesn't know how to respond except by filling the room with a long, triumphant yell, sliding down to the floor, and then abruptly starting to sob while lying on my back on the hardwood.

Gavin stands and lets out a big "WOOO!"

"You. Have. No idea. What this. Means to me," I say in between sniffles and sobs. "I would be honored to accept the role. Thank you."

We talk shortly about logistics before ending our conversation. "Thank you again. I appreciate all of your trust in me. I won't let you down," I say.

"You deserve it, Sunday. Enjoy celebrating—we'll talk more soon."

"Sounds good," I say, and we finish the call.

I jump off the floor to meet Gavin in his celebratory dancing.

"That was the hardest secret I've had to keep in my entire *life*," Gavin cries. "You're going to be a star on Broadway! In all seriousness, though," we stop dancing as he holds my elbows and looks me in the eyes, "I am incredibly proud of you for persevering and pursuing your dream. You truly deserve it, and you will shine on that stage," he says, kissing me on the cheek.

"Thank you," I say. Tears shimmer in my eyes. "I couldn't have done it without you."

*Or Tyler.*

Brittany called me the day after I was offered the role, sending her congratulations. I was stunned, to say the least. Because of her generous phone call, it seemed as though the sincerity of her remorse was validated; she wasn't just asking for forgiveness solely to achieve the role.

The past few weeks, we've been in rehearsals. My costar, Derek Jakes—the option Gavin and I had at the top of our list for the character of William—has proven to be the perfect choice for the role. He is kind, charming, and an incredibly gifted singer. Gavin and I swooned when we saw him during the casting call, but our crushes were soon smashed when I learned that Derek is gay, and Gavin reminded himself that he is already married to Eric. Still, we've all developed a sweet friendship over the last month. Our favorite thing is going to different bars to search for the best pint, as Derek is from

Ireland. His accent and many other beautiful things about him have stirred on many moments of Gavin purring in my ear, "If I wasn't married..." I always follow up his statements with a prompt smack in his chest, and then we burst out laughing.

A week ago, at Gavin and Eric's apartment, while Derek and I were snuggled up on the couch, he asked me where the show's inspiration came from. Although I kept it close to my chest for any other person that might have asked, I decided to tell him the truth. I explained my history with Tyler and our momentous night in the theater. Derek listened intently as I explained our story. He was both empathetic toward and saddened by our ending.

To my surprise, he told me he has worked with Tyler and Brittany in past shows. He and Tyler had done a run of *The Three Musketeers* together in Massachusetts years back and have kept in touch since, making a point to see each other every few months. He assured me that Tyler was thriving in London. It was none of my business to know, but Derek seemed to sense that I needed to hear it. He also told me he wasn't the biggest fan of Brittany's. I didn't have much to say except I was grateful to see growth in her despite all that happened.

Along with Derek, the rest of the cast and crew quickly have become a second family to me. I remember this feeling in my small productions in high school and college, but there is an even greater depth here. They all believe in this story and care about bringing it to life just as much as I do.

In a few short weeks, we'll begin previews where we'll perform the show in front of live audiences but can still tweak and shift minor elements. About a month after that, we'll have our official opening night.

During our first morning break, I slide down one of the walls, sitting on the floor to allow my feet a much-needed reprise from the nonstop dancing and 3-inch heel-wearing. I slip off my shoes and massage my throbbing toes. Derek sits down on the floor beside me, snacking on some chips and chugging water.

"I meant to tell you this before," he says. "But you're doing a remarkable job for a first-timer in this process."

"Thanks, Derek. I'm glad I have you to lean on."

"Right back at you." He shifts his body slightly on the wall, inspecting a chip in his hand. "Were you able to give out all of your opening night tickets?"

The producers allotted each of the main cast member five tickets for opening night, designated for family and friends to be able to see the first show.

"I did. My mom and dad will be there, plus my two sisters and Mick." Mick had visited a few weekends ago. We all went to a local pub so she could meet Gavin and Derek officially.

"Nice," he replies. I notice there's something beneath the surface as he speaks. He's hiding something from me.

"How about you?" I ask, hoping he'll explain the underlying weirdness that's exuding from him.

"Yeah, my boyfriend and a few other friends are coming. My parents are on a year-long exploration of South America, so they'll come to a later show."

"Gotcha. I'm glad your friends can make it. I hope they enjoy the show."

"Me too," he replies with a wry grin, and before I can say anything else, our dance captain calls us back to the floor. Though my feet protest, I slip my heels back on and get a hand up from the ground from Derek.

After rehearsal, Derek, Gavin, and I go to dinner at P.S. Kitchen in Midtown. The vibes are cozy and chic, and everything on the menu is vegan, which Derek and I love, but Gavin will surely complain about. "So, you're saying this isn't real fish?" he'll ask. "No," "Then what is it?" "I don't know, tofu, maybe? You're the one who ordered it!" This is a classic bit from Gavin and me, as he's eaten at many vegan restaurants, for my sake. Deep down, I think he enjoys the food.

While we settle into our seats, I bring up this morning's conversation with Derek. "Okay, so tell me. Why were you acting weird when we talked about our opening night tickets?"

He shakes his jacket off and glances at Gavin with a worried look, to which Gavin shrugs.

"It's no big deal, really," Derek says, placing the jacket on the back of his seat, avoiding my eyes.

"What's no big deal?" My eyes dart between the both of them. Whatever it is, they're both in on it together.

Derek sighs and says, "Okay, fine. I may have given one of my tickets to a mutual friend of all of ours."

I narrow my eyes on him. "And who might that be?"

Gavin coughs, "Tyler Axel."

Derek winces.

"Okay," I say, trying to remain calm while placing my hands outstretched on the table before us, attempting to steady myself somehow. "And is he coming?"

"I'm not sure yet," Derek says sheepishly.

"That's fine. You guys are friends, and you can invite whoever you want!" My voice sounds like I'm riding a roller coaster. You'd think by now I would have gotten better at hiding my nerves after being in hundreds of rehearsals where my fear was bubbling to the surface each second. But when it comes to my real love life, there's no filter. Just raw, uncomfortable *me*.

Derek reaches for my hand across the table. "I know you guys have history, but he is one of my closest friends who just got back from his show in London."

Anxiety fills my belly. I didn't know he was back yet. I stare at Derek with a worried look before Gavin bumps his shoulder, saying, "Go on…"

What else could he possibly have to say? I dart between both of them, wondering what remains unspoken.

Derek adds in one breath, "I also think there could be some reconciling there, based on what Brittany said the day you both auditioned." My eyes go down to the table while my heart rate speeds up. "I don't want to force anything on you or make you talk with him if you don't want to, but I think it could be good for you guys to interact again."

I let out a small, insecure laugh. Our opening night was already going to be nerve-wracking enough, but it instantly just became eight million notches more so. But I would be lying if I said I hadn't hoped

Tyler would come to see the show at some point. He needs to witness the creation that was inspired by him in the first place. But does it have to happen so soon?

Gavin interjects his bold opinion, saying, "And if you guys got back together and got married, your babies would be *so* freaking beautiful."

I look at him with a deadpan expression. "Thanks, Gav."

We move on from the topic and start talking about Gavin's new apartment he and Eric just moved into. While chatting and enjoying our food, a group of women come over to our table and nervously ask me, "Are you Sunday Truelove?"

They then gaze at the rest of the table, noticing Derek and Gavin, and I think one girl comes close to fainting. She leans on one of her friends after letting out a squeal. Derek jumps slightly at the noise, knocking his fork into his cheek, and looks back at her, perturbed.

"I am," I say with an embarrassed laugh. "And this is Derek Jakes and Gavin Russo." I point across the table to my two favorite men.

"Can we get a picture?" one of them asks.

"Of course," I say, and Derek wipes his mouth of the spilled sauce smeared on his cheek from when the woman startled him. The girls squat in front of our table, and we all squeeze in for a selfie.

They say thank you about ten times each and giggle back to their table.

"That was weird," I say.

"First time someone's recognized you?" Derek asks while scooping up a forkful of salad from the shared plate in the center of the table.

"Yep," I respond.

"Have you read anything about yourself on the internet yet?" Derek asks.

"Last night, I started to," I say grimly. "One of the worst decisions I could have made. I saw one nice comment someone posted and got excited, but realized quickly that there are about five rude comments for every nice one."

"Yeah," Derek says empathetically and pats me on the shoulder. "You'll learn quickly to *never, ever read the comments.*"

# TWENTY-SEVEN

*Opening Night*

There's a new buzz backstage amongst the cast. Everyone is excited, but the night simultaneously welcomes a fresh set of nerves. Our show will be frozen after tonight's performance, meaning there will be no more tweaks. The producers were kind enough to welcome Gavin and my input on the final calls. I'm over the moon with how it all has turned out after the changes. It's even better than before, not surprisingly. We placed it in the hands of brilliant creatives who poured their hearts and souls into it, making it a masterpiece.

With the whirlwind these past few weeks have been, it hits me now, staring into my dressing room mirror as I put pin curls in my hair, that I haven't asked Derek if Tyler will be in attendance tonight.

Gavin is backstage, wishing everyone good luck, and I can hear him singing throughout the halls.

"You guys are going to do great! Break legs! But seriously though, because then I can swing in for you and tear the roof off this place." I hear their laughter before he waltzes into my dressing room. Taking a seat beside me, we look at one another through the mirror. I can practically see the pride oozing out of him while he takes the imagery in.

"I never expected that the girl who worked the morning shifts with me at Devoción would turn out to be my best friend, favorite creator, and the catalyst for my writing to make its way to Broadway."

I smile back at him as my eyes glisten.

"We did it," he says with a charming grin.

"Yeah, we did," I choke out.

"Okay, I won't make you cry and ruin your makeup." He puts his arm around me. "But I love you. You're going to kill it tonight. I'll be right there watching and supporting you every step of the way." He turns and gives me a smooch on my heavily makeup-ed cheek, then rests his forehead on my temple. The gesture reminds me of Tyler. If I close my eyes, it's just like he's in this room, comforting me and encouraging me before my big debut. Adrenaline suddenly shoots through me as I remember that he might be here, possibly even sitting in this building at this very moment. Taking a deep inhale, I say, "I love you too."

Once Gavin leaves, my dresser Cindy comes in to help me with my wig and costume. My attire is set, my voice is warm, now it's a waiting game until I hear the call for "places."

Though it isn't my ritual, I decide to try it out for good measure. I scroll through Spotify and find the wildest heavy metal song I can. Connecting my phone to its speaker, I turn up the volume and stare back at my reflection.

My fists begin to pump in the air, and I dance around the room like a lunatic. "YOU CAN DO THIS," I yell at the mirror. "YOU ARE AWESOME," I say while pointing at myself with my thumbs. "YOU KNOW THESE LINES LIKE THE BACK OF YOUR HAND!"

Derek's head pops in as I'm in the middle of an air-guitar solo.

"Am I interrupting something?" he asks with a smirk and steps inside. He looks so handsome in his 1900s-inspired suit with his hair combed back like he's Hugh Jackman in *The Prestige*.

"Hi," I say as I turn the music down. "You know, just trying out a new pre-show ritual."

His smirk lingers, and his eyes narrow in on me. "I wonder where you got the idea for that one."

My cheeks turn pink, knowing he has probably seen or heard Tyler doing this before the shows they were in together. Noticing my sudden embarrassment, he kindly changes the subject. "How are you feeling?"

"I'm excellent," I say with a relaxed sigh. "I knew I'd have nerves, but they're not debilitating. I've got this, like, river of peace flowing through me—which I know sounds weird, but that's exactly what it feels like."

"That's amazing," he responds with a sweet laugh. "Keep holding onto that. You're going to do great."

"Thanks, Derek. You too." As we embrace, the stage manager calls "places" over the loudspeaker. Derek gives me an excited smile and walks out. Seconds later, I realize what I'd forgotten to ask again. I run out of the room, calling back, "Wait! Is Tyler here?" But Derek doesn't hear me. He's already down the stairs, walking toward the other end of the theater to make his first entrance.

As the lights go down in the theater, I emerge from the backstage area, walking into the orchestra seating with my security guard. We find our way to the front-row seats reserved for us. Looking around, I try to spot my family and friends, but the lighting is too low to make anything out.

Settling in my seat, a surge of anxiety runs through my body, but I remind myself that I've done this all before and I can do it again. There is nothing to worry about.

The maroon curtain lifts while the stage lights come up, and the crowd cheers as Derek steps out center stage to begin his monologue.

I applaud with the audience and watch as he recites the lines Gavin and I toiled over for months. Pride bursts in me toward Derek, our creators, and this show as a whole. I find myself beaming in my seat as the voice to my left whispers, "Break a leg."

Turning toward the sound, for a moment, my eyes frantically glance over the swoopy hair and bright blue eyes without registering who is smiling back at me. Stubble has grown on his cheeks, intersecting with the joy lines around his smile. Under the dim lighting, Tyler looks at me with a closed-lip grin and many unsaid words behind his longing eyes.

*Why on earth did I let him slip away?*

Everything fades from view except him and me. I happily stare back at him, now knowing the truth of our story. Tyler always cared for me and valued me. He saw and loved me. He supported me and my dreams. He created and was a part of some of the most sacred and happy memories I've ever experienced on this earth. With a tender smile on my lips, my eyes gaze back into his and I wonder whether he could do it all over again.

Suddenly, the spotlight from above shines down on me. My cue. I turn my head back to the stage as Derek looks up, concluding the play's last scene before us. He makes eye contact with me, and this is the moment where his character, William, begins the journey of falling in love with my character, Lila.

The yellow hues of the spotlight shine on my body as the scene before us on stage freezes in time and time reverses to when my character first enters the theater. With a deep breath, I open my mouth and begin to sing the opening number from my front-row seat.

*The theater doors opened; my face turned red*
*The beauty of the stage was impossible to forget*
*I was led to my seat in the front of the room*
*And all I could think is how I can't wait to see you*
*...and I've never even met you*

*The lights go down, and the show begins*
*You walk past my aisle, the audience frozen*
*Standing center stage, you could hear a pin drop*
*Just for a moment, it feels like my heart might stop*

*And then the beat drops…*

The ensemble members move around the stage, dancing slowly and hauntingly with only their silhouettes distinguishable while they sing the next line.

*This night will be magic*

At this point in the number, I rise from my seat and walk through the aisles. I don't dare look at Tyler—though I've felt his presence the last few minutes as if he were a burning flame, growing brighter and warmer with each passing moment. Instead, I keep my gaze fixed on Derek, who sits motionless at the front of the stage, with his eyes fixed on where I was just seated.

> *The story goes on right in front of my eyes*
> *So close to the stage; I've been spit on a few times*
> *There can't be much more than 2,000 in the seats*
> *I wonder how come you haven't noticed me?*
> *I mean, I'm right at your feet!*
>
> *This night will be magic*
> *All I dreamed of*
> *And though the story is tragic*
> *I'm leaving here in love*
> *By this wonder I've met*
> *I'll never forget*
> *Oh, this night will be magic for me*

I find my way back to my seat. There is an instrumental break as the dancers move gracefully around Derek. The music drops down, and I softly sing the next verse.

*The finale unfolds as the last song is played*
*His love interest dies, they hold each other on the stage*
*He cries in her hair, and I'm starting to sweat*
*In my wildest dreams, I couldn't fathom what comes next*
*I watch in wonderment*

Three ensemble members come out from the wings and make their way into my row. They gently take hold of my arms and legs, lifting me to the stage as though I'm floating to Derek. After gingerly placing me in front of him, Derek and I grasp one another's hands. We kneel, facing each other as the stage slowly rotates so the audience can glimpse all angles of this magical moment.

A spotlight shines on him and me, filling the rest of the theater with darkness. Little twinkling starlights illuminate and grow brighter around every part of the stage, creating a sky-like scenery. Haze pours around us, filling the floor. Each time we rehearsed this scene, I felt a pang in my heart because it replicated the moment between Tyler and me so well. As Derek and I perform it now, I wonder if he feels the significance and sentiment of what is unfolding before him.

*As the final verse leaves your breath,*
*head lifts, gaze moving to me*

*Those blue eyes stare into my soul,*
*and you sing so sweetly*

Derek gazes into my eyes with a loving shimmer covering his dark irises.

This is our Maria and Tony "Balcony Scene" moment. This is our Christian and Satine "Elephant Love Medley" moment. William falls deeply in love with Lila after seeing her for the first time, cultivating a story of wondrous romance even between parallel universes.

Derek sings to me.

*Your presence is magic*
*My heart has just been won*
*And as I look into your eyes*
*I know that I'm in love*
*With a girl I've just met*
*I pray you don't forget*
*That this night has been magic for me*

We rise to our feet, switching into a key change, and finish the song with an explosive chorus as the dancers swirl around us. Derek and I hold one another, singing like never before.

*This night will be magic*
*All I dreamed of*
*And though the story is tragic*
*I'm leaving here in love*
*By this wonder I've met*

*I'll never forget*

*Oh, this night will be magic for me*

He lowers me into a dip and kisses me as the crowd goes wild.

We continue with the story, the audience witnessing Lila and William defy the odds of falling in love within a made-up world. After an hour and a half of the first act, the curtain closes on us right after another romantic kiss between Derek and me. The stage goes black, and the backstage lights pop on. While he's still holding me from our kiss, I break out of character instantly.

"YOU HAD HIM SIT NEXT TO ME?!" I scream-whisper in case anyone can hear us from behind the curtain—*especially* Tyler.

Derek releases a "Hehe," lifting me back to my feet from our dip.

"No, 'hehe'!" I mock. "He whispered to me right before my first lyrics. I almost missed my cue!"

"Yeah…that wasn't the best planning on my part."

Gavin struts onto the stage and asks, "What's all the bickering about, my two favorite lovebirds?"

"Tyler was sitting right next to me before I sang!" I whine.

"Oh, yeah, isn't that great?" he says. "I'd bet he was just as surprised as you, so don't sweat it." Gavin peers from behind the curtain to see if he can snatch a glance at Tyler. While I feel silly, I walk over and look from the curtain's edge with him. We've only opened it a crack because this is a big no-no in theater, especially Broadway. But we see Tyler flipping through the Playbill with what looks to be a small grin playing at his lips, and then he casually begins talking with the couple seated beside him.

"He looks happy," Gavin whispers to me.

I try to sound normal, but my words come out as a squeak. "He does, doesn't he?"

"And so sexy," Gavin purrs.

"*Okay*, that's enough." I close the crack of the curtain.

With a serious look, Derek walks over to us. "I'm sorry it was a surprise, but it seems like there is still something there romantically, and I don't want you both to miss out on it."

I shake my head at his matchmaking antics. "Derek, it's been almost two years. He probably doesn't even think of me like that anymore. Maybe he's even seeing someone!"

"It wouldn't hurt to talk to him," Gavin responds in a singsong voice.

"Let's just focus on this moment. It's our opening night. Don't let my romantic pursuits—or lack thereof—hinder our celebration," I say as I grab both of their hands. "This is our debut on Broadway—well, mine and Gavin's—Derek, you are too cool for us, you three-time Broadway star, you. Anyway. I want to be present *right here.*"

They smile back, and we form into a cheesy group hug. They are essentially just smushing their chests against my face as I stand between their tall frames.

After a bit of stretching, bathroom breaks, and gentle lip trills, it's time for act two.

While I'm in the midst of a scene where my character is lingering in the background, I cautiously sweep my eyes over the audience. I spot my family in the third row. Mick sits with them and smiles as she watches the story unfold. A row behind them sits Finn, Lucas, Rachel, Jacob, and Eric—Gavin invited them all with his five tickets.

Without thinking, my eyes land back on the front row. Tyler stares back at me intently. I quickly return my gaze to the scene, doing my best not to break character with a look of random glee that my face so badly wants to morph into. But it's a serious scene, so I keep my cool.

An hour later, it's our final number. While crafting the show, Gavin and I decided to leave the audience with a happy ending. Nothing else made sense to us. So, with the ups and downs of our characters in the fictitious show on stage, we transport them back to reality—breaking the fourth wall once and for all. Lila and William choose to continue their love story in the real world.

When Derek and I finish our last song together, we take one another's hand and then walk down the steps into the audience. We move past the aisles and exit through the back doors as if our characters were truly stepping out into the world to live their love story in New York City.

Applause erupts through the theater doors at the show's conclusion. Our security guards rush us backstage to take our final bows.

Once we find our way back, Derek and I quick change into our finale costumes. Mine is a long, sequined lavender dress, while he wears a black suit with lilac-colored flowers delicately painted on the jacket. We wait behind the closed doors at the rear of the stage with our hands interlaced.

"You crushed it," Derek whispers to me.

"Thank you. So did you." I beam back.

"Are you ready for your first official Broadway bow?"

"Ready as I'll ever be," I say with a lopsided grin.

We see the ensemble members step out to the front of the stage from the wings. Then the featured actors go out. And finally, as the doors in front of us slide open, Derek and I step out. The audience rises to their feet in a standing ovation.

The scene is overwhelming. Thousands of people clap and cheer for us. We walk to the front as the noise drowns out the background music. I take everything in, doing my best to glance around at every corner of the theater and send my thanks through my gaze. My parents applaud wildly, and I see Mick yelling, "That's my best friend!" to the woman beside her, which makes me cackle.

Once Derek and I bow together, he takes a solo bow at the front of the stage. I applaud him as he gives air kisses with his hands and says, "Thank you" to the audience.

He then turns and extends his arms to honor me as I take my first bow.

Stepping to the front of the stage feels like a literal dream. This moment I've been waiting for my whole life has finally arrived. I am now an official leading lady on Broadway.

My eyes sweep to Tyler. He looks up at me with the sweetest grin, and our story has come full circle. I smile back before sweeping my eyes to the broader audience, bowing in a graceful curtsy as the applause grows louder.

I return to the line of my beloved castmates, and we bow one last time as one body. One family.

Once the music picks back up again, Derek takes my hand, and we dance together while exiting the stage.

# TWENTY-EIGHT

The cast throws a mini celebration backstage with champagne, cake, and techno music blasting. We plan to do an even more elaborate party this weekend, so this is just a quick "We did it!" festivity before heading into our individual dressing rooms to de-makeup, take a breath, and visit with our families and friends before resting to do it all over again tomorrow night.

When I enter my dressing room, my family and Mick are there already waiting. After handing me a gorgeous bouquet of wildflowers, my mom and dad give me big hugs and kisses, telling me how proud they are of me and all I've accomplished. My sisters hug me, saying I did a wonderful job, and then last but not least, Mick pulls me into the tightest hug I've ever experienced while jumping up and down before yelling in my ear, "You were amazing!" I honestly would expect nothing less.

Because it's opening night, I want to greet fans who have decided to stay around and meet the cast at the stage door. Once my family and Mick leave the dressing room, I change into my street clothes and make my way to the exit. A security guard waits for me inside, saying, "You ready?" Flashing a scared grin, I nod and he swings the door open.

Stepping out on the street, I am greeted by hundreds of people calling my name with big smiles. The applause and cheering are alarming. It's overwhelming to receive such praise, but it's wholly wonderful.

I take a deep breath before the guard hands me a silver marker, and I turn to the group at the right of the door to begin signing hundreds of Playbills, taking photos, and greeting each person with a smile. Many say they enjoyed the show, which makes my heart sing. Though all the preview performances went well, I had a recurring nightmare these previous weeks that our opening would go over horribly. It even turned cartoonish when the audience started throwing juicy tomatoes at me onstage and shouting rude remarks toward the entire cast. Thankfully, in real life, that's not the case.

One little girl I take a picture with says she hopes to be like me one day. "Don't give up on that dream," I tell her as I sign my signature on a tote bag she purchased with our show's logo. "And don't be surprised if the journey turns out different than expected. It will all be worth it in the end." With a wink and a hug, I move on to the next cluster of people.

A few fans give me beautiful flowers and small gifts that I plan to place in my dressing room until my run ends. Halfway down the line, my cheeks start to hurt from smiling so much. Derek and Gavin follow me, signing Playbills and taking photos. Just as I reach the last person, I sign their Playbill before looking up because I'm preoccupied with talking to the group before them. Once I finish my autograph and turn to the person, I find myself staring back into the brilliantly blue eyes of Tyler Axel. My heart skips a beat.

"Hi," I squeak.

"Hi." He smiles and bites his bottom lip before saying, "Would you like to walk with me?"

Nodding, I say, "Uh-huh."

I turn to the crowd and shout, "Thank you all for coming!" After giving them a wave and a large smile, I notice Gavin and Derek beaming back at Tyler and I. Derek shouts to us, "Have fun, you two!" I smirk at his remark, while disregarding Gavin who makes kissy faces in our direction. Returning my gaze to Tyler, he takes my hand, and we walk away from the bustling city street.

Once out of sight from the theater, we walk down Fifth Avenue. While we're quiet for a few blocks, I notice that each time I try to sneak a glance at him, his eyes meet mine as if he were attempting to do the same.

"So," I begin once we're walking down a quieter street. "What did you think?"

He takes a moment before responding. "Well, first, I need to say that you were outstanding." Quickly looking into his kind eyes, his sweet laughing lines have come out for me once again—dancing along his eyes and mouth. I smile shyly, and he continues. "Second, I love the story you created." A small laugh comes from his lips. We're both a little coy because somewhere floating above us, it seems we both know that our love story inspired it.

"Thank you," I say and squeeze his hand with mine.

Walking by Bryant Park, we take in the scenery for a moment. Couples walk hand-in-hand, families rush back to Grand Central after a busy day visiting the city, and friends drink late-night coffees with laughter. I sneak another glance up at Tyler, who is just as handsome as ever—if not more. His hair is an inch or two longer than when I last saw him, and it has a few more grays sprinkled in than I remember. The wind brushes it lightly as I stare. He lets out a cackle while watching two boys run and scream from hundreds of pigeons after they have spread their leftover food on the ground. Tyler's face turns to me, and he points his head back to the street to have us continue walking.

I notice that the city feels just as it did the night we stayed out until dawn. It's moving and breathing through the people within it—full of life and wonder. I suppose it's always like this, but because this past year has been so chaotic and busy, the moments of slowing down and noticing these little things were few and far between. It makes me happy to be living back in the unhurried moments with Tyler by my side.

There is a lot unsaid between us, so I begin with the basics, asking him about his recent show in London. We catch up on the last two years, walking a couple of miles with lots of laughter and coy smiles. We're quickly able to default back to our old antics and playfulness that we once had. I'm reminded again of his humor as he tells a story about his London adventures where he hopped on the train and accidentally ended up in a different country. Nothing has changed about his wit or his sweetness.

We reach Washington Square Park, and he leads us to the edge of the fountain where we splashed and lay those many nights ago. Leaning against the side, he asks, "Do you remember the first time we saw each other?" He's looking into the distance with his hands in his pockets.

*Of course, I do. It was one of the best nights of my life.*

"You mean at the dog park?" I ask with slight disappointment as I stare at my lap.

"No, not the park. Before that."

*What?*

I turn to face him. He continues to be in his own little world, reminiscing.

"What do you mean?" I ask.

As this moment has gone unsaid throughout our time of knowing one another, it's as though the secret has become locked up, waiting for the other to one day unleash it. At the same time that it's locked away, it has grown layers of protection, making it more and more difficult to unveil. I've always been so fearful that if I asked him about it, he wouldn't remember, and I would be left feeling foolish. But at this point, I've done more terrifying things these past two years than I can count. I push past the fear and, instead, take up my imaginary pickax and begin hacking away at the protective shell that has calcified over this wonderful moment of ours, bringing it to light once and for all.

"You remember," I breathe.

He turns to me while his eyes move around my face, lips curving into a smile.

"I do."

A heaviness that I wasn't aware I was carrying suddenly lifts from my shoulders. I feel like I can fly again.

"You were in the front row with Finn in a beautiful white dress," he says. "I remember my heart was pounding when I looked up from the floor and met your eyes and..."

"Everything changed."

"Yes."

I close my eyes and bring my fingers to my forehead in astonishment. It feels like my body is being transported back to the moments after our first encounter in the theater.

Mere minutes after our glorious moment, insecurity started to creep in without me realizing it. It continued to grow throughout our relationship and then went into hyperdrive with Brittany's destructive words. Ever since that moment with Tyler, I've wanted to know if I was the only girl he'd done this with, but so much of me desired to be clueless for fear that the truth would devastate me.

But tonight is for truth. Tonight, I no longer need to hold back because of fear. It's now or never. It's time that everything is brought out to the open.

"You must have done that with any girl you found attractive in the front row," I say quietly. As Tyler purses his lips with his brow crinkled, I brace myself for the worst.

"No," he says. "That was the only time I've ever done that. Felt that. Every other night, I'd look at my shoe, or the floor, or a light," he uses his fingers to list the different objects of his gaze.

"Tyler," I put my hands on him to stop him from listing things. "Are you telling me that moment was real? Because Brittany told me—" I cut myself off, not wanting to shame Brittany for our conversation in Tyler's dressing room because of her bravery in eventually telling me what I hoped was the truth.

His face turns serious. "Sunday, I've never experienced anything like that in my life. I remember you were sitting there with the blue lights cast over you like some moonlit wonder," he motions to my face with his hand, and we can't help but share a little laugh. "You didn't notice me look at you toward the beginning of the show. But you stood out to me in the crowd like a…lone firework in a black night sky. I couldn't take my eyes off you. I can picture, even now, the smile you had on your face as you watched the ensemble dance in the first number." He closes his eyes momentarily while saying this and lets out a small laugh as he thinks about the memory.

"After I saw you, something inside of me told me you needed to have the most special moment. So, I intentionally saved that last line for you. Every other night, I swear, I was either looking at the ground or at the mezzanine. But that night, I wanted to sing to you. I wanted to give you a moment that was pure magic."

He turns his body toward me, gently lifting a hand to my face. It reminds me of the last time he held me, with my body recoiling from his touch. This time, I can't seem to get close enough to him.

"And I'm so glad I did because I started falling in love with you that night." Warmth engulfs my body, and my heart leaps at his words. I smile at him with joyful tears forming in my eyes.

"I even scoured the stage door, signing Playbills and taking photos with *every single person* to see if I could find you," he grins softly. "But you had left already. It wrecked me to think that I'd never see you again. Then when you found Jasper a few days later, our stories collided again, and I knew something greater was pulling us together.

"And that night at 54 Below, I thought I'd lost you for good. I confronted Brittany the next night before our show and she lied to me, too; telling me that you were only interested in me for my fame. I was crushed. It didn't make sense, but I trusted her. I even had to have my agent call the production in London to ask for a second chance at the role."

"What do you mean? I thought you planned to go there?" I say.

"No, they offered the role to me, but I turned it down. I didn't tell you because I didn't want you to be upset that I'd turned down a dream role to stay in New York with you, but I couldn't see myself leaving. I just didn't want it. I wanted *you*. But after we broke up, I thought it was best to get away for a while so we could both have time to heal.

"Only the whole time I was gone, all I could think about was you." I half-smile because what he's describing is exactly how I felt during our time apart. With each victory and loss I experienced, my thoughts always turned to Tyler. I wanted to tell him everything. I wanted him to know about my days, about my hardships—any and everything. I wanted him to be there through it all.

"When Derek asked me to come to your opening night," Tyler says, "he assured me that after getting to know you and hearing our story from your perspective, your intentions were always pure toward me."

*Thank God for Derek.*

"I know now you were never pursuing me to enhance your career. You achieved all that on your own, and I'm so proud of you." He smiles. There's a moment of silence between us as I process his words. While many have given me verbal affirmations for my work and growth, the one person I cared the most to hear it from was Tyler.

"I've never met someone so kind and determined and wonderful," he says. "I hope you know I see and value you for who you are. And through your ups and downs, I want to continue seeing you. You are the sweetest gift, and—" he rests his forehead against mine before quietly saying, "I don't want to lose you again."

His arms slide around my middle, and everything in me is beaming with adoration for this man. I thread my arms beneath him, embracing him back.

I believe his words and trust in his intentions, now and forevermore.

"I don't want to lose you either," I whisper back. "Saying goodbye to you was the hardest thing I've ever done, and I'm so sorry."

Hot tears slide down my face. He brushes them away with his thumbs and says, "I didn't know it then, but those words I sang to you could not be more true. You have filled my life with wonder, and I want to do the same for you."

I wait a moment, soaking in what he's just said, before softly shaking my head and saying, "You already have." Then, with a teasing smile, "Also, that was a beautiful rhyme. How very creative of you."

He laughs, and the sound is like hearing a symphony for the first time. I want to hear his laugh every moment of every day. I want to be the one that makes him laugh every day. I want to spend my life from here on out with Tyler Axel by my side.

He draws my face toward him, and his lips meet mine, sweetly and gently—letting the moment linger.

Moments later, his lips leave mine and he looks deeply into my eyes, reminding me of that first night that oscillated with the unknown. The blue rings surrounding his pupils sparkle in the low lighting of the park. As his eyes move around my face, his lips turn up in a smile.

"I love you, Sunday."

His words feel like the sun shining all over my body after a long winter. I've wanted to hear them for far too long. I'm like a tulip opening its petals for the first time as we enter our relationship's spring. My love for him never wavered, it only grew brighter and stronger over our time apart.

"I love you, too," I say back.

He beams and leans in, kissing me again, as we bask in our articulated love. No more hidden moments or unsaid words. No more doubt or distrust. Everything has been uncovered. Tyler can see all of me. He can have all of me. I give him permission to access every part.

"Hey, guess what?" he says as he leans our foreheads against one another again.

"What?" I reply.

*"This night has been magic for me,"* he sings, and I could legitimately melt right onto the dirty park floor. My heart has never been more full.

I sing it back to him, believing this will not be the last time. I will continue to sing to him, and he will continue to sing to me from now until we're rocking alongside one another, old and gray.

Tyler and I dance upon the clouds once again, but this time, even if the clouds disperse, I trust that the stars will hold us up with them above the mountaintops because it's where we were always meant to stay.

# EPILOGUE

*June 11th, The Following Year*
*Radio City Music Hall*

And the Tony Award for Best Original Score goes to—" Brittany Oliver stands on the Radio City stage in a gorgeous purple dress that splits right at her hip. She peels open the envelope and my stomach twists in knots.

A big grin emerges on her lips, as she calmly announces into the mic, "*He Sang to Me*. Music and lyrics by Sunday Truelove."

*Holy crap.*

The crowd erupts into applause all around me. It's utter chaos, but all I can hear is my heartbeat in my ears as hundreds of mouths around me open and close, congratulating and cheering. I rise to my feet and turn to kiss my husband, who wears the brightest smile of them all. He whispers in my ear, "You did it. I love you."

Then I begin the journey toward the stage. Time slows down. I feel every step beneath my heeled feet. People lean in my direction from the aisles, offering their commendations, but I keep my gaze fixed on the stage and drown out the noise surrounding me—pressing forward. I stop at the beginning of the stairs and lift up my emerald green silk dress so I don't trip. Finn designed and customized the dress for me for this special occasion. She is now the CEO of a successful clothing line with Lucas, her new hubby, as their marketing manager.

A kind gentleman takes my arm and helps me walk up the stairs. I turn to see whose hand I hold, and Lin-Manuel Miranda beams back at me. He wears a closed-lip, kind smile. "Congratulations." I feel like I'm dreaming. With wide eyes, I say back, "Thank you." He chuckles and lets me go as we reach the top. Making my way to the microphone, I give Brittany a tight embrace. She whispers in my ear, "You deserve it."

With glossy eyes, I receive the award from her, holding it in one hand and pulling my speech out from my bosom with the other hand. A silly expression falls on my face, and a few audience members laugh.

Looking out to the hundreds of people in Radio City Music Hall, I see those who have gone before me, paving the way for our show, and I have to stifle a sob. Because of the endurance, talent, and creativity of the people in this room, I can stand here today.

"Wow," I say, trying to compose myself though my hands tremble.

"This is such an honor," I start. "I moved to this city three years ago, hoping to make my dreams come true. Though my journey was nothing as I anticipated, it was everything I needed. Along the way, I met some of my best friends.

"Gavin, this award belongs to you as much as it does me." I scan the crowd, finding his eyes as he sits with Eric. They both wear the giddiest smiles with watery eyes. I raise the award in his direction, saying, "You are my favorite person to create with. You are so wonderfully bold and equally brilliant. I would not be here without you." He blows me a kiss with his hands.

"Derek Jakes," I scan the room. "Where is Derek Jakes?" I ask with a laugh before some audience member shout, pointing to him a few rows back from where I was just seated.

"Ah, hi," I say, and he smiles back at me. "Derek, I am immensely grateful we opened this show together. You loved and supported me through my first Broadway experience, and I can never thank you enough for shooting out of the cannon alongside me."

I gaze at the cameras before me. "Mom, Dad, and my sisters— thank you for your continued support and love for me and my craft. I love you all so deeply. Mick, you're probably on your couch, screaming at the television right now. You are my dearest friend. You fought for me when I couldn't fight for myself, and I love you to the moon and back.

"To the cast and crew of our show, thank you. Jamie, thank you for seeing me and trusting me with this story we created. To Finn, Lucas, Jacob, and Rachel, I am beyond thankful for your many hours dedicated to making our show what it is."

I close my eyes, internally centering on the One who brought me here in the first place. "Thank you, God, for blessing me with this story and for every song you've poured out of me through this journey.

"And finally," I open my eyes, sweeping the crowd and landing on the place where he sits.

Tyler.

"Thank you to my husband." Just like he did to me the first night we encountered one another, my gaze meets his, and it's as though no one else is here—only us. His blue eyes shimmer with love as we leap over the stars above it all. This place where we have been living and always will live together.

Memories from the last year flood my mind. Tyler asking me to marry him while in London at Christmastime. We had spent most of our days drinking tea and reading old books at an adorable bookshop he often visited during his childhood. One night as we walked in to do our evening reading, twinkling lights were draped over every inch of the tiny space. He led me to the small fireplace that was decorated with hundreds of pink peonies and red poppies—my favorite flowers. After telling me how much he loved me, he got down on one knee. It was spectacular. We wasted no time getting married. We committed our lives to one another on a beautiful, brisk spring evening in a high-rise building overlooking the glorious Manhattan skyline at dusk with our friends and family surrounding us.

"Ever since our paths crossed those few years ago, you have seen and loved me even more than I thought possible on this side of heaven. I love you so deeply." A small sob escapes my lips. I pull myself together after a deep breath.

"The last few weeks having you in the show with me have been a dream come true." Tyler stepped in after Derek's run, replacing him as William. Each night, we get to sing the songs inspired by our story for thousands of people to enjoy. I never want it to end, but life goes on, and we play our final show in a few weeks because my character is not written to be pregnant.

"I can't wait to raise our baby together," I say, patting my belly with a giggle, and a few people in the audience gasp because we haven't officially announced it yet. The tabloids will be going berserk tomorrow.

"Our story of love inspired these lyrics and this show. I will forever be grateful and humbled that you sang to me on that glorious night." Tyler looks back at me with the most joyful expression while his eyes swim with tears.

I then raise the Tony Award in his direction, staring into his loving eyes, and finish my speech with the words that began our story.

"My life is full of wonder, all because of you."

## *Acknowledgements*

I cannot express enough thanks to all those who helped this book come to life. First, I need to thank God. I am immensely grateful that the true Creator would trust me to reflect His creativity with my own; it is one of my greatest joys on this earth. Thank you, Lord, for how you've carefully sewn moments together that have inspired this book. You are the ultimate author, and I will do my best to continually give you the pen for the story of my life.

To Jennifer Wislocki, thank you for your willingness to take this piece and run with it wholeheartedly. Your selflessness does not go unnoticed. I'm grateful for your constant encouragement of my work and for making it more grammatically correct and typo-free than I ever could have. I won't ask you to edit this part, so hopefully, I do a good job!

To Rachel Fairchild, my BFF, your continual support has meant the world to me. Thank you for every minute you put into this book—critiquing, helping shape scenes, and laughing with me at the silly things I threw at the wall. I am so grateful for your friendship and for your beautiful creativity. You are a light in my life.

To my Momma, you have always taught me to cultivate my creativity and go after my dreams—without you, my life would look radically different. Thank you for continually pointing me back to Jesus, loving me no matter the circumstance, and always listening to my joys, sorrows, pursuits, and dreams. I love you so much!

To Kelly, Gabe, and Dad, I'm so grateful for your encouragement. Dad, thank you for providing for the family so I have the capacity to write books. Gabe and Kelly, thank you for loving me well and celebrating my victories along the way. And to the rest of my family, I'm immensely grateful to have such a beautiful clan of loving, supportive people.

To my friends: Rebekah, I am so freaking grateful God put you in my life. You are a consistent anchor for me and such a wonderful friend. Thank you for sticking by my side through all these years. Chels, thank you for always creating with me and pushing my songwriting to new levels. "This Night Will Be Magic" is dedicated to you! Christa, thank you for being in my corner. From the headshots to the edits, I am forever grateful to you for your many kindnesses. My church family, your creativity and passion for the Gospel is forever inspiring and appreciated. My New York family, thank you for welcoming me in with loving arms and championing my dreams.

To New York City and every single creator who has had a hand in creating my favorite weekend activity, thank you for Broadway. Theater has continually inspired me, given me full-body chills, sparked something fresh, and become the backdrop for one of the best nights of my life.

Lastly, to you, dear reader. I cannot thank you enough for picking up my story. I pray this book is a reminder that though you may not see or feel it, you are known, loved, and valued.

I love you all! Thank you.

Until next time!